At the Edge of the Orchard

Tracy Chevalier

W F HOWES LTD

This large print edition published in 2016 by
W F Howes Ltd
Unit 5, St George's House, Rearsby Business Park,
Gaddesby Lane, Rearsby, Leicester LE7 4YH

1 3 5 7 9 10 8 6 4 2

First published in the United Kingdom in 2016
by HarperCollins*Publishers*

A CIP catalogue record for this book is available
from the British Library

ISBN 978 1 51004 670 2

Typeset by Palimpsest Book Production Limited,
Falkirk, Stirlingshire

Printed and bound in Great Britain
by TJ International Ltd, Padstow, Cornwall

MIX
Paper from
responsible sources
FSC
www.fsc.org   FSC® C013056

At the Edge of the Orchard

ALSO BY TRACY CHEVALIER
FROM CLIPPER LARGE PRINT

Remarkable Creatures

For Claire and Pascale
finding their way in the world

The juice of Apples likewise, as of pippins, and pearemaines, is of very good use in Melancholicke diseases, helping to procure mirth, and to expell heavinesse.

—John Parkinson, *Paradisi in Sole Paradisus Terrestris*, 1629

To the spirit bowed with affliction, or harrowed with cares, a pilgrimage to these shadowy shrines affords most soothing consolation. Behold the evergreen summits of trees that have withstood the storms of more than three thousand years! . . . While lost in wonder and admiration, the turmoil of earthly strife seems to vanish.

—Edward Vischer, *The Mammoth Tree Grove, Calaveras County, California*, 1862

Go West, young man, and grow up with the country.

—John Babsone Lane Soule, 1851 and Horace Greeley, 1865

BLACK SWAMP, OHIO

SPRING 1838

They were fighting over apples again. He wanted to grow more eaters, to eat; she wanted spitters, to drink. It was an argument rehearsed so often that by now they both played their parts perfectly, their words flowing smooth and monotonous around each other since they had heard them enough times not to have to listen anymore.

What made the fight between sweet and sour different this time was not that James Goodenough was tired; he was always tired. It wore a man down, carving out a life from the Black Swamp. It was not that Sadie Goodenough was hung over; she was often hung over. The difference was that John Chapman had been with them the night before. Of all the Goodenoughs, only Sadie stayed up and listened to him talk late into the night, occasionally throwing pinecones onto the fire to make it flare. The spark in his eyes and belly and God knows where else had leapt over to her like a flame finding its true path from one curled wood shaving to another. She was always happier, sassier and surer of herself after John Chapman visited.

Tired as he was, James could not sleep while John Chapman's voice drilled through the cabin with the persistence of a swamp mosquito. He might have managed if he had joined his children up in the attic, but he did not want to leave the bed across the room from the hearth like an open invitation. After twenty years together, he no longer lusted after Sadie as he once had, particularly since applejack had brought out her vicious side. But when John Chapman came to see the Goodenoughs, James found himself noting the heft of her breasts beneath her threadbare blue dress, and the surprise of her waist, thicker but still intact after ten children. He did not know if John Chapman noticed such things as well – for a man in his sixties, he was still lean and vigorous, despite the iron gray in his unkempt hair. James did not want to find out.

John Chapman was an apple man who paddled up and down Ohio rivers in a double canoe full of apple trees, selling them to settlers. He first appeared when the Goodenoughs were new arrivals in the Black Swamp, bringing his boatload of trees and mildly reminding them that they were expected to grow fifty fruit trees on their claim within three years if they wanted to hold on to it legally. In the law's eyes an orchard was a clear sign of a settler's intention to remain. James bought twenty trees on the spot.

He did not want to point a finger at John Chapman for their subsequent misfortunes, but occasionally he was reminded of this initial sale and grimaced. On offer were one-year-old seedlings or three-year-old saplings, which were three times the price of seedlings but would produce fruit two years sooner. If he had been sensible – and he was sensible! – James would simply have bought fifty cheaper seedlings, cleared a nursery space for them and left them to grow while he methodically cleared land for an orchard whenever he had the time. But it would also have meant going five years without the taste of apples. James Goodenough did not think he could bear that loss for so long – not in the misery of the Black Swamp, with its stagnant water, its stench of rot and mold, its thick black mud that even scrubbing couldn't get out of skin and cloth. He needed a taste to sweeten the blow of ending up here. Planting saplings meant they would have apples two years sooner. And so he bought twenty saplings he could not really afford, and took the time he did not really have to clear a patch of land for them. That put him behind on planting crops, so that their first harvest was poor, and they got into a debt he was still paying off, nine years on.

'They're my trees,' Sadie insisted now, laying claim to a row of ten spitters James was planning to graft into eaters. 'John Chapman gave 'em to me four years ago. You can ask him when he comes back – he'll remember. Don't you dare touch 'em.' She took a knife to a side of ham to cut slices for supper.

'We bought those seedlings from him. He didn't give them to you. Chapman never gives away trees, only seeds – seedlings and saplings are worth too much for him to give away. Anyway, you're wrong – those trees are too big to be from seeds planted four years ago. And they're not yours – they're the farm's.' As he spoke James could see his wife blocking out his words, but he couldn't help piling sentence upon sentence to try to get her to listen.

It needled him that Sadie would try to lay claim to trees in the orchard when she couldn't even tell you their history. It was really not that difficult to recall the details of thirty-eight trees. Point at any one of them and James could tell you what year it was planted, from seed or seedling or sapling, or grafted. He could tell you where it came from – a graft from the Goodenough farm back in Connecticut, or a handful of seeds from a Toledo farmer's Roxbury Russet, or another sapling bought from John Chapman when a bear fur brought in a little money. He could tell you the yield of each tree each year, which week in May each blossomed, when the apples would be ready for picking and whether they should be cooked, dried, pressed or eaten just as they were. He knew which trees had suffered from scab, which from mildew, which from red spider mite and what you did to get rid of each. It was knowledge so basic to James Goodenough that he couldn't imagine it would not be to others, and so he was constantly astonished at his family's ignorance concerning their apples. They seemed to think you scattered some seeds and picked the results, with no steps in between. Except for Robert. The youngest Goodenough child was always the exception.

'They're my trees,' Sadie repeated, her face set to sullen. 'You can't cut 'em down. Good apples from them trees. Good cider. You cut one down and we'll be losing a barrel of cider. You gonna take cider away from your children?'

'Martha, help your mother.' James could not bear to watch Sadie work with the knife, slicing uneven steaks too thick at one end, too thin at the other, her fingers threatening to be included in their supper as well. She was bound to keep cutting steaks until the whole ham was chopped up, or lose interest and stop after only three.

James waited until his daughter – a leaf of a girl with thin hair and pinched gray eyes – continued with the slicing. The Goodenough daughters were used to taking over the making of meals from their mother. 'I'm not cutting them down,' he explained once more to Sadie. 'I'm grafting them so they'll produce sweet apples. You know that. We need more Golden Pippins. We lost nine trees this winter, most of them eaters. Now we got thirty-five spitters and just three eaters. If I graft Golden Pippins onto ten of the spitters, that'll give us thirteen eaters in a few years. We won't have so many trees producing for a while, but in the long run it will suit our needs better.'

'*Your* needs. You're the one with the sweet tooth.'

James could have reminded Sadie that it was she who put sugar in her tea, and noticed when they were running low and nagged James to go to Perrysburg for more. Instead he doggedly set out the numbers as he'd done several times over the last week when he'd announced his intention to graft more trees this year. 'That'll make thirteen eaters and twenty-five spitters. Add to that fifteen of John Chapman's seedlings he's bringing us next week, and that takes us to fifty-three trees, three more than we need to satisfy the law. Thirteen eaters and forty spitters, all producing in a few years. Eventually we'll have more spitters than we do now for cider. And we can always press eaters if we have to.' Secretly he vowed never to waste eaters on making cider.

Slumped at the table, her daughter moving lightly around her as she prepared supper, Sadie watched her husband through her eyebrows. Her eyes were red. 'That's your latest apple plan, is it? You gonna go straight past the magic number fifty to fifty-three?'

James knew he should not have used so many numbers to explain what he wanted to do. They bothered Sadie like wasps, especially when she had applejack in her. 'Numbers are a Yankee invention, and we ain't in Connecticut now,' she often reminded him. 'Ohioans don't care a spit about numbers. I don't want to know exactly how many mouths I got to feed – I jest want to put food on the table.'

But James could not help himself: it comforted him to count his trees, to mull over the number, add another Golden Pippin, remove a mongrel spitter that was a result of one of John Chapman's visits. Solid numbers held back the woods surrounding their claim, so dense you could never count all the trees. Numbers made you feel in charge.

Today Sadie's response to the numbers he laid out in his argument was even blunter. 'Fuck your numbers,' she said. 'You ain't never gonna reach fifty, much less fifty-three.'

Disrespect for numbers: that was what made James slap her – though he wouldn't have if she'd still held the knife.

She responded by going for him with her fists, and got in a jab to the side of his head before he wrestled her back into her seat and slapped her again. At least she didn't manage to catch an eye, as she had done once; his neighbors enjoyed teasing James about the shiner his wife had given him. Buckeye, they called it, after the chestnuts so common in Ohio. Lots of wives sported buckeyes; not so many husbands.

The second slap split Sadie's lip. She seemed puzzled by the sight of her own blood, and remained seated, the bright drops spotting her dress like fallen berries.

'Get your mother cleaned up, and call me when supper's ready,' James said to Martha, who set down the knife and went to get a cloth. Martha was his favorite, being gentle and never challenging him or seeming to laugh at him as some of his other children did. He feared for her each August when the swamp fever arrived. Almost every year one of his children was picked off, to join the row of graves marked with wooden crosses in a slightly higher spot in the woods not far from the cabin. With each grave he'd had to clear maples and ash to make space to dig. He'd learned to do this in July, before anyone died, so that the body did not have to wait for him to wrestle with the trees' extensive roots. Best to get the wrestling out of the way when he had the time.

I was used to his slaps. Didnt bother me none. Fightin over apples was jest what we did.

Funny, I didnt think much about apples fore we came to the Black Swamp. When I was growin up we had an orchard like everybody else but I didnt pay it no attention cept when the blossom was out in May. Then Id go and lie there smellin some sweet perfume and listenin to the bees hum so happy cause they had flowers to play with. That was where James and I lay our first time together. I shouldve known then he wasnt for me. He was so busy inspectin my familys trees and askin how old each was – like I would know – and what the fruit was like (Juicy like me, I said) that finally I had to unbutton my dress myself. That shut him up a while.

I never was a good picker. Ma said I was too quick, let too many drop and pulled off the stems of the rest. I was quick cause I wanted to get it done. I used two hands to twist and pull two apples and then the third would drop and bruise and wed have to gather all the bruised ones separate and cook em up right away into apple butter. Beginnin of each season Ma and Pa would get me pickin till they remembered about that third apple always droppin. So they put me on to gatherin the windfalls that were bruised and damaged from fallin off the tree. Windfalls werent all bad apples. They could still be stewed or made into cider. Or theyd have me cookin or slicin rings to dry. I liked the slicin. If you cut an apple across the core rather than along it you get the seeds makin flowers or stars in the middle of the circle. I told John Chapman once and he smiled at me. Gods ways, he said. Youre smart to see that, Sadie. Only time anyone ever called me smart.

James wouldnt let me touch the apples on his trees either. His precious thirty-eight trees. (Oh I knew how many he had. He thought I wasnt listenin when he was rattlin through his numbers but drunk or not I heard him cause he repeated himself so much.) When we was married back in Connecticut he learned real quick how many apples I spoiled. So in the Black Swamp he got some of the children to pick em – Martha and Robert and Sal. He wouldnt let Caleb or Nathan pick, said we were all too rough. He was like a little old woman with his trees. Drove me crazy.

*   *   *

James headed out behind the cabin, past the garden they'd begun turning over now the ground was no longer frozen, and out to the orchard. Upon settling in the Black Swamp, the first thing the Goodenoughs had done after building a rough cabin close to the Portage River was to clear land for the orchard so as to plant John Chapman's apple saplings. Every oak, every hickory, every elm he cut down was an agony of effort. It was hard enough to chop up and haul the trunk and branches to set aside for firewood, or for making bed frames or chairs or wheels or coffins. But extracting the stumps and roots almost killed him each time he hacked and dug and pulled and ground. Prying out a stump reminded him of how deeply a tree clung to the ground, how tenacious a hold it had on a place. Though he was not a sentimental man – he did not cry when his children died, he simply dug the graves and buried them – James was silent each time he killed a tree, thinking of its time spent in that spot. He never did this with the animals he hunted – they were food, and transient, passing through this world and out again, as people did. But trees felt permanent – until you had to cut them down.

He stood in the melting March dusk and surveyed his orchard – five rows of trees, with a small nursery of seedlings in one corner. It was rare to see space around individual trees in the Black Swamp; normally there was either open water or dense woods. The Goodenough orchard was not spectacular, but it was proof to James that he could tame one small patch of land, make the trees do what he wanted. Beyond them, wilderness waited in the tangled undergrowth and sudden bogs; you had to take each step with care or find yourself up to your thighs in black stagnant water. After going into the swamp, to hunt or cut wood or visit a neighbor, James was always relieved to step back into the safe order of his orchard.

Now he counted his apple trees, even though he already knew that he had thirty-eight. He had expected the requirement for settling in Ohio of fifty viable fruit trees in three years would be easy to achieve, but he had been assuming apple trees would grow in the swamp as they had done on his father's farm in Connecticut, where the ground was fertile and well drained. But swampland was different: waterlogged and brackish, it rotted roots, encouraged mildew, attracted blackfly. It was surprising that apple trees could survive there at all. There were plenty of other trees: maple was abundant, also ash and elm and hickory and several kinds of oak. But apple trees needed light and dry soil or they could easily not produce fruit. And if they did not produce, the Goodenoughs must go without. The Black Swamp was not like Connecticut, where if your trees had blight or scab or mildew and grew no apples, you could barter or buy from neighbors. Their neighbors here were few and scattered – only the Days two miles away had been there almost as long, though

13

lately others had begun to settle nearby – and had no apples to spare.

James Goodenough was a sensible man, but apples were his weakness. They had been since he was a child and his mother had given him sweet apples as a special treat. Sweetness was a rare taste, for sugar cost dear; but an apple's tart sweetness was almost free since, once planted, apple trees took little work. He recalled with a shudder their first years in the Black Swamp without apples. He hadn't realized till he had to go without for over three years how large a part apples had played in his life, how he craved them more than whiskey or tobacco or coffee or sex. That first autumn when, after a lifetime of taking them for granted, James finally understood that there would be no apples to pick and store and eat, he went into a kind of mourning that surprised him. His desperation even drove him to pick the tiny fruit from a wild apple tree he came across along one of the Indian trails; it must have grown from a settler's discarded apple core. He could only manage three before the sourness forced him to stop, and his stomach ached afterwards. Later, over near Perrysburg, he shamed himself by stealing from a stranger's orchard, though he took only one apple, and it turned out to be a spitter rather than an eater. He ate it anyway.

In subsequent years he bought more trees from John Chapman – seedlings this time – and grew his own from seeds as well. Trees grown from seeds usually produced sour apples but, as James liked to point out to whoever would listen, one in ten tended to turn out sweet. Like growing anything in the Black Swamp, it took time for the apple trees to thrive, and even those that seemed healthy could easily die over the winter. While the Goodenoughs did have apples within three years of their arrival, they could not be relied on. Sometimes the crop was heavy; other times the apples were scarce and tiny. Sometimes disease killed the trees. For several years James struggled to get thirty trees to grow, much less fifty. More recently he'd had more success, and the previous fall had picked apples from forty-seven trees. Over the winter, however, it appeared nine had died, like a punishment for his hubris.

Luckily no one ever came around to count how many trees they had, as it was too hard to get in and out of the Black Swamp for law officials to bother. None of his few neighbors seemed concerned about the fifty-trees rule. Sadie was amused by the number, and enjoyed taunting her husband with it. Sometimes she would whisper 'fifty' to him as she passed. But James fretted over it, always expecting someone to show up on the river or along one of the Indian trails that criss-crossed the Black Swamp and inform him that his farm was no longer his.

I never wanted to live in the Black Swamp. Who would? It aint a name that draws you in. You get stuck there, more like – stuck in the mud and cant go no farther, so you stay cause theres land and no people, which was what we were lookin for. James was second youngest of six healthy sons, so there werent but a little bit of Goodenough farm in Connecticut for us. We managed for a time but James kept reachin for me at night and the children kept comin. Then his father, an old killjoy who never liked me, started hintin about us moving west where we could settle more land. He got the wives of James brothers to talk to their husbands, which they were glad to do cause they didnt like me either. They didnt trust me round their men. I got something they didnt have. So the brothers started pushin James to be more adventurous than he was. Really they shouldve gotten James brother Charlie to go west. Charlie Goodenough was the youngest and by tradition he was the one shouldve gone. Plus he had the gumption in him. Charlie wouldnt of let mud trap him in the swamp. Hed have bust through it and got out into the open where theres good healthy land solid under your feet, with sun and grass and clean water. But everybody loved Charlie, his wife most of all. It was she took against me the worst. Maybe she had reason to. Damned if she werent the nicest of the wives too.

Then all of a sudden Charlie also said James ought to go – though he looked real sorry when we did leave. Stood longer than the rest, watchin our wagon go down the long track away from the

16

Goodenough farm. I bet he wished it was him beside me headin towards a new life.

Turns out lots of Connecticut farmers had gone to Ohio before us. Too many. We went across New York then took a boat on the lake from Buffalo to Cleveland and started lookin, expectin our pick of land to be laid out before us like a nicely made bed, but all we found were other Yankees – most of them war veterans got their allotment from the government. We made a circle round Cleveland, then heard we was better off goin west to the Maumee River, and even into Indiana. After Lower Sandusky we was headed towards Perrysburg when the road – if you can call it that – got worse and worse. That road was where we met our first enemy. Mud. I never saw anything stick so much. It stuck to the wagon wheels and when they turned they collected more mud like a ball of snow gettin bigger and bigger. Got so we had to stop the wagon every fifty feet to scrape it off. Near broke the horses legs. Finally they wouldnt budge and we had to wait till they recovered. Next day we got half a mile before they stopped again. Along that stretch of road there were inns every quarter mile for all the travelers gettin stuck. The inns themselves were set up by settlers who couldnt get no further.

At last we got to the Portage River and decided that was it, we couldnt go no farther so it looked like wed arrived at our Promised Land. By then everything was covered in mud. Wed been wadin through it and couldnt get it off our boots or off our dresses or out from under our toenails. Sometimes the boys would take off their trousers at night and in the morning theyd be standin up by themselves with the mud dried on em. Had to live with it, and wash in the river. John Chapman was a smart one with his canoe glidin up and down the rivers and creeks easy as you like, stayin out of the mud.

After a time we got used to it. Maybe I jest stopped carin. Id hear new settlers complain bout the mud and think, Theres worse things than mud. Jest you wait.

We arrived in the swamp in early April which is a good time to settle cept theres a rush to plant crops and a garden and build a house. And to do any of those things you first got to clear the trees. They was another enemy waitin for us in the Black Swamp. Oh, there were a lot of enemies there.

Damn them trees. I hate em, God love me I do. Back east we didnt have the tree problem the way we did in Ohio. James and I both grew up on farms that had been made some time before, with houses and barns built and cleared fields and gardens. My mother even had flower beds. Thered been settlers in Connecticut for two hundred years, and theyd been the ones breakin their backs to dig up the trees. Every garden, every field, every churchyard and road had to be made by takin out the trees. Wasnt till we was faced with a slice of land full of Ohio trees that we realized how much work we had to do. Well, James had to do, and the older children. I was carryin Robert in my belly and was too big to use an axe or haul wood or pull at those goddamn stumps. There sure wasnt gonna be any flower beds in the Black Swamp. Any clearin had to be done for a better reason than flowers. It was for feedin you and keepin you warm and dry.

Clearin took so much out of my children that sometimes I think thats what killed Jimmy and Patty, weakened em so the swamp fever got em that much easier. Patty died the first summer, Jimmy the next. I never forgave the trees for that, and never will. If I could Id gladly burn down these woods.

Even when we thought wed cleared all the trees we needed to, they kept growin and growin, pressin in on us. We had to keep an eye out for the seedlings that sprung up everywhere. It reminded me of dirty pots or dirty clothes: you scrub and scrub and get em clean, then an hour later youve burnt oatmeal on the bottom of the pot or smeared mud on your apron, and you realize it never ends, theres always gonna be pots and laundry to do. Trees are the same, you clear a field and they start springin up again. At least theyre slower than laundry. But you think youre payin attention, then a year goes by and you find you overlooked a seedling and suddenly its a tree, with roots that dont want to come out.

I heard theres land out west thats got no trees

on it at all. Prairie. Lord send me there. I tried to talk to James bout goin there, but he wouldnt listen, said weve made a place for ourselves, hunkered down like toads in the stinkin rottin swamp, and here well stay.

A branch snapped behind him in the orchard. My shadow, James thought. He did not turn around but reached out to run his finger along the branch of the nearest tree – a spitter – and feel the satisfying bump of a nascent bud. 'Robert, get me a Golden Pippin from the cold cellar.'

A few minutes later his youngest child returned and handed him a yellow apple speckled with brown dots – the only yellow apple in the Black Swamp that James knew of. It had an unusual oblong shape, as if someone had stretched it, and it was small enough to be held comfortably in his hand. He squeezed it, relishing the anticipation of its taste. It might be wrinkled and soft and well past its prime, but Golden Pippins retained their taste for months, if not their crunch.

James bit into it, and though he did not smile – smiles were rare in the Black Swamp – he shut his eyes for a moment better to appreciate the taste. Golden Pippins combined the flavors of nuts and honey, with a sharp finish he'd been told was like pineapple. It reminded him of his mother and sister laughing at the kitchen table in Connecticut as they sliced apples into rings to be dried. The three trees on the edge of the Black Swamp orchard that produced these sweet apples were all grafts from the Golden Pippin tree James had grown up with. He had grafted them when the Goodenoughs first arrived in the Black Swamp nine years before, from branches James insisted on bringing with them to Ohio. Though grafted at the same time, they had grown up to be different sizes; it always surprised James that the trees could turn out as varied as his children.

Robert was watching him with brown eyes the color of pine resin, still and intent like one of the smarter breeds of dog – English sheep or German shepherd. He rarely needed looking after, and he seemed to understand trees in a way none of the other Goodenoughs did. By rights he should be James' favorite: a son, slight but healthy, clever and alert, the Goodenough child most likely to survive swamp life. He had been born just after they moved to the Black Swamp, and maybe because he was a native to the swamp, the mosquitoes left him alone, looking for foreign blood. Even when he was very young, it was Robert who nursed the Goodenoughs through swamp fever, sometimes the only family member unaffected. He followed his father around, watching and learning from him as his older brothers Caleb and Nathan never bothered to. Yet James found his son's attention discon- certing. At almost nine Robert was too young to judge others, but he often caused James to look at himself, and there he always found fault. However much he taught Robert – how to skin squirrels, how to build a wormwood fence, how to plug gaps between the logs of the cabin to make it warmer, how to store apples so they did not bruise – his son continued to stare at him expectantly. That was why he preferred fragile, floating Martha, who did not seem to want more than James could give.

Now Robert's direct gaze made James feel nailed like a hide to a wall, and he fumbled with the half-eaten Golden Pippin and dropped it. It rolled into dead leaves, catching them in its exposed flesh. Before James could move, Robert had picked it up, brushed it off and held it out to his father.

'You finish it,' James said.

'There's not many left, Pa.'

'That's all right. You eat it.' James watched with satisfaction as his son finished the apple in two bites, his face revealing his shy pleasure in the taste.

'Where do those Golden Pippins come from?' he quizzed his son.

'Connecticut.'

'And before that?'

'England. Your grandparents brought over branches of their favorite apple tree.'

'Where in England?'

Robert stared at his father with his unsettling eyes and shook his head. He was not the kind of boy to bluff if he didn't know. James was glad of his honesty. 'Herefordshire. Now, tomorrow we'll graft. Go and check the grafting clay, make sure it hasn't dried out. If it needs it, add a little water and stir it in.'

Robert nodded.

'You know what you're looking for? You don't need me to check it with you?'

'I'm all right, Pa.' Robert trudged off towards the river, picking up a wooden bucket as he went.

Most springs James Goodenough grafted a few apple trees, turning spitters into eaters, or poor spitters into better spitters. In Connecticut he had learned from his father how to make a productive tree from an indifferent one, and though he had now performed successful grafts dozens of times, he still appreciated the surprise of this re-creation. Their fourth autumn in the Black Swamp, they picked their first crop of Golden Pippins, small and with a thicker skin than those in Connecticut, but edible. James could still recall the first bite he took of one, savoring the crunch and the honey taste with the pineapple finish. The fact that Golden Pippins could grow in the swamp – that a sliver of his ordered life in Connecticut was now tucked into Ohio mud – made him hopeful that one day he might finally feel at home there.

Grafting had always seemed a miracle to James, that you could take the best part of one tree – its roots, say – bind to it the best part of another tree – one producing sweet apples – and create a third tree, strong and productive. It was a little like making a baby, he supposed, except that you had control over what characteristics you chose. If he could graft his children, what parts of himself and Sadie would he choose to put together? Perhaps his steadiness with her spirit – which, though mercurial, was infectious. In the right mood she could make a room full of people dance.

But he could not choose the parts: they came potluck. The Goodenough children were not a combination of the best of their parents, but a sometimes painful mixture of the things that bothered James about himself and what he hated in Sadie, with an added pinch of their own particular characters. Caleb was dour and violent, Sal tetchy, Martha uncertain, Nathan sarcastic. Robert was a mystery – a changeling, James sometimes thought, a child he would not have thought could be Sadie's if he'd not seen him slip out of her womb in a wave of water and blood, landing ashore without even a cry.

Sadie viewed grafting with suspicion, an attitude she had picked up from John Chapman. 'You ain't God,' she liked to say. 'Choppin' and changin' and makin' monsters. It ain't right.' He noticed, though, that she still ate the apples from the grafted trees. Once when he pointed this out she threw the apple she was eating at him and gave him a bloody nose. Afterwards he retrieved the apple and finished it himself. He did not like to see fruit wasted.

*　　*　　*

The first time John Chapman came through we hadnt been in the Black Swamp but a few weeks and were livin half in the wagon half under canvas thrown over a frame James had knocked together. The girls and I were down at the river on the edge of our claim washin clothes when we heard a whistle sounded like that bird they call a bob white. Then along comes this grizzled man, paddlin in a canoe and hallooin us like we was old friends. He had long greasy hair and a beard stained yellow round his mouth from chewin baccy, and he wore a coffee sack belted round the middle with a piece of rope, and holes cut out for the neck and arms. He looked like a crazed swamp man, but we was glad to see him, as there werent a whole lotta folks around and it was a treat to get a visitor, even a crazy one.

He had a second canoe lashed to the first and it was full of pails of little trees. Turned out John Chapman sold apple trees for a livin – little ones, bigger ones and sacks of seeds he gave away for free. Him and James got to talkin right away about apples, which pleased them both no end, and James even stopped work on the cabin and went walkin with John Chapman all over the woods where he was goin to plant an orchard, showin him the bits of tree hed brought from Connecticut and was goin to graft into new trees. John Chapman sold him twenty saplings, sayin it was best to start with them rather than graftin. Its up to God to improve the trees, he said, though gentle like, not forceful about it as hed later become. Would have sold him more saplings but James had so much land to clear he couldnt do it fast enough to get more than twenty trees into the ground.

They was off so long it started to get dark, so I told John Chapman to stay for supper, though we couldnt offer more than some pease and a couple of squirrels Jimmyd shot. Three squirrels dont go far tween nine mouths, and a tenth aint so welcome then. But John Chapman told us he didnt eat meat cause he couldnt stand for somethin livin to be killed jest to keep him alive. Well. None of us had heard such a thing before but it meant we all got more squirrel, so we werent complainin. Even the pease he didnt take much of and drunk water rather than cider.

After supper he walked round as we sat by the fire. That man was a pacer and a talker. Now he werent talkin apples, though. Instead he said, Let me bring you some fresh news right from Heaven. I wouldnt of taken him for one of them types, who got to share their religion like theyre passin round a bottle for everyone to drink from. He started to talk and I confess that first time – in fact the first few times – I didnt understand a word. After a while the children rolled their eyes and wandered off, and James got intent on his whittlin. I didnt mind though cause I liked watchin John Chapman. He didnt want to sleep in the wagon or under the canvas that night but said he was fine in the woods. Wouldnt even borrow an old quilt. Nathan spied on him and came back sayin John Chapman was sleepin in a pile of leaves.

Next day he was gone fore we was up, though he came back a week later with the saplings. We hardly had the money to buy em, havin spent it all to get to Ohio. But James said it was worth it as wed have apples two years sooner than if we planted seeds. Then he was goin to graft the branches hed brought from Connecticut onto some of the saplings, though he never told John Chapman that as hed learned pretty quick how John didnt like graftin cause it tampered with Gods creation.

John Chapman started to pay us visits two or three times a year. Always in the spring when he come up to see how we and our trees had fared over the winter and sell us more if we needed any, and then in the fall when he was checkin on his nursery of trees further up the river. Sometimes in the summer hed stop by too, on his way from one place to another. I liked to think he stopped to see us cause of me, and Id run out to the river whenever I heard him whistle Bob white, Bob white.

John Chapman was a singular man, thats for sure. I never once saw him wear clothes like other men, breeches or trousers and shirt and suspenders. Nor shoes, nor jacket, even when there was frost at night. Dont know what he did for clothes in the winter since we never saw him then. Maybe he holed up like a bear. He was a shaggy man too

– shaggy hair and beard, long fingernails, heels like cheese rinds. Bright eyes though that flashed and followed their own conversation.

He always took the time to talk to me, once hed figured out no other Goodenough was gonna listen to his God talk. When he found out I could read a little he used to lend me bits of books hed cut up and given to settlers up and down the rivers. All fired up from his visit, I would take the pages gladly, but once hed gone I couldnt make head nor tail of what was written on them. I never told him but I preferred the revivalist camp meetings we went to now and then when the mud was dry enough and we could walk to Perrysburg. Got to meet a lot of people there and be entertained by a God I understood.

What I liked best about John Chapman was that he didnt judge me like some I wont name did. He never said, Sadie youre drunk. Sadie youre a disgrace. Sadie youre draggin this family down in the swamp. He didnt take the bottle from me, or hide it, or empty it so I had to drink vinegar instead. John Chapman understood the power of apples and the things that come from em. It was he who showed me how apples could be the cure for another of our enemies. That was the swamp fever.

Swamp fever came alongside skeeters. They started bitin in June, but in August they swarmed so bad we had to wrap sheets round our heads and wear gloves, even in the heat, and burn smudge

28

pots day and night so the smoke drove em away. Even then they still got us, bitin so much that our faces and hands and ankles – anything not covered by our clothes – swelled up, hurtin and itchin at the same time. I never seen anything like it. It was enough to drive a person wild as a cat. Patty and Sal had it the worst. Poor Pattys face was so swollen she didnt look like a Goodenough no more, but like a swamp creature.

She was the first to get the fever. Begun to shake so hard her teeth cracked. I held her down in bed and doused her in water, tried mayweed and catnip and rattle root, but nothin worked. Jimmy was taken the next year, and baby Lizzie after that, then baby Tom, then Mary Ann. Did I get that order right? Hard to keep track. Some years we were spared. Sometimes I wished it would take me. I birthed ten children and got five left.

Only Robert werent never touched by swamp fever. But then he never was like the rest of us. I birthed him two months after we settled in the swamp. I was wonderin if Patty or Mary Ann was up to helpin me through the birth, as in those days there werent no neighbors close by. James would have to do, though I never liked men to be at a birth, it was bad luck. As it was I didnt need James or the gals or nobody – I was only jest settlin down with the pain when Robert slipped out so he almost dropped in the dirt. We had walls by then and canvas on the roof, but no floor yet. Robert didnt cry at all and he looked

29

at me right away like he could see me, not all dazed or squinty or squally like the others. He grew up like that too – would give me a straight look that made me a little scared of him and ashamed of myself. I loved him best cause he seemed to come from a different place from the rest of us. Maybe he did. I could never be sure, though I had my suspicions. But I could never show it, couldnt hug him or kiss him cause hed give me that look like he was holdin up a mirror to me to show me jest how bad I was.

Robert had to look after the sick ones during the swamp fever. One October John Chapman come through when all but Robert and Sal was laid up, shiverin and shakin and rattlin the beds till I was sure our neighbors could hear us even though they were a couple miles away. John Chapman had planted stinkin fennel for us near the house to use when we was poorly, but neither that nor nothin else seemed to stop us from rattlin and shakin – nothin cept time or death. This time he helped Robert and Sal with the animals and the cookin, and he picked all our apples for us.

Sadie, this is what you need, he said when he come in with a sack of spitters.

I didnt know what he meant and didnt care at the time cause I was so cold and shaky I jest wanted to die right there.

John Chapman took some of our spitters away in his canoes and paddled all the way down to Port Clinton and come back with five barrels of cider.

It wasnt hard yet, that would take some weeks, but John Chapman said to drink it and it would drive the fever out. So I drunk it and you know, I felt better. James said I was improvin by then anyway without the help of the cider. That smart remark of his was the beginnin of our apple fights that last to this day. He didnt like John Chapman payin me attention, was what it was, so he cut under whatever the man said. But John was a man of the woods, hed lived with swamp fever for many years, so why wouldnt he know what he was talkin bout? I ignored James and listened to John Chapman. He told me soft cider was fine against skeeters but hard cider was better and applejack best of all.

Id never made applejack, and he told me how. You put a barrel of cider outside in the winter, and the top where the water is freezes, and you throw away that ice, then do it again and again till youre left with just a little in the barrel, but its strong like its got fire in it with jest a little taste of apple behind it. James wouldnt drink it, said it was a waste of good cider. I didnt care – that was more jack for me. And John Chapman was right – when it was in my blood the skeeters didnt like it and left me alone, and the swamp fever didnt come. The problem was keepin enough jack around to last till August when it was really needed. We needed to make more jack, meanin we needed more trees – spitters, not the eaters from Connecticut James loved more than his own wife.

31

Golden Pippins. I didnt understand why he thought they taste so good. Went on bout honey and pineapple when all them apples tasted like was *apples*.

The next morning was a gray, rainy day, and James was teaching Robert how to graft. He had shown his son the process before, but now that he was almost nine, he was old enough to take in and retain information and make it his own.

Other years Sadie came out to watch James graft and make harsh remarks about ruining perfectly good trees. Today, though, she was still asleep, stinking of the applejack she had drunk the night before. Since John Chapman's departure she had been drinking steadily. She was an unpredictable drunk – angry and violent one minute, crying and petting the children the next. Sometimes she would sit in a corner and talk to one of her dead children – usually Patty – as if they were there with her. The living Goodenoughs had learned to ignore Sadie, though Nathan and Sal enjoyed the petting.

'We ready?' James said to his son. 'You got the scions?'

Robert held up the bundle of branches James had cut from the centers of the Golden Pippins when pruning them in November; he'd carefully stored them in the cellar behind wooden boxes of apples and carrots and potatoes, sticking the ends in a pile of soil for the winter. He'd hidden another bundle in the woods in case Sadie discovered and burned the cellar scions as she had one year, claiming she'd run out of kindling.

Lined up neatly on the ground were the tools and materials they needed for grafting: a saw, a hammer and chisel, a knife James had sharpened the previous night, a pile of strips torn from one of Sadie's old aprons and a bucket of grafting clay made from a mixture of river clay and horse dung, plus the contents of Sadie's hairbrush over a few weeks, which he'd had Martha gather without her mother's knowledge. He had also brought one of the sacks of sand he'd dug up a few years before from the Lake Erie shore, making a special trip to get it. Golden Pippins particularly favored sandy soil, and James would need to fork in sand around the grafts now and then.

Though they were ready – tools and scions and clay and sand and son – James did not move yet, but stood in the light rain with his trees. He could almost see the branches unclenching after the frozen winter, the sap starting to circulate, buds emerging in tiny dots like foxes poking their noses from their dens, testing the air. Colorless now, in a few weeks those dots would show green, signaling the leaves to come. Growth seemed to happen so slowly and yet each year leaves and blossoms and fruit came and went in their cyclical miracle.

The process of grafting did not take long, but like everything he did with apple trees – planting, winter and summer pruning, picking – James was methodical. Now, however, he must be bold. 'All right,' he said. Picking up the saw, he stepped up to one of the spitters – a mediocre producer, planted from a John Chapman seedling four years back – grasped the trunk at waist height and sawed rapidly through it, trying not to look at the nascent buds dotted along all of the branches he was cutting off, for those buds would have produced leaves and flowers and fruit. He always did this fast, as it was the destructive part, and he did not like to dwell on it. He must also move quickly before Sadie came out and witnessed the sacrifice of the source of her applejack. When she saw only the results – two sticks bound to a trunk with a ball of clay surrounding the join – rather than the act, she was not so likely to lose her temper. Confronted with something new, it could be surprisingly easy to forget what had been there before, like a man's freshly shaved beard drawing attention instead to his long hair.

The cross-section of the sacrificial tree was about three inches across – enough for two scions. 'This needs to be good and flat,' he said to Robert, scraping the surface with his knife. Then he took up the hammer and chisel. 'Now we make a cut about two inches deep, straight across.' As James hammered carefully, the feel of the handle, the tinking of metal against metal, the presence of his son at his elbow, the dripping trees, all made him think of being with his father in Connecticut, learning so that he too could create good trees and pass on the skill, over and over along the chain of Goodenoughs stretching into the future. It was not always easy to feel a part of that chain while living in the Black Swamp, especially when a child every other year was being sacrificed to it, but when he was working on apple trees, he could feel its unique tug.

James cut the ends of two Golden Pippin scions into wedge shapes. 'Look here,' he said to Robert, showing him the ends. 'A graft'll be more likely to take if there's a bud eye at the base of the wedge – see there? – where the bark begins again. Buds attract sap. You get that sap circulating through the two bits of wood, that knits them together into one tree.'

Robert nodded.

They were inserting two scions into the cross-section cleft when Sal appeared. James wished she hadn't arrived at this delicate moment in the process, with him holding open the cleft with the chisel and directing Robert to fit the scions so the bark matched that of the root stock and a bud eye was just above the surface. Only when both scions were in the right place could he withdraw the chisel so that the cleft closed around them. They had already tried it once and pulled the scions back out to cut new ends that would fit better. James did not need the daughter who reminded him the most of Sadie to come and sit nearby on a stump, and then not even watch what they were doing, but pick at the dry mud on the hem of her skirt. If she was going to be there, he wanted her to care about grafting.

'Your Ma up?' he asked, with the vague hope that a question might lure her over. Who could not be interested in the surprise and magic of grafting?

But Sal did not look up from her futile picking – any mud she removed would soon be replaced by more. 'Just for some water. Said her head hurt.'

'You getting dinner on?'

Sal shrugged, a gesture she used often. Even aged twelve she had learned that it was no good caring about things too much, and she held the world at an arm's length. 'Martha's doin' it.'

'The boys still working in the barn?'

When she did not answer, James said, 'You go and dig up the garden, then.'

'It's raining.'

'That'll make the ground easier to dig.' James renewed his grip on the chisel. Robert was fumbling with the scions, turning them to find just the right position. 'Go on, now.' When Sal did not move, James pulled the chisel from the cleft and stepped towards her. 'Git!'

Sal got up, but slowly, making it clear she was not moving because of her father's command. The memory of her mother's split lip the night before and the violence her father was capable of appeared to have no effect on her. Smirking, she sauntered back to the house rather than towards the garden. Noting the insolent set of her shoulders, James wondered when exactly he had lost authority over his family. There was no one moment, he decided, but an accumulation of Sadie's drinking and their fighting and his fixation on his trees. And John Chapman: his canny eyes on James, a judgment about his stewardship that the Goodenough children sensed. Only Robert seemed still to respect his father, and Martha was young enough to do what her father ordered.

We're sinking into this swamp, James thought. Eventually the mud is going to cover us and the Goodenoughs will all disappear.

'Pa,' Robert said, 'you think that will take?'

James looked down at the graft. The cleft had closed so snug around the scions that they appeared to have grown out of it naturally, with tiny buds set just above. He knew. Sometimes with just a glance you could tell. 'Yes, that's a good one,' he said, surprised that his one moment of disregard, when his attention had turned to his daughter, seemed not to have mattered. The graft would take without his total devotion.

He and Robert bound the graft with strips of cloth, then packed the clay around it in a clumsy, protective sphere that resembled an oversized wasps' nest. It would remain in place until summer. In just a few weeks they would be able to tell if the graft had taken: if the buds on the scion began to grow, that meant the sap was flowing from the tree on the bottom to the branch on the top. Then it would produce leaves, flowers and, in a few years, fruit.

When they were done, James showed Robert the last step of grafting, opening his fly and peeing near the new trees. They would do so for a few days until the area around the grafts was marked, to keep the deer away so they would not graze on them while the leaves were young and tender.

They grafted fifteen trees that morning, five more than James meant to. He kept finding promising-looking scions in the bundle, and feeling the press of the spitters dominating the orchard, and wanting to redress the imbalance, and so they kept going, Robert silent over the fact that they were taking five extra trees out of production for two or three years. Something had taken James over – that compulsive desire for creation overriding everything else. He would, he must, make the very best apple trees he could.

You should see em, Ma, Sal said. Theyre out there butcherin your trees like hogs.

Sal had always been a tattler. I knew she was lookin out for me more than any other Goodenough did, but that didnt make me like her more. Shed come to me and say, Ma, Marthas wet the bed, Ma, Nathan ate all the bacon, Ma, Robert let the fire go out. She wanted everything to be fair, when the best lesson she could learn was that life aint fair and theres no point expectin it to be.

My head still hurt from the applejack but I got up and looked out the window to see what this tree massacre was all about. Id forgotten James was graftin. The days smudged together so it was hard to keep track. Couldnt see nothin – they must have been in a far corner of the orchard. It was rainin and I didnt want to go out in it and have the drops hammer on my head when there was already a fearsome hammerin goin on inside. But I was curious too. So I said Ill look but you go on and dig up the garden, Sal, you know it needs it and you dont need me to tell you what to do, big gal that you are. Sal made a face but she took up the hoe and went out.

I put a shawl over my head and followed her out into the rain to see what James and Robert was doin. I stayed off to the side so they couldnt see me. They wouldnt have noticed anyhow, they was that intent on their trees. Seein them bent over a little stump, their heads almost touchin, made me want to throw rocks. It was like when the Goodenough wives back in Connecticut had their heads together by the fire, talkin and laughin and leavin me out.

Sal was right: they were butcherin the trees. Whatever numbers James had told me over and over, he couldnt have meant this many of my trees were gettin the chop. This meant war. I wanted to rage and shout and hit and kick. But I didnt. Stead I would wait for John Chapman to come back. Hed know what to do with those balls of shit James was hanging on the apple trees.

And a few days later he did come back in his canoe, glidin up the river and whistlin Bob white,

Bob white. Thank God for my John Appleseed –
and the bottles of jack he brought with him, cause
he knew I needed them, for the skeeters. They
wouldnt start bitin for a few months but I could
look after the bottles till then.

He brought the trees him and James had talked
about but didnt unload em right away from the
second canoe. Instead James wanted to show him
his devil work on the trees and took him down to
the orchard. So he saw what unnatural business
my husband had been up to. I wanted to hear
what John Chapman would say about it, but I had
to hide cause James didnt like me listenin to his
apple talk. So I snuck down along the edge of the
orchard behind the old dead brambles that barely
hid me.

John Chapman was canny and didnt say nothing
at first bout them shit balls hangin on the trees
and all the butcherin and ruinin that had gone
on. He was a businessman after all and he had
trees to sell.

You know I got a dozen good saplings in my
canoe you could have instead of seedlings, he said.

I dont want saplings, James said. Just fifteen
seedlings.

My saplings are strong, they wont die on you.
Theyll be producing fruit in three years – maybe
even two years.

We dont have the money for saplings.

I will take credit. Youre trustworthy and not
moving anywhere. Pay it back when you can.

With interest, you mean, James said. My husband aint as dumb as all that.

I see you have been doing Gods work for him again, John Chapman said, noddin at the grafted trees.

So?

Those trees will never be as strong as those grown from seed.

What, the ones you want to sell me?

Trees are stronger left to grow themselves. Man does not need to tinker with them.

So no pruning either? No thinning out trees so others grow stronger? No mulching with straw to protect em from the cold? No spreading ashes to help em grow?

God will take care of all that.

I am taking care – of the trees, of my family.

I do not think you are taking care of your wife.

I liked how John Chapman brought the conversation back to me. I liked that they were fightin about me. May have sounded like it was about trees, but it was me. I aint had men fight over me much. Maybe a little when I was just ripe. But not after ten children and nine years in a swamp.

You want to talk about trees or my wife? James said. Its one or the other.

There was a silence, then John Chapman said, Fifteen seedlings will cost you ninety cents.

James whistled. Thats a cent more per seedling than last year.

That is my price.

Thats the price I gotta pay to stop you takin an interest in Sadie?

Its you who chooses to see it that way. I am simply selling apple trees.

Bring em down, then. Ill send Robert to help you.

They went off and I was left sittin in the dead brambles, wonderin why of the three of us, I probably felt the worst.

James kept a close eye on his wife while the new grafts were vulnerable to her attention. He made a point of working near the orchard, beginning to plow the small field behind it where they would grow oats. But Sadie made no move to look at the grafts; she remained digging in the garden with Sal and Martha.

One morning when James woke he saw a muddy foot poking out from under the quilts. He glanced over at Sadie asleep beside him, then jumped up and went straight outside without even putting his boots or coat on, and ran to the orchard. One of the cows was loose among the trees, and in its wanderings it had rubbed up against seven of the fifteen graft balls, knocking them off and snapping the fragile splices. All that was left were the stumps of the root stock. The Golden Pippin scions had been trampled and chewed.

After he had shut the cow in the barn, James went back to the cabin and stood over the bed. Sadie was still asleep, her face happier and more peaceful than it should be. Or maybe he just saw what he wanted to see. He did not wake her and beat her. He did not say anything to anyone, not even to his helper Robert. Instead he mixed up more grafting clay, got out the scions he had hidden in the woods, and regrafted the trees. There was still time for them to grow, and perhaps Sadie would not notice if he did not make a fuss about it.

That night he plowed her as hard as he dared. She seemed to like it.

I was sore in the morning, snatch and head, and had to sit back down on the bed cause I felt dizzy all of a sudden. The jack can make my mornings a misery – though if I have a nip of it first thing that helps. Fight fire with fire as my Pa used to say. I wanted to ask someone to bring me a drop but for once the house was quiet. Only Martha was in, so light on her feet you couldnt hear her cept she was hummin to herself while she moved round the table and fire. She was like a little mouse waitin for me to drop a crumb for her. If I asked her for jack shed get it but hold it out so timid with her mouse paws that Id feel worse than I already did. Martha was the runt of the litter, the only weak one left who hadnt died. She hummed all the time, hymns to block out the sound of Deaths footsteps behind her. Rock of Ages, Sometimes a Light Surprises, Blest Be the Tie That Binds and that goddamn Amazin Grace. Save a wretch like me indeed.

Dunno where she knew em from – I didnt teach her. Probably it was our neighbor Hattie Day, a woman who knows her hymns and how to lord em over us.

What you makin, honey? I said to her, thinkin if I used some kind words then I could ask for the jack more easily.

Pie, she said.

I could see callin her honey made her brighten like a lantern shone on her. So I used it again. What kind of pie, honey?

That second honey was a mistake – it come out false and Martha knew she wasnt my honey.

Apple pie. Im goin to get some now, she said, then wiped her hands so there was flour up and down her apron, and ran away, leavin me all alone.

Quick before she come back I went to the bottle and took a swig. That would have to do. Dont know why I didnt want Martha seein me drink, but I didnt.

It wasnt often that no one was in the house but me. It made me nervous, I liked people around even if I didnt always want to talk to em. Back east there were too many Goodenoughs nearby and I had to hide in the hay sometimes for a little peace. Not here. The hay wasnt sweet and dry like Connecticut hay. Swamp liked to get in and rot it.

I looked around the empty room. Sal and Martha kept it neat, Ill say that for em. Wood stacked, floor swept, fire burnin clear, dishes stacked on the shelves. Up in the attic theyd have made the beds all smooth. Quilts not aired cause of the rain, but they could go a few days without airin. End of the day thered be mud tracked everywhere, a pile of muddy boots by the door, food on the floor where Caleb and Nathan dropped it. But for now it was all prepared and ready for a day of battlin the Black Swamp. We werent livin with the land, but alive despite it. Cause it wanted to kill us every chance it got, either the skeeters or the fever or the mud or the damp or the heat or the cold. At least the house was warm enough, easy to do now the winters back was broken. Sometimes durin the cold spells when the snow was high against the house, all seven of us would be huddlin by the fire wrapped in quilts and not movin the whole day cept to feed the animals and the fire and ourselves. I was glad those days were done, cause my family drove me crazy then.

Martha had already made the pastry for the pie and rolled it out on the table into a perfect circle. Jest like her. Sal or me wouldnt of bothered but left it ragged, but Martha would crimp the edges all even with her little fingers and weave a pie top that looked like checkered cloth.

I was still lookin at the pastry when she come back with her apron full of apples – spitters wed kept back from the cider press for cookin. I frowned. You gonna put some sugar in with them?

Martha peeped at me with her startled eyes. No, Ma. None left.

I already knew that when I asked her. I knew

45

what we had and didnt have. We had thirty-eight apple trees and no sugar. So what you doin with spitters? I said. Pie will be too sour to eat.

Martha didnt say anything, jest tucked her hair behind her ears like she always does.

Go back and get some of them Golden Pippins.

Martha peeped again. There arent many left, Ma.

You heard me. Go on and get em. Take those back. I nodded at the spitters shed tumbled onto the table.

Martha looked over her shoulder towards the orchard, but of course James couldnt hear. Pa wont like it, she said in a small mousy voice to go with her mousy eyes and paws.

Dont matter. You do what I say. Bring em all back here. All of em.

So she did. She took away the spitters and brought back the rest of the Golden Pippins. Funny lookin apples. Theyre little but long too, like someones pulled on em. Then she chopped em all up for the pies. Didnt say a word, but wept little mouse tears.

I couldnt wait for dinner so I could see James face when he bit into that pie. First though we had to get through the pork chops and pickled cabbage and corn pone and apple sauce – made back when we still had some sugar. James looked mighty pleased when Martha brought out the pies – gave her a big smile cause he likes pie. She served everybody a slice but herself, though nobody noticed but me. They didnt know about the apples. Course none of them cared about apple taste like James. Caleb and Nathan jest gobbled theirs down. Sal picked at her piece cause she was wet and cold from hoein in the rain and wanted to complain about that rather than enjoy some fresh baked pie by the best pie maker in the family. Even Robert ate his slice without a word, cept for a smile at his sister.

I ate mine with my eyes on my husband. James looked so contented with that first sweet taste. Only slowly did it come to him that these were his special apples, the ones he said tasted like honey and nuts but jest tasted like water to me. He squinched his face and said, What apples are in this pie?

Martha kept her eyes on her empty plate. Golden Pippins, she said so soft only I could hear. But James didnt need to ask – he knew his apples.

Whyd you use those? You know youre not supposed to cook with those. Thats what spitters are for.

He was waitin for her to say somethin but she didnt.

Are there any left?

Marthas tongue was frozen, and it seemed like the rest of her was too. Finally she managed to shake her head. I was shovelin my pie in faster and faster, expectin her to look at me any second and then James would know I was behind it and who knows what hed do then. Not knowin made me nervous and happy. But Martha didnt say another word, didnt tell him she had been obeyin me, even though it was gonna hurt her.

It did hurt her, cause he whipped her. Id been all set to laugh and tease him about wastin his apples in the pies, but whippin Martha kind of took the fun out of it. I finished my slice, but I wasnt really tastin what I was eatin. To be honest, pies are better made with spitters anyway, even without the sugar. The tartness holds up better than the sweet when its baked.

He was whipping his daughter but he was thinking of his wife. With each red strap mark that appeared across Martha's narrow buttocks and twig-like calves, James grew angrier at himself for punishing her when he should be aiming his blows at Sadie. He knew she was behind Martha's using Golden Pippins for the pies. But Martha would never admit it. In all her short life she had never tattled on anyone, preferring to take the blame. Her brothers and sisters always took advantage of her silence – all except Robert. He and Martha were both quiet, though it was not the same kind of quiet. Robert was stronger, and would stand up to someone he felt was wrong. He looked straight at people with his bright brown eyes, and his level gaze unsettled them so that they didn't dare blame him for something he did not do. Martha had watery gray eyes and never held a gaze; she tended to hunch over and keep her eyes on the ground, reminding James of a willow tree with its spindly dangling branches. This morning Sal had braided Martha's hair in a fishtail plait that did not suit her thin locks. The braid hung down her back like a frayed piece of twine with a kink in its tail, and every time James looked at it as she leaned against the wall, awaiting the strap, its wispiness made him strike her harder than he had intended. She didn't even cry properly, but was silent while tears dripped down her cheeks. Her siblings were silent too, watching the whipping, mostly indifferent. Only when James saw Robert grimace did he cease.

Sadie was smirking into her pie. 'War,' she said, and got up to go to the bottle of applejack.

Is this a war? James thought as he escaped the airless cabin. Because if it was, he would surely lose, as his wife was more experienced than he was at cruelty and ruthlessness. It was also easier to go on the offensive, as she did, than to defend, as he must his trees.

Nonetheless, he took precautions. If he was to protect them, he would do so thoroughly. Taking precious time out from plowing – turning it over to Nathan and Caleb, who as predicted did not plow straight furrows and chipped the blade – James built around each graft a shoulder-high fence made of hickory branches sharpened to points at both ends and driven into the ground. He told the family that peeing around the trees wasn't enough and they needed the fences to keep the deer away; but they were equally effective at stopping Sadie, or at least slowing her down. To

49

get to a graft she would have to pull out some of the sticks. Unfortunately it meant that James could not get close to the grafts either, depriving him of the pleasure of inspecting them closely for progress. He could only peer at them from several feet away, when what he wanted to do was squeeze the buds and scrape his nail along the scion's bark to see if it was greening. He still did not feel secure enough, and so he ringed the older Golden Pippins with deer fences as well, though they were mature enough that deer were unlikely to want their tougher leaves. Even as he built them he worried that the fences might send a signal to Sadie, tempting her to mischief she had not even thought of.

Luckily spring was such a busy time of year that she was unlikely to visit the orchard. There was too much to do: plowing and planting fields of oats and corn, digging and planting the kitchen garden, repairing roofs, cleaning out the barn and the house. While James worked with Nathan and Caleb in the fields, Sal and Martha dug the garden, and Robert swung between garden and field, helping whoever needed it most.

Because she did not like digging and did not mind making her daughters do it, Sadie mostly stayed out of the garden, and spring-cleaned the house after the long winter, throwing back the doors and windows, sweeping and scrubbing and beating and dusting. This was when she could be bothered. Sadie had never been very house-proud, not even back east. She was even less interested in it in Ohio, where it was harder to keep clean. She would get an idea into her head that something needed to be done – the quilts aired, for instance. Then she would make a great show of stringing a rope between two trees and bringing out the quilts to hang up and beat. Inevitably she would carry too much at once, and drag the ends through the mud so that they had to be scrubbed – not by Sadie, who never liked to fix what she had broken. Sal, or more likely Martha, would have to boil water and wash out the mud. By then Sadie would have moved on to another task, such as scrubbing every surface with so much vinegar that the sour acrid smell drove the family outside again. She moved between extremes: attractive when she was loving, which wasn't often these days; or, more often, unpredictable, vicious or indifferent. James had to remind himself of the lively girl in the blue dress who had wrapped her legs around him and laughed. That Sadie was long gone, left somewhere in a field in Connecticut, the dress faded to the color of the sky.

At least she did not touch his grafts. After the declaration of war and the letting loose of the cow, she let it drop – typical of Sadie. James did not trust her, though. She might be addled with applejack most of the time, but she did not forget grudges. Indeed, she seemed to relish holding tight to them.

One April day after they had finished plowing and planting the fields, James was walking through the woods along one of the old Indian trails they didn't use much, looking for muskrat push-ups he could set snares near, when he became aware of a green haze overhead. The leaves on the trees had come out, small and new and creased like a summer quilt that has been folded away during the winter months and needs a day or two of shaking out to become smooth. Although he knew that unless God had other, apocalyptic plans, it would happen every year, James was always caught off guard by the leaves' appearance. He thought he had been keeping a close watch, yet they still managed to surprise him so that he never caught the midpoint between closed bud and open leaf.

With his eyes on the leaves, he stepped into a mudhole that slopped over the top of his boots and stank of rot. James cursed and stopped to shake them out. This was why his children often went through the swamp barefoot – it was easier washing your feet than getting boots clean of swamp mud. But James hated the squelching clay between his toes, and preferred the civility of shoes.

When he stood up again he noticed, just off the path, a gray-brown boll plastered around the sawn-off branch of a wild apple tree, a small wand sticking up out of it. It was the tree he'd once eaten sour fruit from when he was desperate for the taste of apples.

He stepped up to the graft, but didn't even need

to examine it to know it was Robert's work, for it looked exactly like a graft James himself would have made. There was no one within a hundred miles who could copy him so well. Not only that: the graft had taken, with buds on the scions close to bursting into leaves. He couldn't be sure until it flowered, but he suspected the blossoms would be tinged the pink of Golden Pippins. Robert was thinking ahead, cultivating an apple tree out of Sadie's way. James smiled at his son's foresight.

Though he should have gone on to look for signs of muskrats – the drag of their tails, the underwater entrance in the stream he was following – James instead did something a settler would never normally do during the busy springtime when food stores are still low and there is so much work to be done. He did nothing. Lowering himself onto a damp log, he sat and looked at the green fuzz taking over the trees, at the birds flitting through the branches as they built nests, at the trout lilies and trilliums and Dutchman's breeches at his feet and at the graft his son had created at a safe remove from Sadie and her wrath.

Gradually he relaxed on the log in a way he never could around people. He liked to note the cycle of the trees through the seasons, with their leaves unfurling to an intense green, then flaring and browning and falling. Trees did not talk back, or willfully disobey, or laugh at him. They were not here to torment him; indeed, they were not here for him at all. James' sitting under them did not matter one way or another, and for that he was profoundly grateful.

He contemplated the grafted Golden Pippin before him, and wondered how long it would manage to grow before the Black Swamp got to it with mildew or mold or rot. Humid swampland, full of grasses and reeds and trees run wild, was not ideal for an apple tree – though the wild one had managed somehow.

James sighed and looked down at his hands, roughened and scarred from years of the worst kind of hard work – the futile kind. After nine years he knew he should have gotten used to the life here. The Goodenoughs were old-timers compared to all the newcomers whose axes rang through the woods as they fought the trees. They were now the people new settlers came to for advice on how to drain a field to grow barley (Grow potatoes), on how to keep the skeeters at bay (Wear mittens in August), on whether the numerous bullfrogs were tasty enough to eat in a pinch (You'll find out).

At last he got to his feet. He would not tell Robert he'd found the grafted tree. There were few secrets in a family who lived in such close quarters, but he would keep one now.

As he walked back towards the farm he was overwhelmed by the need to look at the grafts in his orchard. They had shown no sign of budding on the top scions as Robert's already had, but it was hard to tell with the spiked deer fences keeping him away. Now with the leaves emerging all around in the woods, he had to know if the grafts had been a success.

He spotted it from the edge of the orchard: an applejack bottle tipped upside down and hung over one of the fence spikes. James' stomach twisted. Drawing closer, though, he saw that the grafted trees were still intact, and in fact were all budding above the graft. Their leaves would open soon, to join the rest of the greening woods.

The upended bottle was a reminder that Sadie was watching them too.

James always said the best part about May was that the apple blossoms were out. He would say that. For me the best part was goin to Perrysburg for the first time since November. It was only twelve miles away but with the state of the roads it might as well be a hundred, we were that cut off. By May the snow was gone and the mud was bad but not as bad as April. And our stocks were real low then – wed been livin on bacon and squirrels and corn pone for months. It was always hard in the spring how everything was growin but we had so little food to eat. Id been dreamin of bread made with flour and of eggs – fox got most of the chickens – of coffee and tea and of a stir of sugar to go in it. Needed some lettuce seeds, some tomato seeds. Besides that, our boots all had holes and the plow blade needed mendin. Id run out of white thread and was havin to repair quilts and shirts the mice got to with brown. James wanted nails. We needed a couple of chickens.

And all of us wanted to see other people. The Goodenoughs were sick of the Goodenoughs. Who wouldnt be, trapped in that cabin all the long winter. Back in Connecticut the winters were hard but there was family all around and plenty of neighbors too. If I got sick of one of those Goodenough wives I could go into another room and sit with another one. If James drove me crazy I could talk to Charlie Goodenough. I could run down the road to a neighbor or to my mother or sisters. Here the neighbors were too far to run to in the snow and cold just for fun. And they got that mad-eyed look from the mud and the cabin fever. None of them were people I wanted to spend my days with, though James said I was too picky. Why dont you visit with Hattie Day, he kept sayin. Ill tell you why. That woman was dull as a bucket of water. I sat with her once to sew and fell asleep over my patchwork. Id brought Sal with me and she had to kick me to wake me up. After that Sal and I got the giggles while Hattie Day jest sat there frownin. Looked over her specs perched on the end of her piggy nose and told us it was time for us to git home before dark even though the sun still had hours left in the sky.

Perrysburg had some life to it – a few stores, a blacksmith, a tavern or two, a school. And people. Thats what it had. Every time I went I sucked up the people, starin at their faces till they made a face at me to stop. I could see em laughin at us swamp folk with our backwater ways and the mud we shed from our clothes. I didnt care, I was that glad to see other people.

Best of all was that there was a big camp meeting every May, went on for days in tents pitched jest outside of town. We stayed a night or two, depending on James mood. They got preachers talkin all day and all night and I stayed up listenin to the God talk and singin the hymns. Bein at the revival set me up for a time, gave me a reason to smile. It wasnt the God talk that made me so happy, though I liked that well enough. It was the other people, especially the ones that stayed up late like me. At home nobody ever wanted to stay up with me, so at the meetings I was glad to be with my other night owls. Wed sing and share bottles – though lots of the preachers frowned on whiskey or jack and we kept the bottles low so they didnt see. James and the children would go to sleep back in the wagon and Id jest carry on all night with my new friends.

It was always hard to leave the camp meetings. Id have stayed a week if I could but James never wanted to. Hed start talkin about gettin back home practically the minute we left the farm, fret about the corn or the trees or the snares hed set. Or he worried about the children left behind, that theyd set fire to the chimney or the cow would get loose or theyd get bit by a rattler. After a time all those worries would take him over and wed have to go back.

We always left two behind. We had to, to protect our property and feed the animals and milk the cow and keep the fire goin. We had to leave one of the older ones, Nathan or Caleb, who could shoot an Indian or a fox or a rattler if they had to. Then we left another to keep em company and run for help. Nathan and Caleb took turns each time we went but the younger children drew straws. Sals a cheater and never had to stay behind. The last few times Martha drew the short straw. Typical of that gal.

She drew the short straw this time too and you should of seen her face. Ill stay back, Robert said. You go in my place, I dont mind.

Martha gave him a smile made me want to kick a cat. No, I said, that would jest defeat the purpose of drawin straws. Otherwise you might as well volunteer to stay every time. Straws means its fate and no ones fault, so no one gets the blame.

But—

No, I interrupted him. And dont you ever talk back to your mother or youll get a whippin will send you straight to Sandusky.

He gave me that Robert look cause he knew I would never whip him. But he didnt argue with me. Sorry, Martha, he said. Im selling some squirrels tails and Ill buy you some candy. You want lemon or peppermint?

Lemon, she said real quiet. Fool should of chose peppermint. The taste is stronger.

We took the wagon for sleepin in and for the

58

supplies but we walked most of the way to Perrysburg, takin turns to ride and rest our feet. Wed learned what we didnt know when we first tried to come through the swamp – you keep the wagon light on the corduroy road and it dont get stuck so much. Also we had a pair of oxen now that were used to swamp ways – the old Connecticut horses died, one of a leg broke goin through the logs laid across to make up the road, the other cause it was jest too damned tired of all the swamp work it had to do. The oxen were big and dumb but they knew how to step along a rough corduroy road.

I didnt mind walkin cause we were goin some-where and it was sunny and there was other wagons and people walkin to Perrysburg for the same reasons as us – supplies and the camp meeting. So I talked to em while James jest nodded and kept to himself. Made me some friends along the road I promised to find at the camp. Heard there was plans to start to macadamize this road in a month or two. Meant it would be easier to get around. Easier to leave too.

Closer to Perrysburg the road was better and the oxen went easier and I was tired so I rode a while settin next to James while Sal and Nathan and Robert walked a little behind. We was quiet, content for a change. Jest for a little while I could forget James and me were havin a war.

I hear theyre settin to start fixin this road soon, I said.

James grunted.

Be work there for some. Nathan and Caleb could work on it, bring in some money. Jest while we can spare em till harvest.

James still didnt say anything. I could tell he wasnt really listenin to me.

Then he said, Sadie, you ever think about goin back?

I was so surprised I didnt say anything for a minute. Back where? I said then though I knew what he meant.

Back east.

I didnt know whether I wanted to lie or tell the truth. No, I said finally.

Well, I been thinkin about it.

Damn. I looked out at the trees along the road. The leaves were all bright and there were still some dogwood flowers out. A yellow butterfly was flappin over the road like a little leaf got caught up in the wind. Suddenly everything looked different. Why? I said.

Its too hard here. Theres always something dying.

We didnt lose any children last year. Thats somethin.

We lost nine trees.

I begun to laugh. Thats what this is about? Those goddamned trees? Five of our children died in this swamp and you want to go back because of trees?

James gritted his teeth so his jaw flexed and I felt the thrill I got when he was angry. Are we goin to fight right here on the road with people all around? I thought. Cause there were people ahead of us and behind us, and they would all get to see the Goodenoughs go at each other. If I was lucky Id give him a buckeye he could show off in Perrysburg.

But he didnt hit me. He surprised me again. This is a hard life to be passing on to our children, he said. I will feel guilty about that all my life, that we could have made it easier for them by staying in Connecticut. Then there wouldnt have been so many died, and so much death and hard work in their futures.

Theyll be all right, I said. Five children. That aint so bad. Sides, we got nothin back east. Your familys got no land for you.

I was surprisin myself by defendin us stayin in the Black Swamp. So many times over the years Id wished we could load the wagon and head back. But too much time had gone by, and when I thought about Connecticut it didnt make me smile. Instead I remembered how the wives all hated me. I could even admit now that Charlie Goodenough had probably been relieved to see the back of me. There was nothing to return for. Besides, we had five children buried in the swamp. We couldnt leave em.

Sadie, James said, that swamp is defeating me. I cant even grow fifty apple trees.

Numbers again. Dont worry bout that goddamn number, I said. Nobodys countin but you.

★   ★   ★

Perrysburg always made James feel a little better and then a little worse. Seeing the small collection of rough buildings after miles of trees and marsh reeds made his heart beat faster. Here was smoke from chimneys. Here were right angles and pine boards planed at a mill. Here was whitewash. Here were curtains in windows, and windowpanes rather than paper greased with bear fat. Here were planks to walk on over mud, hitching posts, the sound of laughter, even the tinkle of a piano. Here were women wearing brightly colored hats and dresses with hems that weren't muddy. Here was civilization that did not rely on Goodenough sweat to make it happen.

Very soon he felt worse, though. For all the hardships of the swamp, there was a purity to it that Perrysburg lacked, or had destroyed. Buildings had been raised with no thought to the surroundings. Bits of wood had been left where they fell – splinters from planks, ends hacked off and strewn about, stumps half-chopped and then abandoned. Piles of earth left from excavated cold cellars had been rained and snowed on so that they solidified into ugly miniature mountains. Here and there were smoldering piles of leaves and rags. The outhouses stank of shit. No one cleared up the horse dung from the street. The planks outside the saloons were slick with spit and piss and puke. When anticipating a trip to Perrysburg, James always managed to forget about this aspect of the town. Now as he looked about him from the safety of the wagon seat, he had a sudden desire to be back on the farm, in the orchard, where the apple trees were blooming. It was the most beautiful time of the year there and he was missing it to come and be among people and their dirt.

The Goodenoughs scattered the moment James pulled up: Sadie to look over the merchandise in Fuller's General Store, Nathan and Robert to trade their squirrel tails, Sal to look for other girls. James would ride on to the blacksmith to drop off the plow blade, then bring his own furs to the trading post. He reminded Sadie that they would not have much to spend. She gave him a look. 'Got to get flour and thread and nails and sugar. Fabric for new shirts for Caleb – he's grown out of everything we got. Shoes need mending. We need seeds.'

'No ribbons, that's what I meant,' James said. 'Brown sugar, not white. And leave the shoes – we won't need 'em for the summer. We can get 'em fixed in the fall.'

Sadie snorted and disappeared inside. Now that he had forbidden ribbons, she would probably buy some.

He left the plow blade with the blacksmith, frowning at the cost, and arranged to pick it up the next day. That would mean only one night at the camp meeting, James hoped – though he knew the repaired blade could wait at the blacksmith's for a few days. He was always looking for reasons not to stay at the camp. All those noisy people praising the Lord made him uncomfortable.

He went on to the trading post to see what he could get for the furs and pelts he had brought in the wagon, a bundle that represented the winter's hunting and eating: muskrats, beavers, rabbits. Nathan and Robert were already there, watching the proceedings and jingling the few coins they had made from their squirrels. From all over the area, men and boys were bringing in skins. Like the Goodenoughs, most of the swamp people brought in muskrats and beavers and deer, but a few had made more exotic kills: a polecat, a few wolves, a fox with a bushy red tail. One brought in a black bear skin, and everyone stroked it, though the greasy musk was so strong and persistent that James smelled it on his hands for the rest of the day.

As they were leaving – James disappointed with the prices he got, for he was not a good haggler – a ragged man with a ginger beard entered and threw down the pelt of a panther. 'There!' he cried, triumphant. 'Betcha ain't seen many of these!'

They hadn't, and stopped to look: the sleek midnight fur, the cat's fangs frozen into a snarl, one eye gone, the other dead yellow. Nathan stayed behind with the crowd to admire it, but Robert followed his father out. James was not sentimental about animals; he'd killed to eat – pigs, chicken, deer, wild birds, rabbits, boars – without hesitation. But the cat's snarl made him sad.

He grew uneasy as they approached Fuller's. It was bad enough that he would have to tell Sadie he'd gotten less than expected for his furs, so that even buying brown sugar was out of the question. He was also nervous about going into the shop at all. Though run by men, and with plenty of male customers, general stores were still a woman's domain, something James had felt even back in Connecticut. The gossip, the laughter, the emphasis on the look of things – the yellowness of the corn-meal, the redness of the check cloth, the shininess of the silver pins – seemed to him to be misplaced priorities. He understood the pragmatism behind it – pale cornmeal was not as tasty; tarnished pins left marks on fabric – but James could not take an active interest himself. Stepping inside the shop, he noted that most of the other men there were standing around the edges of the room and remaining silent as well.

Sadie was in the center, a few women gathered around. That was not new: she always found her way to the center. Her voice could be heard even from outside the store, and made him wince. She was talking about apples. As he sidled in she was saying, 'Don't know why he's got such a sweet tooth he has to have eatin' apples all the time instead of spitters. Cider's what we need, not apples to eat. Don't it feel good to have those barrels full of cider lined up, and the bottles of applejack. And the vinegar, of course.' James suspected Sadie tacked vinegar on to the list because of the reaction of a short woman standing nearby, who jerked her head at the mention of applejack. It was Hattie Day, the Goodenoughs' closest neighbor. Two more different women you could not imagine in the same room: Hattie Day was short and stout and shapeless, with a broad, smile-free face and a sideways look that implied many thoughts, all held back. She had unfortunate taste in hats; today she was wearing a stiff straw one with a straight brim that sliced across her forehead, trimmed with tiny white silk flowers that had gone gray from swamp life. James did not notice women's hats much, but he could see it did not suit her. Even Sadie's ragged bonnet was better than those limp gray flowers.

But he would not judge. The Days had been their neighbors for seven years, and Hattie had set aside her own wordless judgment many times in order to help out the Goodenoughs, whether through fever or flood or hunger or one of Sadie's rages when she ran out of applejack. The Days were prudent farmers, John Day a good hunter, and they had no children, so they always had enough to spare.

It wasn't all one way. Sal and Martha had been sent over on wash day to help Hattie. James and the boys had helped John Day build a bigger barn and harvest corn and hay. But the Days seemed to be in control of their farm, and treated the Goodenoughs' help as if they could get by without it – which they probably could. James never talked to John Day about apples, or offered to trade scions or help him to graft eaters. He couldn't help envying how the Day farm seemed steadily to grow, with a little more land cleared, an extra cow bought, a smokehouse added, a pantry filled with more jars of food than they could eat in a year. The only way in which they did not expand was children – which made the other expansion irrelevant in James' eyes. For all his envy of the cows, the army of jars and an orchard planted with exactly fifty apple and pear trees, he would not want to switch places with them.

'I'll tell you what I did,' Sadie continued now to the group of women. 'We only had a few eaters left, and I used 'em all up in a pie! You should've seen my husband's face when he tasted it. You'd of thought he was eatin' his own children, the way he went on about it!'

The women around her laughed, except for Hattie Day, who seemed to take a step away from Sadie's words, and began examining bolts of fabric. Her move away was not subtle enough, though. James could have told her there was nothing Sadie hated more than to have someone choose not to listen to her. Leaving her admiring circle, she followed the one person not taking in every word. 'What would you do if your husband was crazy about apples, Hattie?' she said.

Hattie Day gazed at Sadie. 'I would be glad my husband was growing something good and plentiful to eat,' she said. 'It's a hard life in the swamp.

Least he can do is enjoy his apples.' She turned her back on Sadie and went over to the shopkeeper, pointedly engaging him in conversation. Sadie stood alone for a moment, the other women smirking behind her at such a public slight.

It was a rare feeling, but James pitied his wife. She had never really learned how to get along with other women, he'd noticed. Those worthy of her did not take to her, and Sadie usually ended up with the sycophantic or the unsound. She'd had a terrible time with his brothers' wives: seeing her with them was like watching someone pet a cat against its fur.

He looked down, then stepped towards her as if he hadn't seen her or heard what she'd said about him and the apples. 'Got the fur money,' he said. 'You can get some sugar, and a ribbon or two.'

'White sugar?'

'Yes, white sugar.' It was worth the further debt he would get into, just to see her rare grateful smile. Women might shun her, but James would not.

Id never been to a camp meeting till we moved to Ohio. They aint something New England Methodists ever needed – we had our churches to go to every Sunday. But there were no churches in the Black Swamp, only one in Perrysburg. Imagine wadin through all that mud or snow or with a fever to get to a church twelve miles away, then find out the preacher was sick or stuck somewhere.

So we got our religion readin the Bible, and once or twice a year at camp meetings held out in the woods outside of Perrysburg. People came from all over, and like us Goodenoughs they were straight out of the swamp and starved of company. Wed gone when there were a thousand people gathered, maybe even two thousand, sleepin in wagons or under canvas strung between trees.

This time we left our wagon and went into the woods to find a place to set. James hung back cause he was always like that at camp meetings, leavin it to me to fit us in. It was crowded with people settin all over, spreadin out quilts to claim their place. Looked like there werent no space but I found a little opening between two families and spread out a Goodenough quilt – a frayed old nine-patch I would have to get Martha to mend again – and though they gave us the side eye, the people next to us shifted a little and we squeezed ourselves in. Five minutes later another family done the same thing, and by this time we were old hands and had the right to grunt and roll our eyes at them for makin it more crowded. But for the most part people was that happy to be with others that no one stayed mad for long.

At the camps everybody brought food and cooked over fires, some families for themselves, others pitchin in together. Course James wanted the Goodenoughs to keep to ourselves, while I was all for joinin with others. But I was the cook so I decided what we were goin to do. Near us there was a big pot hung over a fire, and I added a knuckle of ham to it without askin James or anybody else. Once Id done that the women tendin the pot got a whole lot friendlier, welcomin me in to cook and chat. I sent Nathan and Robert off to look for firewood. Nathan complained that with so many people around and hundreds of fires, there wouldnt be wood close by and theyd have to go a long way to find any. But I made em go anyway, and Sal went off to find some other gals, and James went out to the road to stand by the wagons and listen to the other men without sayin a word himself. Then I could relax and start to enjoy myself.

There were so many people campin that we were a ways from the platform where the preachers stood so everybody could see em and hear em. Once Id made sure people had seen me do my share of stirrin the pot and Nathan and Robert had brought back armfuls of wood, I slipped off to hear some God talk.

I hadnt been to a camp meeting since the previous summer, and the only God talk Id had since then had been John Chapmans, with all his big words like correspondences and redemption and regeneration. These preachers were very different from him. They was usually Methodist ministers, but now and then youd get a stray Baptist or Congregationalist preacher come through and get a turn to speak. We wasnt picky that way. In fact of all the preachers I liked the

Baptists best. The Methodists I was used to from my childhood, and they talked a long time without sayin anything new. But the Baptists shouted with fire straight from their bellies – straight from God, I expect. Also they asked questions and we could call back to em.

When Id pushed my way up so I was close enough to hear I knew I was in luck and it was a Congregationalist preacher – they was almost as good as the Baptists. I couldnt see him but I heard him ask: Where do you think God is today?

Hes here, people round me answered.

Where did you say He is?

Right here with us.

Does He ever leave you?

No he does not.

Is He in your heart?

Yes he is.

Is He in your hands?

Yes he is.

No! *You* are in *His* hands. Where are you?

In His hands.

Right away I got that soarin feelin of not havin to think or make any decisions, jest answerin with the crowd what the preacher and God wanted me to say. Thats what I loved about camp meetings – lettin go of my whole life so I didnt have to think about James or the children or what we were gonna eat or the hardship of livin in the Black Swamp. I could jest be.

Course it helped that I had a little jack in me by

71

then. Somewhere between the cookin pot and the preacher Id managed to get handed a bottle, and I took a big gulp cause I didnt know when Id get another chance. It was powerful strong jack, stronger than what I was used to. It cut a path straight to my belly then spread out all over so that I tingled to my fingertips and toes. It loosened my tongue too so it was easy to shout back at the preacher.

Then he got us to sing, and I liked that even better. The hymns were different from what I knew back home but they were easy enough to pick up, and more fun to sing too. I sang real loud:

> This night my soul has caught new fire
> Halle, hallelujah!
> I feel that Heaven is drawin nigher
> Glory hallelujah!
>
> Shout, shout, we are gainin ground
> Halle, hallelujah!
> Satans kingdom is tumblin down
> Glory hallelujah!

I jumped as high as I could when I sang, Shout shout. People round me were singin too, but I noticed a couple of women were givin me those side eyes looks I knew too well, and the men were laughin and I knew it was at me. The good thing about camps is theyre so big you can jest move and after a few minutes youll be with new people who are more welcomin.

I made my way round, callin and singin and movin, and then there was another bottle and I stayed a while havin a spree with those friendly people till they turned on me all of a sudden like a mean dog and I had to move on.

Preachers changed a few times – some quieter, some talked so long I fell asleep and someone poked me awake cause I was snorin.

Then along came a real Baptist preacher who was the best of all. He was jest a little man but with a long brown beard ended in a point. He had on a yaller checkered suit, and though he was in the sun and sweatin like a man choppin wood, he still kept his jacket on. He stood completely still on the platform and started off real soft so at first I couldnt hear him. Then he got a little louder, sayin: I feel the Lord now. Do you feel the Lord?

Yes, a few people said.

I feel the Lord now, he repeated. Do you feel the Lord?

A few more said, Yes I feel the Lord.

He jest said it over and over. I feel the Lord now. Do you feel the Lord? Each time he was a little louder.

Yes I feel the Lord, I said all of a sudden. It jest popped out of my mouth without me even thinkin.

Then the preacher started to shake a little bit – his hands, then his arms, then his chest. And he was repeatin himself over and over and shakin a little more and a little more until he was head to toe shakin, and then we were all of us answerin,

73

Yes, I feel the Lord, over and over like a wave. And I couldnt help it, I started to shake too, it was like a force took me over. My teeth started chatterin like I had the swamp fever, and my arms were jerkin so I hit people round me without meanin to. But they was flailin too, we were all shakin together and sweatin and crying and shoutin, Yes I feel the Lord! Id never felt so good in all my life, not even when I went with Charlie Goodenough way high up in the new hay in the barn and lay with him. I was full of joy, and full of the Lord.

And in the middle of all that jumpin and jerkin and shoutin I opened my eyes, which had sweat rollin into them and stingin them, and I looked across the field of writhin witnesses to the Lord and I saw Robert standin still. It was easy to see him cause he was the only person not movin. And he was lookin at me.

His look made me want to stop, cause there was no God in it, jest a boy lookin at his mother and thinkin, Why, Ma?

I couldnt stand that, cause I didnt want to stop. So I turned my back on him. I turned my back on my son. Then I started jumpin and shoutin again, but it wasnt the same as before – not at all. Suddenly I saw myself the way he saw me, and it was so ugly I had to sit down in the middle of all those people and cry. Real tears now, not what the preacher had wrung from me. These were the real tears from God.

★   ★   ★

James found the talk by the wagons tiring after a while. He liked to listen, and he had thoughts of what he'd like to say about the weather, or the corn crop, or the road being macadamized, or the rascals in Congress. But he never quite had the courage to speak them aloud. By the time he had formed words to his liking, the conversation had moved on.

Then one of the men in the circle James was hovering near commented, 'Lost eight apple trees this winter.'

Without thinking James said, 'I lost nine.'

'Four,' another said.

'Two, but I've got my eye on a third that's still not blossomed.'

'I didn't lose any. Luck, I guess. If there is luck in this swamp.'

'What kind you got? Seek-No-Further? Fall Queens? Milans?'

'No – Early Chandler. From back east. I grew it from seed.'

There was a pause, then James said, 'I grafted fifteen Golden Pippins this spring.'

'Golden Pippin,' the first man repeated. 'Never heard of it. Where's it from?'

'A tree from Connecticut, and before that, England. My grandparents brought it over. It's a yellow apple, an eater.'

'What's its yield?'

'Usually ten bushels a year.'

'Not bad. And the taste?'

'Honey and nuts, then pineapple at the end,' James answered almost automatically. He had been describing that taste all his life.

'You grafted them, you say?'

'I did.'

'You use wax on the strips?'

'Don't need to. Clay's enough, as long as you mix hair into it to keep it from breaking.'

'The grafts take?'

'Yup.' James almost added that the grafts had blossomed, but decided he'd better not overstate their success.

The talk moved on, but those few minutes were enough to elate him for several hours – all the way through the long evening and into the night of preaching and singing, eating stew and listening to folks talk. His good mood was ruined only when he was making his way through the woods towards the wagon to get to sleep, and stumbled upon Sadie, skirts up, being pumped by the ginger man who'd brought in the panther fur to the trading post. They were both so drunk they didn't notice him, not even when he held his lantern high to shine down on them. He watched them for a moment. Then he knocked the man off Sadie like he was flicking a fly off a piece of pie. The man didn't fight back, but lay in a slump and started to snore. Sadie looked up at her husband in the lantern light and laughed.

'We're going,' he said. 'You coming?'

'I ain't finished yet.'

James said nothing more, but turned away

and continued threading through sleeping forms all over the ground. It was hard not to step on people, and his boot caught hands and ankles and shoulders, leaving shouts and mutterings in his wake. He did not respond, for he was in no mood to apologize to anyone.

He found the oxen tethered in the field where he'd left them, asleep on their feet. James patted them for a moment before blowing into their nostrils, resisting the urge to yank them; he must not take out his rage on innocent beasts.

The oxen were reluctant to start up again in the dark. A handful of oats and an apple – a spitter but they didn't seem to mind – at last roused them, and James led them over to the wagon, where the children were asleep under the nine-patch quilt. He raised his lantern and studied it for a moment. The quilt had come with them from Connecticut nine years before – new then, finished in a hurry by Sadie and his sisters, for they had decided to go west suddenly. James knew the squares well, even in the dim lantern light. They were made up of fabric from dresses and aprons and old sheets and other scraps of family: a worn yellow bonnet of his mother's, a blue skirt of Sadie's that had torn, his brother Charlie's breeches, also torn. His whole Connecticut family was sewn into it in quick, uneven stitches now unraveling in places. There were tears between the squares where the stuffing was coming through. But despite its ragged appearance, it was a comfort.

James did not wake his children, but once he'd hitched up the team of oxen and they began to move up the road, Robert sat up. Soon he had joined James on the seat.

'We going home?'

'Yes.'

James was grateful it was Robert who'd woken. Nathan or Sal would have peppered him with questions. 'Does Ma know?' was all Robert said.

'She'll make her own way back.'

They said nothing for a time, sitting in the dark, only the light of the lantern hanging on the wagon to guide them. 'Pa,' Robert said after a while, 'what about the plow blade and the supplies we left in Perrysburg? Don't we have to pick them up?'

James let the oxen continue on for a minute before he pulled up the reins. 'Goddammit.' In his haste to get away from Sadie he had not thought about anything other than getting home as fast as possible.

'It isn't far, Pa,' Robert said. 'Just a turning a little ways back.' He sounded like a parent soothing a child.

James held the reins in his hands and listened. A deep darkness settled around him that would not shift for many hours. There was no moon, and the stars were very bright – a poetic rather than a practical light. He sighed, thinking about having to wait outside the blacksmith's until the man opened for business.

But there was nothing he could do except to turn

the wagon around and start back, feeling foolish. Luckily it was only Robert he had to feel foolish in front of. When they reached Perrysburg, Robert joined his brother and sister back in the bed and soon slept as well. James remained awake, sitting and trying not to think about his wife.

His children did not stir until the dawn chorus, which James noted was as loud in town as it was in the swamp. Then Sal sat up, hair in her eyes, looking like a younger Sadie. 'Where's Ma?'

'At the camp.' James studied the blacksmith's windows in the dim pink light the sun gave off to announce its arrival.

'Why ain't she with us?'

James did not respond.

'Where are we?'

'Perrysburg.'

'Camp ain't far. I could go back and get her.' But Sal did not move, despite knowing she was her mother's best chance. She was not a girl who would do more than the minimum required of her. She looked at her brothers, asleep on either side of her, and chose Robert to nudge awake. 'Go and get Ma,' she said. Robert did not sit up, but turned his brown eyes on her.

'Robert isn't going anywhere,' James said. 'No one is. We're waiting here for the blacksmith and the store to open so we can pick up our supplies. Then we'll head home. Your Ma can come when she's ready.'

'But she don't know the way!' Sal began to snivel.

It was true that Sadie had never been good with directions. There was only one road towards the Portage River, but she might find it hard to tell which turning to take off of it to get to their property – the old Indian trails all looked the same if you didn't know them well, and if you were drunk. James had a vision of Sadie wandering in the woods and a grim smile crossed his face. 'She'll work it out.'

Sal lay back down but continued to sob; she seemed to enjoy the drama of it. Nathan still slept – he could sleep through the loudest thunderstorms – but Robert got up and rejoined his father. James reached into a burlap sack at his feet, pulled out two cold johnnycakes, and handed one to his son. As they ate, they watched the rim of the sun squeeze up over the trees to start another day.

'How long do you think the blacksmith will be, Pa?' Robert asked.

'An hour or so. He's a big man – he'll want a big breakfast.'

Robert nodded.

James glanced behind him to make sure Nathan and Sal were asleep. Then he cleared his throat to dislodge the words that were stuck there along with the johnnycake. 'I saw the graft you made out in the woods,' he said quietly so that Sal would not hear.

'You think it will take?'

'It already has. That was good grafting.' James rarely praised his children. He had never felt he had to.

'What if Ma finds it?'

'She never goes out there.' Even as he was saying it, though, doubt wrenched at the part of him where he kept his love of apple trees. Robert's graft was on one of the Indian trails near the main path to their cabin. If Sadie got lost coming back – which she was likely to do – she could easily take that path and stumble upon the graft. And if she were angry and scared, he knew just what she'd do to the tree.

'You want me to go and get her?'

Everythin was hurtin. My head from the jack. My throat from the screechin and callin to the preacher. My snatch from the wild ginger man. And I was lyin in some brambles that scratched me every time I moved.

After a bit I managed to turn my head, then propped myself up on my elbows so I could see what was goin on round me. Everywhere there were people busy makin themselves presentable after the night – women brushin and braidin their hair, men pissin in the woods, people makin fires and mixin cornmeal into patties to fry. I smelled bacon somewhere.

I seemed to be the only one still on the ground, the only one hurtin all over, though I was sure some of these people had done things last night to make parts of them hurt too. Why was it I was always the one to get caught out? Everybody else could sin and still have smooth hair and an innocent smile

81

in the morning. But me, I had my skirt up round my knees and hair like Id been dragged through a hedge, my breath stank and only God had any idea where my bonnet was.

I pulled my skirt down and twisted my hair into a bun and held it with a twig cause Id lost my hairpins. Then I stood though my head hurt even more and brushed my skirt off. It had some blood on it and dirt and other things I couldnt do much about. I didnt look at anyone though I could feel them givin me the side eye again. I jest started walkin through the camp, tryin to find a way to the wagon. There were so many people though and it was so big and my head hurt so that I didnt know where I was.

I thought I was goin to cry. Then I saw Hattie Day busyin herself foldin a quilt. And I went up and took the other end to help her and I said, Hattie, I know you dont like me but please can you jest show me the way to where all the wagons are. She looked at me with a drop of pity in her eyes and pointed. Normally I hate pity from anyone, but this time I thought maybe a drop would do me no harm. So I thanked her and handed her the ends of the quilt and headed in the direction shed showed me.

I got out to the road at last and walked along the long line of wagons but I couldnt find ours. I was tryin not to panic but my teeth were chatterin and my hands were shakin even though it wasnt cold.

My family was gone. I could feel it. I was all alone. That made me stop in the middle of the road and jest stand there. A wagon was comin towards me and a man was shoutin at me to get out of the way, but I couldnt move. Tears was runnin down me on the inside and the outside.

Ma.

I turned round and there was Robert. Of all of my family I was glad it was him that found me, cause I loved him best even when he made me feel the worst. Robert was the Goodenough with the most future in him, the one the swamp wouldnt get.

He held out his hand and said, I come to fetch you.

I was still cryin and I let him take my hand and lead me away like I was a child.

AMERICA

1840–1856

Smithson Fery
Kingsvill
Canada

Janery 1, 1840

Godenufs
Blak Swamp
Portig River
Neer Pearysburg
Ohio

Deer Brothers and Sisters this is yor brother
Robert. I hav lernt my letters. The captin of
the bote I am working on Lake Eery taut me.
Now the lake is froz I am at Kingsvill in
Canada. I hope yoo ar all well and the fever
did not take any one this yeer. Yoo can rite
to me I wate for a letter.

Yor brother Robert

Winston Hotel
Detroit
Mishigin

Januery 1, 1841

Goodenuffs
Blak Swamp
Portedge River
Near Pearysburg
Ohio

Deer Brothers and Sisters,
It is 1 yeer since I wrote. The ~~boot bote~~ boat
I werked on ~~broke~~ broak in a storm and I am
not on the lake any mor. Detroit is all rite. I
am washing bottles in a Hotel.
How are everywon. How are the appl trees.
Martha if you still no yor letters you can rite
me at the Winston Hotel, Detroit.

Yor brother,
Robert

Terre Haute
Indiana

January 1, 1842

Goodenoughs
Blak Swamp
Portage River
Near Perrysburg
Ohio

Dear Brothers and Sisters,
Greetings and happy new yeer. I have lerned my
letters better from Mr Jonah Parks who I travel
with now in a wagon selling medisin. I work
for him as Detroit had two many people. We
are mostly on the ~~rode~~ road going town to town.
I like it, it sutes me better than a ~~sity~~ city.

Maybe you have writ to me at the hotel like
I sed last yeer but I had no letter. They were
not good people ther so maybe I did not get
it becus of them.

Do you no I saw John Chapman once. I
asked him for news of the family and the
farm, but he sed he did not go to the Black
Swamp any more, he is mostly in Indiana.
That was a shame for I wood like news of
the family.

Do you remember John Chapman gave us a ride in his dubble canoe once? I still remember how they ~~rode~~ road so smooth through the water.

Mr Parks is a good man and if you rite to almost any town in Indiana he will get the letter. Xcept Lafyett and Bloomingtown ~~were~~ where he wood be arrested, so do not write there.

Yor brother,
Robert

Gilbert Hotel
Racine
Wisconsin Territory

January 1, 1844

Goodenoughs
Black Swamp
Portage River
Near Perrysburg
Ohio

Dear Brothers and Sisters,
I am sorry I did not write last yeer as I did the other new years, but the law caut up with me and Mr Parks and I was in ~~jayl~~ jale. When I got out I went farther west and am in Wisconsin where I work in a hotel stables looking after horses. It is good becus the horses keep me warm at night as the winters are ~~vary~~ very cold in Wisconsin, colder even than the Black Swamp. I have not ben here yet in the summer but they say there are not so many skeeters.

How is the farm. Some times I recall the Golden Pippens. I miss the taste. There is a Golden Pippen tree I grafted off one of the Injun trails northwest of the farm. I wood like to no if it is alive and did it ever grow fruit. Maybe you can find it.

You can write me here at the hotel. I would like a letter.

Your brother,
Robert

Fort Leavenworth
Near the Missouri River
Missouri Territory

January 1, 1847

Goodenoughs
Black Swamp
Portage River
Near Perrysburg
Ohio

Dear Brothers and Sisters,
It has been 3 yeers since I last wrote. I have gone west since then and am now working at the army stables. The summers are hot here and the winters very cold. I do not want to be a soljer so I do not think I will be ~~here~~ heer two long.

It has been over 8 yeers since I left the swamp and you are all grown. Maybe Caleb you found a wife already. Maybe even Nathan or even Sal two. Maybe I am uncle Robert. I have been a lot of places but I still think about the farm in the Black Swamp. I would like to ~~hear~~ heer the news if you write here soon they are good at delivring letters to the fort.

Your brother,
Robert

Rancho Salazar
Texas

January 1, 1849

Goodenoughs
Black Swamp
Portage River
Near Perrysburg
Ohio

Dear Brothers and Sisters,
I am writing on New ~~Yeers~~ Years Day from
Texas, where I have been working on a ranch
now for almost two years. I did not meen to
come here but fell in with a rough bunch and
it was hard to get away. We came down the
Santa Fay Trail then got work on a ranch run
by an old Mexican who never left even when
Texas was its own country.

It is steady work but hard and I do not like
cattle much. They attract two many flys. Also
the land is a desert, ~~very~~ vary hot and no
trees. We are far away from anyone so I can't
give an address where to rite which is a shame
for I wood like a letter.

I am all ~~rite~~ right but when I make ~~enuff~~
enough money I am going to Californie. A

man here has been there and told me about trees called redwoods that are 300 feet tall and it takes 20 men arms streched out to circle it. I did not beleeve him but I want to see for myself. I miss trees. Also there is gold in Californie and that is a temptashun. I ~~here~~ heer you can make 200 dolars a day gold mining where ~~here~~ heer I make 5 dollars a month.

I will rite again from Californie when I have an address to rite to there. Do not forget me. I have not forgotten my family in the Black Swamp.

Your brother,
Robert

Miller General Store
Nevada City
California

January 1, 1850

Goodenoughs
Black Swamp
Portage River
Near Perrysburg
Ohio

Dear Brothers and Sisters,
I hope you are keeping well. How is the farm.
Some of you must have children there now.
I try to imagine that sometimes.

Well I did make it to California like I said
I wood. It was a long trip like so many have
~~maid~~ made. I picked up the overland trail in
western Kansas and followed it thru the
Rocky Mountens to Salt Lake City and then
the Sierra Nevada mountens. There were
thousands of people heading along that overland roote and many died on the way, there
were graves all along it. But I am used to an
outdoor life so it wasn't too bad for me. I got
to see the mountens and they were something.
Also the buffalo, which I ate once and didn't

take to. I scrached my name on Independense Rock which is a big block of granitt neer the South Pass. That is what everyone does who passes by. If one of you goes overland to California you can look for me on that rock.

I am on the western side of the Sierra Nevadas, where there is gold in the rivers that flow down from the mountens. I am working in one of the mining camps. There is snow on the ground but I still pan for gold every day, sometimes alone, sometimes we work together using a ~~sluise~~ sluce or a rocker. I have found a little bit, mostly flakes. Just down the river from me a man yesterday found a chunk of gold worth $1000. That is what we are all looking for.

I get down to Nevada City pretty reglar for supplies if you want to write. I would surely like to ~~heer~~ ~~here~~ hear from home.

Your brother,
Robert

Miller General Store
Nevada City
California

January 1, 1851

Goodenoughs
Black Swamp
Portage River
Near Perrysburg
Ohio

Dear Brothers and Sisters,
Happy New Year to you all. I am still here in California, mining for gold, same as last year, tho I have moved up and down the river some. I have found plenty but not made much money becus it is so expensive to live here. The minute I am paid for my gold I pay it back for supplies. ~~Flower~~ Flour and bullits and oats and stabling all costs more than anywhere I have ever lived. I do not think I will be mining for much longer as the gold fever does not suit me. Sum men are taken over by it and even when they have found gold they are never satisfyed.

If you are going to write, send it quick as I will not be here too much longer.

Your brother,
Robert

Greenshaw Hotel
Sacramento
California

January 1, 1853

Goodenoughs
Black Swamp
Portage River
Near Perrysburg
Ohio

Dear Brothers and Sisters,
It is two years since I last rote. I left the mining becus it ~~brakes~~ breaks a mans spirit to chase gold. Now I am working on farms and ranches, usually neer Sacramento but I go other places too.

I saw the giant redwood trees they talk about. They are really something, very tall and strait and dark among all the smaller trees. I saw the ocean too. It is a little like Lake Erie but the waves are bigger and the water tastes salty.

The Greenshaw Hotel will hold any letters for me if you want to rite.

Your brother,
Robert

Mrs Bienenstock's Guest House
Montgomery & California Streets
San Francisco
California

January 1, 1854

Goodenoughs
Black Swamp
Portage River
Near Perrysburg
Ohio

Dear Brothers and Sisters,
Happy New Year and I hope that everyone
is helthy welthy and wise.

I have had a good year becus I met a man
called William Lobb. He collects plants and
trees and seeds and sends them to England
where they like California pines and some
plants as well. I did not no there was work
like that as a plant agent. That is what I am
now I am helping Mr ~~Lob~~ Lobb.

We saw giant trees up in a place called
Calaveras Grove. They are like redwoods
with there red bark, but even wider. I wish
you could see them you wood be amazed at
how big they are. The base of the trunk wood

fill the kitchen of the house in the Black Swamp. I think they must be the oldest trees on the Earth. They made me feel small, but it was the best feeling I ever had, better than church or a good meal even.

I move around a lot collecting seeds, but I always come bak to San Francisco, and Mrs Bienenstock is good at getting letters to me wherever I am. I guess by now you have long forgotten me, but I have not forgotten you.

Your brother,
Robert

Mrs Bienenstock's Guest House
Montgomery & California Streets
San Francisco
California

January 1, 1856

Goodenoughs
Black Swamp
Portage River
Near Perrysburg
Ohio

Dear Brothers and Sisters,
Every New Years day I think about what to ~~rite~~ write to my family back in the Black Swamp. Sometimes I do not write because it is too hard and takes so long. It has been over 17 years since I left the Swamp and I never had a letter back. I do not know if any one is still alive and so this is my last letter.

I am still collecting seeds and plants for Mr Lobb. He has taut me a lot and I am very greatful to him. I will be alright here. I have a job working with trees and that is better than I ever expected to do.

I hope that you are all right wherever you are.

Your brother for the last time,
Robert

CALIFORNIA

1853–1856

Robert Goodenough was working in a field north of Sacramento when he first heard about giant trees that were even bigger than redwoods.

He and a handful of other men were raking up hay ahead of a summer storm that growled way in the distance but never seemed to get closer. It was just one of dozens of jobs Robert had taken since quitting gold mining two years before. He didn't mind the sun on his back, the sweat stinging his eyes, the endless repetition. He had coped with such things many times before. Life was often simply the repetition of the same movements in a different order, depending on the day and the place.

What he could not stand was the constant chatter of the man raking to his right: hours of dull stories about the gold he had found and drunk away, or the high prices to be paid for anything in California, or the trials he'd had on the overland trail to get here from Kentucky. These were all familiar tales to Californians, only enlivened by an unusual style of telling or a twist in the tail. The raker had neither of these, but doggedly pursued his stories with more persistence than he did his raking.

Robert gripped his own rake harder and harder to keep himself from punching the man to shut him up. Then the raker commented, 'I'm goin' to git myself back to Kentucky one of these days real soon. I had enough of California. Seen all there is to see. Seen the biggest gold nugget in the world, weighed twenty-three pounds. Seen the ocean and didn't think much of it. Seen the red trees nice and tall, but I miss hickory and dogwood and tulip trees back home. I don't need to see more. I'm done here.'

'Bet you ain't seen the big trees over at Calaveras County,' said the man working on the other side of the raker. 'Now those are some trees. Take your average redwood and triple it across, that's how big they are.'

Robert paused in his raking. 'Is that by the Calaveras River?'

'Naw – up the Stanislaus River a ways,' the man replied.

'Up the Stanislaus? You mean down it, don't you?'

'I mean what I said.'

'East up it? Not west?'

'Yup, east.'

'How far up the river?'

'Don't know. Up into the hills.'

'But there aren't redwoods up in the mountains. You only find them on the coast.'

The man shrugged.

Robert fixed him with his bright brown stare that he knew rattled people. 'You actually seen them?'

Now the man frowned, annoyed to have his authority questioned. 'Heard about 'em from somebody when I was in Sacramento.'

'The only trees I need to see are the dogwoods next to my daddy's farm,' the raker interjected. 'Them's the prettiest trees you ever saw in the spring. I got me a pain jest thinkin' 'bout 'em.'

Robert took up his rake again and pulled the hay into a pile that would eventually grow into a haystack. He asked no more questions, for he had no interest in pursuing rumors about giant trees that had not actually been verified by eyes on trunks. The other man could easily be repeating descriptions of redwoods Robert had seen along the coast. Anyone would remark on their height and call them giant. Robert had seen trees he estimated were at least 350 feet high. And a trunk three times the width of the average redwood: what did average mean? Robert had seen tall redwoods and also small ten-year-old trees that were like pines but with red bark.

Yet the man's words stayed with him. Vague about the size, he was at least clear that the location was up in the hills of the Sierra Nevadas rather than down on the coast. Robert had not seen redwoods further than fifty miles from the ocean, and puzzled over the idea that there could be any so far inland.

When the harvest was done and it came time to move on, he did not go north or west to look for work, but headed south and east, crossing the Mokelumne and Calaveras rivers, and reaching the Stanislaus River without even acknowledging to himself that this was his destination. He began to follow it up into the hills towards its source, and soon the rumor was substantiated. 'There are giant trees all right,' a man who worked for the Union Water Company told him. 'Found by a hunter supplies meat to the company. Was chasing a grizzly up there and came upon a grove of the biggest trees anyone'd ever seen. He's dined out on that story for the past year. Thought everybody had heard it by now. Where you been?'

The man had also not seen the trees himself, but could give detailed instructions as to how to find the grove, which convinced Robert there was something to the story. He still thought the trees must be the redwoods he was familiar with, just unusually wide ones, and far from the coast.

As he got closer to Calaveras Grove, talk grew louder and louder until it seemed every person Robert met couldn't wait to tell him about the mammoth trees. It was strange that no one had actually taken the time to go and see them. But then, Robert knew others didn't care about trees in the way that he did. Finally he reached Murphys, a mining town set up by the Union Water Company about fifteen miles from the grove, and there found someone who had visited

110

the trees. The man said little about them. 'You got to see for yourself,' he explained, shaking his head as if disbelieving his own memory. 'I can't describe 'em.'

In the morning he saddled his horse – an unpredictable speckled gray he'd bought off a miner after Bolt, his constant companion since Texas, got stolen by Indians. He hadn't named the gray, and wasn't sure he ever would, since naming something tied you to it and made it more painful to lose, as he'd discovered with Bolt. Apart from his other caprices, the gray was not fond of climbing higher than foothills and balked and sidestepped much of the way up to Calaveras Grove. The road was in surprisingly good condition, for two brothers had staked a claim on the land where the giant trees grew and built the road for the visitors they intended to attract.

When Robert arrived at the edge of Calaveras Grove, he dismounted and stood, hand on his horse's neck anchoring him. In his travels Robert had seen many things that had given him an ache deep in his chest, like a splinter of sadness needling into his heart: prairie that swept far out of sight; a single elm tree that made the sky behind it seem like the bluest he'd ever witnessed; a tornado cycling across the green-gray horizon; snow-covered mountaintops that hung overhead like white triangles. Now he was seeing another.

Two enormous trees stood on either side of the track, a natural entrance to the wood beyond. They were not as tall as redwoods Robert had seen on the coast, but they were much wider – as wide at their bases as a cabin. They dwarfed a person with their girth and the volume of wood they thrust towards the sky. If you stood far enough back to take in the whole of the trees, you didn't feel how enormous they were. If you came up close, though, you couldn't see their lowest branches.

Robert left the gray and walked up the path, feeling as he did that he was shrinking into a speck beside the two trees. He put a hand on one to steady himself. The tawny red surface was spongy and thickly fissured, a fibrous bark that shed easily and turned into red dust Robert later found in his clothes and his hair, under his fingernails, on the back of his neck, in his saddlebags. The forest floor around the trees was thick and springy with thousands of years of rotting needles, muffling his steps. And it was quiet, for there were no branches anywhere near him to rustle in the wind. Branches only started to grow from about a hundred feet up, and the bulk of them were so high over his head that it strained his neck to look at them for long. They were small in proportion to the gigantic trunks.

Robert had no words for the awed, hollowed-out feeling that swelled inside him.

The speckled gray did not like the trees. Robert might admire them, but the horse saw anything outside the normal range of nature as a threat, and protested by snorting and stamping and rolling his eyes. Robert had to catch the reins – the gray kicking at him as he did – and lead him away to a spot out of sight of the giant trees, among the ordinary evergreens. There he hitched him to a young fir, away from the larger sugar pines, which sometimes let drop their heavy sticky cones that could break bones. It took some time to calm the horse.

When he was quiet at last Robert left him and went back to the grove. It was also full of pines, but dotted among them were the gigantic trees, some nearby, some in the distance. Many of them were as big if not bigger than the sentinels at the entrance. The grove was no longer quiet and empty as it had been when he'd arrived. Some of the men who had described Calaveras Grove to Robert had mentioned that there was work going on up there: the owners were building a hotel for visitors to stay in, as well as other attractions. To get deeper into the grove Robert had to go past a group of men who had just appeared and begun to hammer and shout. He moved reluctantly towards them.

Then he saw the stump, looming several feet above him. A ladder leaned against it, and Robert climbed up and gazed at the surface. It was twenty-five feet across and rough, though a man was busy filing it smooth while two others were building a set of stairs that would take people more easily to the top of it. Robert studied the hundreds of rings radiating out from the center. He did not step onto the stump, vowing to himself that he never would.

His vantage point at the top of the ladder allowed him to look around. From there he could see the whole of a long, long trunk of a tree, extending from where it had been felled far into the woods, so large that Robert had not even noticed it when he walked past it. Closest to him the bark had been stripped, and the trunk looked naked and vulnerable. Further along it other men were scrambling around, building on top of it a basic cabin and a long low house, with the trunk serving as the floor.

Robert climbed back down from the stump and walked around it. Next to it was a huge chunk of the trunk, almost three times Robert's height, that had been cut from the rest of the tree and isolated. Nailed to the side was a hand-painted sign reading 'Chip Of the Old Block.' Its flat surface was scored with deep grooves, made, Robert supposed, by whatever they used to cut down the tree. He could not imagine how that had been done, and the small part of him that was not horrified by the desecration was fascinated by this technical challenge.

Now he followed the full length of the trunk, counting over a hundred paces from the stump to the jagged end where the tip must have shorn off as it fell. He hailed one of the workers to ask what they were building, and discovered the structures would soon be a saloon and a bowling alley. Robert had been many places, but had never heard of a bowling alley. According to the worker, they had them back east.

'How'd you bring down such a big tree?' he could not resist asking, though he did not add, 'and why?'

'Auger pump,' the man explained. 'They brought one up from a mining camp, added an extra length to it and drilled holes into the trunk all the way around.'

'I was there,' another worker added, glad to have an excuse to stop sawing. 'It was a few months back. Took twenty-two days, and even when we finished drilling, the tree didn't come down. Wouldn't come down even when we drove wedges into it. Even when we butted it with another tree. Nothing. Then we went off for dinner and crash! Down it came. Spooked deer and brought rabbits out of their holes. I never saw birds go so crazy.'

'Want work?' the first man said. 'We need the help.'

Robert shook his head, for the first time in his life turning down work. He did not want to be paid to climb all over a felled redwood.

The man grunted. 'You're the second fool to turn your nose up at good money today. You two brothers?' He jerked his head towards a tall man with a dark beard and hair sitting on a rock off to the side of the trunk. He was studying the tree intently, occasionally writing something in a note-book perched on his knee. As Robert watched, he jumped up and picked his way through the tree's branches, which were scattered around the trunk, some detached by the fall, others still part of the trunk. Their needles were surprisingly still green, though it had been cut down some months before. The man squatted by a branch, felt the needles, then took a magnifying glass from his pocket and looked at them through it. After a while he sat on the ground, the needles in his lap, and began to sketch. He seemed unaware of being watched.

Robert found his behavior almost as interesting as the giant trees themselves. He had never seen someone look so hard at a tree before, noting every aspect of it. Now the man was on his feet again, picking up small cones and bringing them up to his magnifying glass before dropping them. Now he was on his knees, scratching at the shaggy bark on the trunk. Now he was walking along the trunk in long, even strides, counting.

Robert did not join him immediately, but left the workers and went to stand some distance from the man. He would let him approach when he was ready. The man finished measuring but continued to walk back and forth, gradually getting nearer. Robert smiled to himself: it was like waiting for his gray to settle and allow himself to be saddled. The man's black hair was tinged with gray but was surprisingly glossy, as if he used macassar oil in it, and it was short and stood straight up, in contrast to most frontier men's long hair, pressed down by their hats and lank with grease and sweat. His beard closely followed his cheeks and jaw. As he drew closer, Robert took in the low brow and deep-set eyes and long nose making a decisive T in his strong, stubborn face. He was probably in his late forties, a good twenty years older than Robert; but it was not easy to tell, for traveling aged men in different ways. Robert himself was lean and wiry, but with a face as rough and scarred as the redwood stump. Only his clear brown eyes remained youthful, tagged with crow's-feet from squinting in the sun.

Eventually they were standing side by side. The man held a cone in his hand in a familiar manner that suggested he did so often. This is a man who knows trees, Robert thought. 'I counted one hundred and two paces,' he said.

'Ninety-five,' the man corrected. 'Though I am a little taller than you, so I'd take fewer strides. I estimate it's three hundred feet long – three-twenty if the tip were still on. Not as tall as the coastal redwoods, but still tall. But its girth is what is so extraordinary.'

'Are these redwoods different from those along the coast?'

'These are not redwoods,' the man replied, firm as a schoolteacher. 'Never call them redwoods. They're sequoias. Same family but different genus and species. They're wider but not as tall as redwoods. The canopy shape is different: sequoia branches are shorter and hug the trunk, while redwoods' upper branches grow straight out, their lower spread out and then down. And the needles – see?' He leaned down to pick up a branch that had been shed. 'Completely different. The sequoia's are like scaly strings. Redwoods have flattened needles more like those of pines. And the cones.' He handed Robert a green cone he held; it was about the size of a chicken egg. 'Redwood cones are smaller than these – maybe half the size.'

In this rapidly delivered lesson Robert detected an English accent, sifted through gravel. It was not a fresh-off-the-boat accent, but had tinges of Spanish in it, and of traveling to many places where a man's mouth was pulled in different directions.

'It's much dryer here than where the redwoods grow near the coast,' Robert remarked, wanting to keep the conversation alive.

The man nodded. 'Heat's opening up the cones so the seeds come out. Like this.' He picked up a dry brown cone and shook it. 'See, the seeds are almost all gone.' He tossed the dried cone into the undergrowth. 'Can only collect the green ones.'

'Are you? Collecting them?' Robert noticed for the first time that there was a sack at the man's feet.

The man frowned – though it didn't change his face much, as his brow was already low and tight across his nose. His eyes were so narrow that Robert doubted he would ever glimpse their true color. 'You with the Laphams?'

'Who?'

'The brothers who staked a claim on this grove. You working on that?' With his head he indicated the building activity behind them.

118

'I don't know anything about that. I've just come to see the trees.'

The man picked up the sack, dropped the green cone in, then turned his back, bent over and picked up another one.

'I don't even know what bowling is,' Robert added.

The other paused, then tilted his head slightly to one side as he responded. 'It is the most ludicrous game imaginable. You set up little logs in a formation, then roll a wooden ball at them to knock them over. Apparently these trees are not enough entertainment for visitors; they must have other attractions to keep them occupied.' He held out his hand. 'William Lobb.' Robert shook it. 'Now, are you going to help or just rest your feet?'

They started with the felled tree, scrabbling among the branches for any green cones they could find. The sequoia cones were distinctive and easily discernible from pinecones. Like chicken eggs, they were round at one end, tapered at the other, and fit snugly in the palm of the hand. The scales were arranged close together in a way that made them look like someone had scored a pattern of diamonds onto the surface.

Lobb was so familiar with the cones that Robert was astounded to learn he had arrived at Calaveras Grove to see the giant sequoias only a few hours before Robert himself. He would soon discover, though, that Lobb was a walking encyclopedia of plants. He had seen so many seed cones in his time that when he found a new one he naturally slotted it in among the cones he had already catalogued in his head, adding to and comparing his knowledge.

Robert collected half a sack of them from around the tree, then William Lobb rummaged through them, pulling out a few that were half-chewed. 'Chickarees got at them,' he explained, throwing them into the bushes. 'Don't collect those. You ship 'em like that and they'll germinate on board, or rot.'

Robert frowned, puzzled by everything Lobb had said, but not wanting to ask too many questions. He grasped at the most immediate. 'Chickaree?'

'Pine squirrels – those noisy little things you see all over. Listen a minute and you'll hear one.' They stood still, and soon a chattering began in a small sugar pine nearby. Robert looked up and watched the tiny squirrel with its reddish fur, pale belly, and dark stripe separating the two.

'They spoil too many cones.' Lobb threw a half-eaten cone at the chickaree and it flashed out of sight.

When they had stripped the branches of the fallen sequoia bare they moved further into the grove to the standing trees. There were about a hundred giant sequoias in Calaveras Grove, scattered among other trees within the area of a mile or so. Each one they arrived at astonished Robert more rather than less. Though freakishly large, somehow they did not announce their presence, except with a flash of orange in among the younger trees, until you were up close. Robert wanted to stop at each, steady himself against it with his hand, and look up. William Lobb was less inclined; as Robert discovered later, he had seen many unusual trees in his travels, and while he appreciated them he was also unsentimental, and brisk about his business.

There were fewer green cones around the live sequoias, as they mainly clung to the branches. Robert was beginning to think it would be impossible to fill the sack when William Lobb stumped off to his pile of equipment and returned with a shotgun. After loading it, he raised it, aimed high into the tree, and fired. There was a crack, and in a moment a branch swung loose and slowly tumbled down, knocking against the trunk and other branches, and showering them with needles and cones. Robert ducked. The Englishman chuckled. 'Best part of the job.'

He left Robert to pick up the cones and went back to his equipment, returning with a spade and some metal pails. 'We need a few seedlings,' he explained. 'Often the seeds won't germinate in a new country and climate, but seedlings might continue to grow.' He tramped through the undergrowth several times around the tree before he was satisfied he'd found a healthy foot-high seedling. Then he began cutting into the thick duff around it, made up of decomposed needles and red dust from the bark. 'Course it's much harder to transport them,' Lobb grunted as he worked. 'Often they don't survive the crossing.'

'Crossing what?'

'The ocean. Won't like being brought down to San Francisco much either. Worth collecting some, though, especially with a new species.' He lifted the seedling and lowered it gently into a pail, adding soil around it and tamping it down with his fingers. When he was satisfied he picked up his spade again to find another.

Robert had collected all the cones he could around the tree, and began looking for seedlings to help out. It turned out not to be as easy as he had expected. Few seedlings grew under the giant trees, as there was little sunlight. Those that did grow were not what he first thought. When he pointed out a potential seedling, Lobb shook his head. 'That's incense cedar. Lots of them here.' He gestured at taller, thinner trees around them with red bark and deep furrows similar to the sequoias. 'Go and feel the bark of that one. See? Much firmer than the sequoia. And the needles may be scaly but they're flatter than a sequoia's, like they've been ironed.'

They moved on to another sequoia, William Lobb handing Robert the gun to shoot down more branches. Robert took careful aim, aware that he was being judged and must not miss. He was used to hunting – it was how he ate his way across America – but he had never deliberately aimed at the branch of a tree. When he pulled the trigger, the slug struck the sequoia branch and it cracked but did not fall.

'One more'll do it,' Lobb said. 'Right at the base.'

This time the branch fell, as well as another shower of needles and cones.

There was a shout from the distant builders, and a man detached himself and hurried through the trees towards them. William Lobb swore under his breath. 'So much for that. Fun is always paid for, one way or another.' He picked up his spade and began cutting the matted turf around another seedling, which to Robert looked like an incense cedar. Clearly he had a lot to learn.

Lobb did not look up as the man arrived, short and sweaty and out of breath, though he had not come far. Robert did not have William Lobb's insouciance. He stopped picking up cones and stood with the sack at his feet, his hands dangling in guilt, though he was not sure what he had actually done wrong.

'Here, now, what was that shooting for?' The man fingered a long moustache that cut the lower third of his round face from the rest. He wore a ratty silk top hat pushed back from his forehead and a shirt with the sleeves rolled above his elbows, its whiteness revealing his trade: he was a money man, not a worker. 'What are you doing there?'

Lobb continued working. 'Digging.'

'Yes, but *what* are you digging? And *why* are you digging? And shooting too. There is no gold here, sir, if that's what you're looking for,' the man added, pulling a grubby handkerchief from his pocket and wiping his hands and then his brow. 'Perhaps you're new to this business and misunderstand the nature of gold, but I assure you there is none under these trees. You're better off going to the river and following it down a ways. Though I've not heard of any gold found in the Stanislaus for a good two years.'

He stopped, expecting William Lobb to stop too. But Lobb kept slicing the ground around the seedling, then lifted it and placed it into one of the pails. Robert went back to picking up cones. The man fingered his moustache again, then held out his hand. 'Name's Lapham. Billie Lapham. I got a claim on this land.'

William Lobb ignored his hand. Robert felt a little sorry for Billie Lapham with his hand left suspended in the air, so after a moment he went over and shook it.

That seemed to perk up the money man. 'Which is why I want to know when someone's shooting on my land, and digging on my land, what it is they're doing,' he continued.

'This is not your land,' William Lobb said.

'Oh, it is, it is. I got the papers. I can show you, back at camp.'

'This is Indian land, if it's anyone's.' William Lobb spoke as if he hadn't heard Billie Lapham. 'Those Miwoks encamped just south of here – they've been here longer than you. It's theirs, or it's God's land – take your pick.'

'No, it's mine, mine and my brother's. We're building, see, for the tourists. A saloon, a bowling alley, and farther back we're extending the cottage to make it into a hotel. The Big Trees Hotel.' Billie Lapham listed these achievements proudly. 'Wait a minute, is that *trees* you're digging up?' William Lobb had placed another sequoia seedling in a pail. 'You can't dig up trees! What are you gonna do with them?'

Lobb paused. 'What, aren't there enough trees here for you? I noticed you don't seem much concerned about the big ones since you've gone and cut one down to make it into – what? The floor of a bowling alley.'

'Well, now, it wasn't me that cut it down! It was others decided to do that.' Billie Lapham wiped his hands again. 'But there were good reasons why they did that. *Educational* reasons. People want to see how big the trees are, and it ain't so easy, standing up close to 'em, did you notice? With a stump that big, though, and a trunk that long, you get a better idea of the size and scale of the thing. I figured with it already down like that I might as well make something out of it! The Great Stump is gonna be a dance floor, you know. And they only cut down just the one. We'll protect the rest.' He must have been criticized before to be so well versed in his defense. Then he tried to flip the argument. 'And I want to protect what's growing too.' He gestured at the seedling in its pail. 'If you dig these up and take 'em away, we won't have them in the future, will we?'

William Lobb stopped digging; it seemed incredulity halted his spade. 'You think these giants' – he waved at the trees around him – 'are going to let these little ones survive? There's no room. Look around you! Once these trees established themselves, nothing could grow to any height under them. I'm doing these seedlings a favor – giving them a chance. They might actually grow up somewhere.'

'Wait a minute, now,' Billie Lapham protested, smoothing his moustache. He was a man full of twitches. 'You planning to plant 'em somewhere else?'

What else would a man do with seedlings he'd dug up? Robert thought but kept to himself, smiling into the sack of cones.

'I can't allow that,' Billie Lapham continued. 'Oh, no! You're stealing trees here to grow a grove to compete with this one. No, sir, I can't allow that. Not at all.'

William Lobb grunted. 'Even if I planted a grove a mile away, it would take a good five hundred years before it would look anything like this one. Your bones and my bones would be dust long before that. Anyway, you can rest assured these trees won't compete with this grove: they're going to England.'

Billie Lapham looked taken aback only for a second. 'England! You plant redwoods there, nobody'll come from there to see Cally Grove trees.'

To this ridiculous argument William Lobb did not bother with an answer. A fourth seedling landed in a pail, a little more roughly than the previous three.

'They're sequoias,' Robert murmured.

'What?' Billie Lapham turned to Robert as if only just noticing him. 'What did you say?'

'They're not redwoods – they're giant sequoias.' Robert found he enjoyed correcting Billie Lapham, even if he did not really know what he was saying.

'Of course they're redwoods.' But William Lobb's indifference to his authority had clearly shaken Billie Lapham's confidence. 'They got to be – the ads I'm running in the papers say they are.'

'An advertisement does not decide what a tree is called,' William Lobb said. 'The California Academy of Sciences decided it is a different genus from redwoods and have named it a giant sequoia, with a Latin name to follow shortly. Redwoods are coastal, and tall and relatively thin, though still huge compared to other trees. Sequoias are in the foothills, and are wider and shorter.'

'Look here, now.' Billie Lapham cycled through all of his nervous tics, smoothing his moustache, then wiping his hands and brow. The gestures seemed to give him strength. 'Are you planning to dig up more than them four pails? 'Cause I'm gonna have to charge you.'

William Lobb stopped digging and stabbed his spade into the ground, close enough to Billie Lapham's feet to make him jump. 'I'm done here,'

127

he said to Robert. 'When you've filled another sack, bring them over to the stables.' He pulled up the spade, took the four pails and hooked them over the handle. As he strode off, holding the spade horizontal so that the pails hung in a row, the seedlings bounced in time to his step.

Robert watched him go, aware that Billie Lapham had now turned towards him. It occurred to him that William Lobb had handed him his second job – negotiating with the owner of Calaveras Grove. Robert was not a negotiator, but if it meant working for Lobb, he would have to do it. From watching animals he had learned that he must not show weakness. And so, as Lobb had done, he did not look at Billie Lapham but continued to toss cones into the sack. At the same time, he considered the situation from the other's point of view. Robert had never owned land, but he thought back to the Goodenough farm in the Black Swamp. If someone had come along and dug up apple seedlings on their property, and gathered seeds from windfalls, how would his father have responded? What would he have expected? A payment, at the very least. Robert tried to recall what John Chapman had charged for seedlings, so long ago. He thought it might have been five cents a seedling. Not that such figures really helped: California prices had been blown all out of proportion by the demands of the gold rush. When he was a boy back east, with a dollar fifty you could buy a whole barrel of hard cider. Here that amount would buy you one dinner in Sacramento. A pound of flour had been ten cents; now it was forty. Tobacco that cost six cents in New York was a dollar in California. But then, two years ago men were making a thousand dollars a month from gold, more than his father would have made in ten years.

It was impossible for Robert to place a value on trees; to him they stood apart from commerce. In pondering the price of a sequoia seedling, he recalled that John Appleseed himself – the consummate tree salesman – had been inconsistent about his prices. For no reason he had sometimes charged James Goodenough six cents a seedling rather than five, yet had also been known to give away bags of seeds.

It had been some time since Robert had thought about apple trees. He had not allowed himself to – when he did it made him feel sick and empty.

He did not want to value each sequoia cone or seedling. And he did not want to haggle. There must be another way. Robert looked up at Billie Lapham, who was once more mopping his brow, readying himself for the negotiation. Before he could touch his moustache as well, Robert said, 'We'll pay you five dollars for the seeds and seedlings we're collecting from Calaveras Grove.'

Billie Lapham stroked his moustache. Clearly he didn't know the value of the trees either. 'All right,' he said, then seemed surprised at himself for agreeing. 'Wait a minute – where would you collect 'em if I said no? There ain't no giant redwoods – sequoias – anywhere else. Are there?'

'You've already agreed.' Robert stood and held out his hand. Billie Lapham hesitated, then took it. Obviously he was not much of a haggler either.

Robert spent the rest of the day collecting cones while William Lobb took more notes and sketched the trees. Lobb also gathered branches, needles and bark, carefully preserving their structure. 'These I'll dose in camphor and send to Kew to be studied,' he explained.

'"Q,"' Robert repeated. 'What's that?'

'A botanical garden outside of London – the finest in the world. They collect and study all sorts of trees and plants. I always instruct Veitch to send them new discoveries. They'll want to see the sequoias.'

Robert nodded, trying to imagine people interested enough in plants to study them. But then he thought of his father grafting the apple trees, how methodical he had been, and it didn't seem so strange.

They camped just beyond Calaveras Grove rather than near the others – 'so I don't have to listen to braggarts all night,' William Lobb muttered. After they'd eaten and were sitting by the fire, Lobb smoking a pipe, Robert shyly asked if he could look at the leather notebook the Englishman had been using all day. When Lobb handed it over he held it to the firelight and leafed through the many notes and the drawings of the Calaveras Grove sequoias. Overviews Lobb had done of a whole tree, sitting several hundred feet away in order to see it from different angles. Drawings of the trunk, the bark, various branches, the needles, the cones, the habitat under and around it. He had also sketched clumps of trees, and several sketches that could be put together into a panorama to give an idea of the size and scale of the whole grove. In some of the drawings Lobb had included a small figure standing next to the sequoia, wearing a hat similar to Robert's own. He had never seen himself in a drawing, and though it was unsettling, he was pleased to be in William Lobb's notebook. There were also sketches of the cones, as well as notes about their collecting: the date and location and elevation of where they had been picked up.

'What will you do with the seeds?' Robert asked, handing back the notebook.

'Send 'em to England.' Lobb stowed the notebook away. 'The English will go crazy for these trees. They already love the redwoods I've sent back, and lots of the California pines. These sequoias will be the kings of many an estate in Bedfordshire or Staffordshire or Hertfordshire – if they survive.'

'Is the weather the same?'

William Lobb snorted. 'No! Plenty of rain, not much sun. The redwoods seem to be doing all right, though: some of the seeds I collected a few years ago have been growing in England. But these – it's dry here, with fires that pop the cones open so the seeds can get out. That will never happen in England. And it's high up here – the beginning of mountains such as England doesn't have. It will be a gamble. But if they take . . .' He tossed a pinecone into the fire.

'What do the English do with the trees?' Robert persisted.

'Plant 'em on their property.'

'Don't they have trees in England?'

William Lobb chuckled. 'Of course. But they want new and different, you see. The wealthy landowners have been busy creating "tableaux" on their grounds.' At Robert's blank look, he added, 'They lay out trees so they look like works of art rather than just letting nature grow as it will. Now they're demanding conifers, for they love exotic trees that remain green all year round. They set off the broadleaf trees, with their changing colors, and provide structure and life when everything else is bare. There are few native conifers there – only the Scots pine, the yew, the juniper. So I've been sending as many as I can from California. Some of them are even creating "pinetums" on their property where they plant and show off a variety of conifers.'

'You send trees to England.' A thought was stirring deep in Robert's mind, like a fish swimming below the surface of a lake.

'Yes, saplings sometimes, though they often don't

132

survive the journey. Seedlings are better – being smaller they don't snap off so easily. But you may as well send seeds, that's best. Even then, many seeds never grow. You might plant a hundred and get twenty seedlings from them, and of those, five might grow into saplings, and two into trees. That's why I have to collect so many cones – as many as my horse can carry. Your horse too, if you've the time to ride to San Francisco. I assume you do or you wouldn't be out here just to look at trees.'

It took Robert a moment to understand William Lobb was asking him to work for him for longer than just that day. Before he could answer, Lobb added, 'I'll pay you, of course. It's worth my while to be able to collect and carry twice as many cones.' Clearly he'd thought Robert's hesitation was over money.

Actually Robert would have helped him for nothing. He had been hesitating because the thought was now surfacing. 'Have you ever heard of a Golden Pippin?' he asked.

'Of course.' William Lobb had finished his pipe and was taking off his boots. He seemed unbothered by the swerve in conversation. 'I'm more of a Cornish Gilliflower man myself, though. I prefer my apples with a bit of red on 'em.'

'Are Golden Pippins common in England, then?' Robert tried to hide his disappointment. From the way his father had talked, he'd always assumed that Golden Pippins were very rare, known only to the Goodenoughs.

'Common enough. Not as common as a Ribston Pippin or a Blenheim Orange, but easily found. You know George Washington had them brought over to Mount Vernon? They didn't thrive, though – not the right climate.'

'The Goodenoughs' trees did.'

'Did what?'

'Thrive. We grew Golden Pippins in Ohio, and Connecticut before that. My grandparents brought branches from England and grafted them, then my father did the same when he went to Ohio.'

'Really?' For the first time, William Lobb looked at Robert with genuine interest. 'Your father was a grafter, was he?'

Robert nodded.

'My brother and I used to do a bit of grafting at Killerton, back in Devonshire. What was the yield of yours?'

'Ten bushels a tree.' Robert allowed himself to think about the Golden Pippins for the first time in years. 'Have you ever tasted a pineapple?'

'Pineapple?' William Lobb chuckled. 'I ate them every day in South America. Got tired of them. Why?'

'That's what our Golden Pippins tasted of: first nuts and honey, then pineapple. That's how Pa described it, anyway. I never tasted real pineapple. Not sure he did either.'

William Lobb was staring at him. 'Where did the Goodenoughs come from in England?'

Robert frowned. He wanted to say he couldn't

remember, but he knew that was not an acceptable answer to someone like William Lobb. He tried to think of what his father had said, so long ago. 'Herefordshire,' he dug out at last.

Lobb suddenly laughed, a great bark, almost a shout. 'Pitmaston Pineapple,' he announced.

Robert raised his eyebrows.

'Pitmaston Pineapple,' William Lobb repeated. 'That's what your father grew. It was a Golden Pippin seedling that originally grew in Herefordshire, had an unusual taste and a local following. Several years ago a man growing it in Pitmaston exhibited it at the London Horticultural Society. Gave it the name "Pitmaston Pineapple" because of the pineapple finish. I've read about it but never had one. Been out of England too much to keep up with apples.'

'I didn't know apples could change their taste.'

'Well, they go from sour to sweet sometimes.'

'I know. One in ten seedlings turns out sweet.' Robert repeated his father's words.

William Lobb nodded, pleased. 'If they can change from sour to sweet, there's no reason why other tastes can't change: from lemon to pineapple, for instance.' He pulled a blanket from his bag.

'So an English tree has come to America,' Robert spoke his thoughts aloud, 'and now you are sending American trees to England.'

'True. There is a commerce in trees, just as in people. But a Pitmaston Pineapple growing in Ohio?' William Lobb chuckled, wrapping his blanket

135

around him in preparation for sleep. 'That's almost enough to make me go there, just to taste it!'

In the morning they collected more cones, then loaded their horses with what they had gathered. The gray did not like carrying the four bulging sacks, which were light but bulky, and spun round and round to try to fling them off. The clanking of the pails that held the seedlings also made him skitter sideways. Lobb watched these antics with amusement while his own horse – a big buckskin mare with black stockings, seeming dumb but probably as smart as her owner – stood stolid and indifferent, though she carried more complicated baggage. In the end Lobb had collected four sequoia seedlings and two larger saplings, all in pails which he hung all over the horse so that she resembled a traveling trader, bumping and jangling with her load of tin. This was apart from saddle-bags and a leather box of drying specimens that hung from her and bumped her side. Lobb had to ride with care, sitting ramrod straight, but like his horse he seemed used to it.

Robert found it hard to leave Calaveras Grove, not knowing when he would come again to see the giant trees. When he glanced back at the tawny bark beyond the smaller trees, his chest felt tight. He was glad, then, to be riding with William Lobb, as it forced him to look and think ahead.

They took the road down to Murphys, a route that should have taken only a few hours but with

William Lobb took the whole day. He was constantly distracted by what he saw, and stopped to inspect what looked to Robert like nondescript flowers, taking quick notes and making sketches and pressing them between the pages of his notebook. Some of them Robert knew: lupines, pussypaws, cow parsnip. But others he was unfamiliar with, like the fiddleleaf, a purple-flowered plant with sticky oval leaves that Lobb was keen to collect. Still others even Lobb didn't know. It occurred to Robert only later that this might have been the first time anyone paid real attention to some of those flowers – that Lobb was studying them and in fact would eventually give them their name.

He also had Robert dig up a few more seedlings – not of sequoias, since they had moved out of range, but of incense cedars and ponderosa pines. He watched closely as Robert placed the spade near the first cedar seedling, paused, moved it a little further away, then hesitated with his foot on the top of the blade. 'Go on, lad,' Lobb said. 'A firm foot and a clean slice is what you want.'

Robert cut swiftly through the duff, four slices around the seedling, and pulled it out in a square of dusty, needly soil.

'That's right. Now, pop it in the pail.'

He directed him in digging up three more seedlings, then must have felt Robert had mastered it, for he moved on to showing him how to press flowers for drying. By the end of the day Robert was beginning to understand the rudiments of plant collecting.

From Murphys they traveled along other roads and paths that led through the foothills of the Sierra Nevadas onto the flat plain of central California. The shift from the conifer-dominated mountains down through the hills covered with dried golden grass and clumps of evergreen canyon oaks meant there were few opportunities for collecting, as the oaks were of no interest to the English. William Lobb was dismissive of them. 'No reason ever to send scrubby things like these to a country famous for its oaks. Ah, the oaks of England – now there's a tree. If redwoods are the backbone of California, oaks are of England. Huge, gnarled, full of personality. Do you know Charles II hid from soldiers in an oak tree in Shropshire? The tree was so popular that afterwards people killed it by taking bits of it as souvenirs. A lesson for Billie Lapham in that.'

It turned out William Lobb was quite a talker. He and his brother Thomas had grown up in a quiet village in Cornwall, and both had then gone on to have remarkable lives as plant collectors. Over the ride to Stockton, Robert heard all about Lobb's travels, to the northern and southern parts of California, but also further afield, to Panama, Peru, Chile, Argentina, Brazil – indeed, all over South America. He heard of snow and steep mountain passes, wars and assassinations, illness and delay. Robert himself had had adventures, of course; it was impossible to cross America as he had without incident. He had been thrown in jail and hidden from Indians and almost drowned crossing rivers and been stalked by wolves and wildcats. But Lobb's travels were several notches more exotic, made even more so by the matter-of-fact way he described the harsh landscape and blizzards and brutal sun and the encounters with locals and the shootings and the government revolutions.

He underscored his stories with bitter and sarcastic remarks about James Veitch, the English nurseryman who had sent William to South America and California and Thomas Lobb to Asia to discover and collect plants. 'He hasn't got a clue what Tom and I have to go through to get plants for him – to make money for him. I doubt he's ever set foot on a ship, or camped in snow, or ridden for twenty hours a day. He complains when the stagecoach from Exeter to London gets stuck in the mud! Dolt.'

Mostly, though, Robert heard of plants: long lists of Latin names he didn't recognize, not even when William Lobb showed him sketches in his notebooks. *Passiflora mollissima. Embothrium coccineum. Tropaeolum lobbianum. Crinodendron hookerianum. Tropaeolum azureum. Araucaria imbricata.* The common names were equally exotic. Passion flower. Firebush. Lantern tree. Flame flower. Blue nasturtium. Monkey puzzle. The last name made Robert smile. 'A Chilean pine,' Lobb explained. 'Peculiar looking. Doesn't have needles, but thick shiny spines grow all over the branches and on the trunk too. Someone looking at one growing in Cornwall said it would be a puzzle for a monkey to climb it – those spines are sharp, draw blood. Silly, really, as there aren't any monkeys in Chile. But that's how they are back in England – lump all the faraway countries together, have 'em share plants and animals. At least the name's a good one.'

As he listened, Robert began to understand how limited his knowledge of plants and trees was. He knew birches from aspens, beeches from hornbeams, maples from sycamores. But he could not tell all of the Californian pines apart, the gray pine from the coulter, the bishop from the knob-cone from the Monterey. William Lobb spent a long time by the fire that night describing the pyramid shape of the bristlecone fir, its beautiful dark green color, its singular cones with their leafy bristles. Robert had never even heard of it, much less seen one.

That night he lay wrapped in his blanket, head on his saddle, and let the names stream through him. Begonia. Rhododendron. Amaryllis. Mallow. Fuchsia. He didn't know any of them, and wanted to.

By the time they reached Stockton they had lost one of the sequoia saplings, which snapped off when the buckskin shied at a partridge fluttering out from the undergrowth. Lobb was sanguine about the loss. 'I fully expect to lose the other one as well,' he said. 'If we don't lose it on the way to San Francisco it'll likely die on board the ship taking it to England. The seedlings stand a better chance. But seeds are best.'

From Stockton they took a steamboat down the San Joaquin River to San Francisco. Robert had seen these steamers going up and down the rivers between Sacramento or Stockton and San Francisco, but never been on one himself. Nor had the gray. Predictably, he rebelled against the floating sensation under his feet, rearing and kicking as Robert led him on board and managing to knock over the other sequoia sapling and trample it. 'That's one to your horse, one to mine,' William Lobb remarked, throwing the broken tree into the river.

The gray continued to buck and kick in the rickety stalls until Robert held him around the neck and put a sack over his eyes. At last the horse grew calm, and Robert was able to rejoin Lobb on deck.

As the boat paddled down the river, they stood together and watched the scenery pass by. Miles and miles of flat, fertile land stretched out before them: grasses browned from the long summer sun, broken by oases of green where there was water and people had settled and built farms. Occasionally they saw groups of Indians walking with baskets full of acorns, or riding in groups, a long string of horses paralleling the river. They stopped and watched the boat, which was still a novelty even though there had been steamers up and down the San Joaquin for several years now. Young boys fishing abandoned their poles and ran along the bank, racing the steamer. Robert could feel himself being pulled west, a sensation he'd had for much of his life.

'Where do you stay when you're in San Francisco?' Lobb asked as they watched the boys on the bank grow tired and turn back.

'I've never been.' Robert was ashamed to admit that he had been in California almost four years and not yet been to its biggest city. Gold had been like a magnet that held him fast to the Sierra Nevadas, even when he was no longer mining it.

'Ha! You'll either love it or hate it. I can guess which.'

They crossed the San Francisco Bay and headed towards the shore, Robert marveling at the wide water, the hills, and the hint of ocean beyond. Landing at one of the quays, he and William Lobb were swept up into the bustle of hundreds of men loading and unloading ships from all over the world. They did not linger, however; Lobb led them away from the docks and into the city.

Riding through the streets, Robert discovered that of all the cities he had been to – Detroit, Indianapolis, Chicago, St Louis, Salt Lake City – San Francisco was by far the worst. Its geography should have made it beautiful and eye-catching, for it was shaped by hills and water so that every part of it boasted a dramatic view. Instead it turned out to be a rough, muddy, smelly place, stripped of trees because they got in the way of the rapid building needed to house the burgeoning population, which had grown from one thousand to thirty-five thousand in four years. Buildings were laid out in a rough grid pattern and crammed together in rows that tiled up and down the slopes. There was no grace to all of these right angles so at odds with the city's natural surroundings.

They passed dozens of saloons, with men staggering in and out of them, and riding fast up and down the streets like water pouring through a sluice. Robert recognized the greedy, impatient, desperate, careless character of miners on a spree, here to spend their earnings since there was little to do up at the mining camps. They seemed to need to match the speed of their spending with their earning, and had come to San Francisco to drink and whore and gamble ferociously; then, pockets empty, they would clear off back to the camps in the hills and on the rivers in pursuit of gold once more. Robert was not sure it was a good idea for a city to be so full of deluded dreamers.

William Lobb clearly had no interest in the city apart from its docks. He was not a gambler or a drinker, and he had given the few women they'd come into contact with little more than a glance. Indeed, he did not seem to like people much. 'This city is a horror show,' he announced as they rode, 'but its docks are essential. Two or three times a year I pack up seeds and seedlings and saplings and dry samples to ship to England.'

'Where are we going?'

'Corner of Montgomery and California. I've got an arrangement at a boardinghouse where I can store equipment and seeds and plants. Here it is.'

They pulled up in front of a house where a woman was leaning in the doorway, smoking a cigar. Tall and broad-shouldered, with red cheeks and scrubby, colorless hair, she wore a filthy pinafore that managed to make her look less rather than more feminine, and she did not wear a cap or hat or bonnet. There were few women living in California, and one way to do it was to ignore what was expected of you. The rules were different here: there were none. That was why many people were tempted to stay: the strict boundaries set by their families and communities and churches back east were nonexistent here. Robert had met many husbands who had decided not to return to their waiting wives, who reveled in the gambling and the whoring and the freedom.

The woman did not move, but let the men get down from the wagon and come to her.

'Hello, Mrs Bienenstock,' William Lobb said. 'Is there a bed available for this lad? He's helping me.'

'No vomit on my stairs,' Mrs Bienenstock directed at Robert. 'You get sick inside my house, you're out.'

Robert nodded; there was no other response to such a statement.

'We've got a special consignment,' Lobb continued. 'It won't be here for long – just till I find a steamer heading for Central America.'

Mrs Bienenstock puffed on her cigar. 'The *Uncle Sam* leaves for Nicaragua in two days. Market Wharf.'

'Not the Nicaragua route. Panama's more reliable.'

'The *Columbus*, then. Pacific Wharf in four days.'

'Excellent. We'll just get these in, then I'll go down to the docks and sort it out. Thank you, Mrs B.,' William Lobb added deferentially. Robert suspected his landlady was one of the few people he treated with such respect.

Lobb's room was at the back of the house, with a north-facing window. It was naturally dim, made darker by black cloth hung over the window, and was stacked with tin cases sealed with wax. Robert looked around the room, baffled. Lobb chuckled. 'Here,' he said, breaking open a case so Robert could see the contents: hundreds of labeled packets of plant seeds. 'Some hold dried specimens as well,' he explained. 'I'll send all this off to England shortly. Look, the cases are lead-lined to keep out moisture and light so the seeds don't germinate. That's why I keep it dark in here too.'

He took Robert next to the small yard at the back of the house, a scruffy patch of land full of scrap and garbage that smelled of shit from the outhouse. Mrs Bienenstock clearly focused her energy on the inside where the rooms were clean, there were no fleas, and the guests were cowed by her enough to behave. 'I keep seedlings and saplings I've collected back here,' he said, gesturing to rows of pails of tiny trees. 'Mrs B. waters them for me – easy money for her.'

Once they had added the pails of sequoias to the others out back, and brought the sacks of cones to Lobb's room, the Englishman left to go back to the docks, and Robert was free to explore the city. The saloons and brothels did not appeal, however; instead he asked Mrs Bienenstock where he could go to see the ocean.

'Seal Rocks,' she replied as she ran a heated iron across dried sheets in the kitchen. 'Take Broad Street west and keep going even when it turns into a track.' She nodded her approval. 'You can't get up to much mischief there!'

Robert was relieved to find that Seal Rocks was well out of the city, away from the miners and the dirt and the noise. There were no buildings there at all, just the beginnings of a fort being built further along the point. Robert and the gray followed the track till it ended and the ground fell away and the Pacific opened out below him like a vast watery sheet reflecting an equally vast sky. Robert had seen the ocean before but it always astonished him. After thousands of miles locked into a land sucked dry of water, here was more water than he could ever imagine in one place.

The gray was not so astonished, but responded to the wide open space as he had at the sight of the sequoias: he neighed and bucked and kicked out until Robert turned him around and led him a few hundred yards inland, where he left him to graze.

He came back and sat on the cliff edge and watched the ocean for over an hour. Off the shore there were large rocks sticking out of the water that looked like giant seals' heads with their pointy noses facing the sky. Real seals lay on them, lolling in the sun and barking.

Little by little, Robert's awe at the sight of the ocean was joined by an undertow of sadness. He had reached the end of the country, and was as far from Ohio as he could get; he could go no further. The thought of having to turn around and face east filled him with such guilt and despair that he felt sick with it. Robert had tried to lead an honest life, even when surrounded by dishonest people, but no matter how cleanly he lived now, he knew he had made one mistake that he could never escape. That knowledge would follow him, east or west. All of this running made no difference.

Suddenly there was a roiling and spraying about a mile from shore, and an enormous tail appeared, fanning out and dipping below the water. He gasped, and watched the tail come and go as the whale swam towards the horizon that Robert himself would never reach. It was another reminder that he had to stop now and find a way to live with himself out here, or go back east and face what he had done.

* * *

Robert and William Lobb spent the next three days preparing and packing the specimens, mostly out in the yard with the weather fine – though Lobb first spent his own money on a sack of lime for the outhouse so that they could work without gagging.

He demonstrated to Robert how to lay the sequoia cones on a canvas sheet in the sun to let them dry. Each held dozens of tiny flat seeds which would be much easier to transport once shaken from the dried cones. 'I'm showing you how, but I'm not going to do that with these cones,' Lobb said. 'We can't wait for these to dry – that's three weeks of waiting when someone else might send some sequoias off to England before us.'

'Are there other tree collectors?'

'A few. Some I've even worked with here and there. Andrews and Parry are all right. I'm not worried about them. It's Bridges or Beardsley or the Murray brothers who are more likely to beat me to it.'

'Have any of them been up to Calaveras Grove?'

'Not that I know of – but I wouldn't put it past them! They could have gone up there just after us, and arrived back today and be on the *Columbus* tomorrow, same as us.' Clearly it was a matter of honor for Lobb to land sequoias on English soil first.

Given how casually they had handled the cones while collecting them at Calaveras Grove, William Lobb was unexpectedly fastidious about packing them. 'The success of plant collecting lies primarily in the packing,' he proclaimed. 'Doesn't matter what you've collected if it arrives in England dead or rotten.'

First they padded the lead-lined tin cases with old newspaper Mrs Bienenstock had saved for them. Then they put in the sequoia cones. Robert would have dumped them in by the handful, but Lobb placed each cone until they made an even layer, then put another layer on top of those, and another layer. When the box was full, he took a sack of sand he'd dug up from a beach and kept in his room, and poured it into the box so that it filled all the spaces between the cones. 'Absorbs damp,' he explained. 'These cases'll be around water for a few months. If the seeds get damp they'll rot or germinate. Can't have that.' Finally they sealed the cases with wax.

William Lobb decided the seedlings must be shipped in a Ward's case, and brought the wood and glass materials into the yard to build a small one. If it was constructed properly any plants inside were protected from wind and sea spray and could be brought on the ship deck to get some sun. They filled the bottom of the case with soil, then planted the sequoia seedlings, as well as a few other plants Lobb had growing. They watered them, then shut the glass lid. The Ward's case would not be opened again until it reached England.

Robert puzzled over this for some time. 'How do they stay moist?' he finally asked as William

Lobb dripped a lighted candle along the seams of the case.

'Condensation,' Lobb replied without looking up. 'The water can't escape through evaporation, so it remains in the case. A plant can live months in a Ward's case, as long as it doesn't get smashed. It's people who are more likely to damage the plants than anything else. I once had specimens survive in Ward's cases all the way from Brazil, only to die from being left too long in the cold on a London dock. Seeds are always a better bet, as long as they don't germinate.'

The next day Robert and William Lobb took their cargo down to Pacific Wharf, where the *Columbus* was docked. It would steam to Panama City, then the cargo would be carried by wagon across the Panama Isthmus to Aspinwall, where another steamship would head up through the Caribbean to New York. There the cases would be transferred to a ship bound for Southampton, on the south coast of England. In all the trip would take two to three months.

Once they had stowed the Ward's case and the tin cases down in the hold and were back on deck, William Lobb took out his pipe, filled it with tobacco, tamped it down and lit it. 'Go and get anything still in the wagon, would you, lad? I've got my hands full.'

Robert thought they had brought everything but he went back as directed. On the wagon bed he found a leather trunk with a brass plate fixed to one side, the initials *WL* engraved on it. He ran his finger over the letters and frowned. Shouldering the trunk, he hauled it on board.

William Lobb was standing in the doorway of a cabin, and gestured for Robert to put the trunk at the foot of the bed. When he straightened, Robert looked at his employer puffing away on his pipe.

'Aren't you coming back to Mrs Bienenstock's?' he said at last, since it looked as if William Lobb wasn't going to speak.

'No, Robert.' It was one of the few times since they had met that Lobb used his name. 'I'm going back to England. I'm not expected for another year, and Veitch'll be surprised to see me. But this is the most exciting find since the monkey puzzle. He'll never believe me about the size of those sequoias unless I describe them to him face to face, and show him my drawings. In a letter he'll just think I'm exaggerating. This way I'll get a chance to look after the Ward's case, make sure it gets out into sunlight now and then, and doesn't get smashed or abandoned.'

'But—'

'Mrs B. will set you straight. Now, I've got a thing or two to settle with the captain. They always try to shortchange me on fresh water. See you in a year or two, if the sea doesn't get me, or a grizzly bear you!' With those words William Lobb strode away, leaving Robert standing lost on deck.

He did not wait for the steamship to set out,

but walked in a daze back to the boardinghouse. He had assumed that once the *Columbus* sailed, he and William Lobb would saddle their horses and ride south towards the mountains around Monterey, where Lobb would teach him about pines. Now he had to discard that dream. All he wanted to do was saddle up the gray and ride away – away from the boardinghouse and San Francisco, away from redwoods and sequoias, away from the Monterey and ponderosa and bristlecone pines he'd hoped William Lobb would show him. The problem was, you couldn't go west of California, and Robert had never run anywhere but west.

In his room he packed his few things. But when he went to settle up with Mrs Bienenstock, who was in the kitchen grinding coffee beans in a hand mill, she shook her head and he knew William Lobb had paid it. More than that: she had money for him, and instructions. 'You take his room, long as you don't mind how small and dark it is,' she said. 'Not so bad now those cases are gone. I'm supposed to pay you. You can have it all now, or regular like a salary. Which do you want?'

Robert stared at her, unable to speak. Mrs B. shook her head again and turned the handle faster. 'We better make it regular.' When he didn't move, she added, 'Come on, man. Time to paddle your own canoe. Go on, put your things in there. I'll get you some fresh sheets.' As Robert went to obey her, he thought he heard her chuckle.

William Lobb had left his room neat and empty apart from a stack of brown leather notebooks and a letter. The notebooks were similar to the one Lobb had used at Calaveras Grove. That notebook full of sequoia drawings was gone now, of course: Lobb would have taken it with him back to England to show to his employer. But the other notebooks were full of everything he needed to know about California conifers.

He opened the letter – the first he had ever received. It consisted mostly of a list.

September 13, 1853

Goodenough—
Please collect the following:
5 sacks each of Pinus radiata, muricata, ponderosa and attenuata + 3 seedlings each
3 of Abies bracteata + 3 seedlings
10 of giant sequoias + 5 seedlings
4 of Sequoia sempervirens + 5 seedlings
3 of Pinus lambertiana + 3 seedlings
5 each of Abies grandis, procera, magnifica and concolor + 3 seedlings
I have marked on the enclosed map where best to find them. Many you can collect near San Francisco or Monterey, but for the last listed you will need to go far north to the Oregon mountains and bring the cones back by ship to San Francisco.
Send all consignments to
William Lobb Esq

Veitch and Sons' Exotic Nursery
Mount Radford
Exeter
England
Use Adams Express, on my account. When you ship specimens, always send me two notes – one on the ship carrying the cargo, the other separately on a different ship – to alert me of their arrival.

Yours faithfully,
William Lobb

He sat for a long time, rereading the letter and studying the list of trees. Lobb had not asked him if he would collect for him, but simply assumed he would. That assumption did not bother Robert. Given the choice between the aimless sort of existence he'd had the last few years, picking up farming and ranching here and there, and collecting trees for an employer, there was no doubt which he would choose. And he was flattered that William Lobb felt he was up to the job – indeed, had spent the last several days training Robert.

He smiled to himself. He was becoming a tree agent.

For over a year Robert collected for William Lobb without hearing a word from him. He worked hard to gather the quantities demanded in the letter, traveling in a wide radius around San Francisco, making another trip to Calaveras Grove – hiring mules to bring the sacks back to the city – and going north for the first time to the Oregon mountains. The gray finally resigned himself to climbing and carrying sacks of cones, though he still kicked and bit when his owner tried to hang pails of seedlings on him, and Robert had to devise leather pouches to put them in instead.

It turned out plant collecting was a solitary occupation. In the past Robert had enjoyed being alone, or so he thought. Actually he had rarely been alone for long: working in hotels, in stables, on ranches and farms, and as a miner, he had always been around others. Now, out in the woods or up in the hills or out on the flat central plain, he could go for days without speaking to anyone. His throat seemed to close up and he had to keep clearing it, singing songs aloud or reciting the Latin names of plants, just to check that he still had a voice. *Araucaria imbricata. Sequoia sempervirens. Pinus lambertiana. Abies magnifica.* He was surprised at how much he missed people. Sometimes he deliberately sought out miners' camps, just to sit with others around a fire. When he needed familiarity, he went back to San Francisco so that he had Mrs Bienenstock to talk to – or at least to be around, as she was more a grunter than a talker. Robert did not say much either, but they sat in the kitchen together, reading the newspaper, or out on the steps of the house, where she smoked her cigar and he watched passersby. Once she offered him a cigar and he made the mistake of inhaling. She chuckled about it for a week.

By the following spring he had collected and packed and sent three shipments of specimens and seeds, ticking off everything in Lobb's letter. He didn't know what to do then, and asked Mrs Bienenstock. She didn't even look up from mopping the kitchen floor, cigar clamped between her teeth. 'Do it all over again.' So he did.

His next round of collecting was what brought him riding down a Sacramento street on a late spring day just as the sun came out from behind a cloud and lit up a woman in a yellow dress. She was standing by a wagon and watching as men loaded it with sacks of flour. Robert pulled up the gray with a start at the sight of Molly Jones.

Robert had met Molly five years before on a Texas ranch where she worked as a cook, with a side line in prostitution. She seemed equally at home in both roles, though she never called herself a whore. Sleeping with men was just another task, like scrubbing pots or gutting chickens. Robert had even seen her pause in the middle of preparing a pot of stew to step into the pantry with a cowboy and lift her skirts.

Molly had curly black hair, wide blue eyes, a substantial bosom and a cheerfulness that did not always match her circumstances. Robert had seen her continue smiling as she passed a corpse by the side of the road or after a customer gave her a black eye. 'Robert Goodenough,' she repeated the first time she heard his name. 'Now I am *sure* that ain't right. I'm gonna have to check jest how good you *are!*' And she did, that night, finding him and leading him back to her room, which had the most comfortable bed on the ranch, and relieving him of his ignorance of women. Her bosom smelled like bread. 'First one's free,' she said afterwards, lying along her arm and smiling. 'You can go now, honey,' she added as Robert sat on the side of the bed, hands hanging between his knees, unsure of the etiquette. Molly was helpful like that.

For a week Robert was in love with her, with her yeasty smell, her frizzy hair that would not stay in a bun, her lips a dark red like she had just been eating blackberries. Really he was in love with being so close to a person that you were actually inside their body. He could not get enough of that feeling, and visited her bed three more times that week. Between bouts they would lie in bed recovering, and Molly would ask him about his past. Robert dodged the difficult questions, said nothing about why he had left Ohio, about having to grow up fast, about being cold and hungry and tired most of the time. If he did not talk about it, he did not have to think about it, and could keep a dark curtain pulled shut between then and now. Instead he entertained her with funny stories about Jonah Parks, the charlatan medicine man he'd worked for in Indiana, like the time they went to jail after Jonah Parks stole a wooden leg and accidentally tried to sell it back to the owner. Molly loved that story.

She was more forthcoming about her own past: a childhood in Georgia, a mother dead in childbirth, a drunk father, a brother and sister killed by Indians while Molly hid in a haystack and watched. 'You got to smile,' she said. 'Otherwise you'd cry all day.'

After the fourth bedding, Molly took his money and said, 'No more for a while, or you'll run through your pay, with nothin' to show for it at the end.' It was her way of warning him off feeling more for her than he should, and Robert knew she was right. He still went to bed with her occasionally, but he did not try to get to know her better.

Sometimes, though, when he was wrapped in his blanket during a starless night, or chasing the horizon across an endless plain under the brutal Texan sun, he remembered the dazed feeling he'd had during that feverish week of love, riding among the cattle with the sensation that everything in the world – every scrubby plant, every outcrop of rock, every cow and horse and man and cloud – all connected up along a path that led back to one woman, standing in a kitchen making biscuits. While he was feeling it he had not thought he could ever feel any other way. Once it was gone, though, he wondered how something so strong could fade to a ghostly trace, like a river that had flooded but now dried to a trickle, leaving behind only a flood mark of debris. For the feeling did fade, Molly became just another worker at the ranch, and when Robert left for California, he said goodbye to her as if they had barely met and certainly not shared a sweaty bed. For her part, Molly remained buoyant. 'Maybe I'll go to Californie too,' she said. 'Find me some gold and put my feet up. That'd be the life, wouldn't it? Maybe I'll do that.'

It seemed she had done what she'd threatened. Robert sat on the gray on the Sacramento street and studied her. Molly was thinner now and more weathered – crossing America did that to a face – but still looked cheerful. She was turned away from him, and he could have ridden past and pretended their paths hadn't crossed, and never seen her again. He thought about it, and then he called her name.

Molly gave a shout when she saw him, ran over as he dismounted and hugged him, laughing, then pressed his face to her bosom. It sagged a little now but still smelled like bread. 'Why do you look so surprised?' she cried when she'd let him come up for air. 'I told you I'd get to Californie.'

'You – are you prospecting?' he asked. It was hard to imagine Molly as a miner. And finding gold was harder now; most of what was left required extraction with heavy equipment and cooperation rather than one man with a pick, a shovel and a pan. Many miners had joined together into companies. The rest had turned reluctantly and headed back east, or stayed and become sailors or ranchers or farmers or merchants or pimps or whores or hustlers. California had once been a huge land with a few Indians and Californios living there; now it held hundreds of thousands of Americans, come for gold and looking for something else to replace that dream.

'Me a miner?' Molly laughed. 'You think I'm gonna get these hands dirty? Naw, I'm cookin' at one of the camps up French Creek, off the Cosumnes River south of Hang Town. You know it? I jest come to Sacramento for supplies. Miners don't want to spend a minute away from their work, so they pay me good money to feed 'em. I'm keepin' an eye out for which one's found the most gold *and* managin' to hold on to his money. That's the one I'll stick with. Ain't found him yet.'

She's a cat, Robert thought, landing on her feet. He was glad to hear she had work and a plan, and had avoided the gold fever that took over so many and ravaged them. But he was a little uneasy too: he thought he'd seen a flash of desperation behind Molly's cheerfulness when she first caught sight of him, more pronounced than the simple pleasure of running into someone she knew. It was not easy for a woman in California, there being so few of them, and so many volatile men, but Robert preferred to think that Molly could take care of herself. He did not want her to want something from him.

'So how about you, honey? You prospectin'?'

'I did for a while, but I'm not now.'

'Didn't think so. You sure don't look like you struck rich. No watch, no new boots. And your horse . . .' Molly made a face at the speckled gray. 'What happened to Bolt?'

'Indians took him.'

She chuckled. 'Shame. They got a good eye for horses. What, they left you this flea-biter, did they?'

The gray seemed to understand her, for he jerked his head and whinnied.

Robert explained that he'd left prospecting and begun collecting trees for William Lobb to send back to England. Molly stared at him. 'What do they want with our trees? Don't they have their own?'

Robert shrugged. 'They don't have so many pines there.'

'You put 'em on a ship goin' thousands of miles and they pay good money for 'em?'

Robert nodded.

'That's the silliest damned thing I ever heard.'

Robert smiled. It was a common response when he told people what he did. 'You ever hear of Calaveras Grove, sixty miles south of here?'

'Heard of it. Never been. There's a hotel up that way, ain't there?'

'Yes, and trees bigger than anything you could ever imagine. Think of the biggest tree you've ever seen—'

'An old pecan tree, back of my Pa's cabin in Georgia,' Molly said immediately. 'I used to sit at

161

the bottom of it and jest look up and up. I loved that tree.' For just a moment she dropped her cheery mask and became pensive.

'Take that pecan and triple it in size, both how tall and how wide. That's a sequoia.'

'Well, now, I'd like to see that. Maybe I'll go to Calaveras Grove and see those trees.' She sounded like she had back in Texas when talking about California. They exchanged a few more words about people they'd both known in Texas and what had become of them. The men had finished loading the flour and were waiting for Molly, picking their teeth and spitting tobacco on the ground around the wagon.

'Well, good luck with your seed collecting, Robert Goodenough,' Molly said at last. 'I can see trees suit you better'n cattle ever did.'

'I guess.'

'Come and see me if you're ever up near French Creek.'

'Are you still making those biscuits?' Molly's biscuits in Texas had been famous for their fluffiness.

'Of course.' Molly winked. 'Remember, the first one is free.'

Robert had thought he would never get to French Creek and take up her invitation. There were no redwoods or sequoias there, only some sugar and ponderosa pines he could collect but which he could also find just as easily closer to San Francisco. There was no reason to go.

Nonetheless, three weeks later he made the trip. Molly was so glad to see him that he knew then the flash of desperation he'd noticed in Sacramento had not been imagined. Indeed, it was in her eyes when he arrived and when he left. In between she kept him near her, brought him into her bed and had him take her over and over until he had slaked his pent-up energy. When they were not in bed he helped her cook, for he had no desire to mine or watch others do so.

Being at French Creek reminded Robert of the prospecting fields he had left three years before: the relentless focus on gold that made men both crazed and dull, and the many nights around fires spent talking about the minutiae of equipment – whether a rocker box caught more gold than an individual pan, or where to buy a balanced pickaxe – or endlessly analyzing the latest rumors of gold elsewhere that could empty out a camp by morning. He hadn't liked it then, even when he took part in it, and he detested it now, when the gold was harder to find. The miners still working were more ruthless, even when they were meant to be cooperating.

They treated Molly far worse than had the Texas cowboys, who had been grateful to her for her food and her bed and her cheerfulness. The miners only cared about gold: how big the nuggets, how abundant the flakes, how easily they could find it. They were never satisfied with what they got, and always worried that they had missed the bigger nugget, the better claim. Anything that stood in the way of their search, even things they needed – food, sleep, sex – was at best dispatched with quickly. At worst, they turned violent, taking out on these necessities all their frustration at not discovering the gold that would cure their fever. They threw meat at Molly's feet if it was too tough, spat weak whiskey in her face, swore at her. Yet she put up with it, watchful, waiting for the man most likely to allow her to live with her feet up as she wanted. She worked, and took men to bed, and was beaten, and waited.

Her bedroom at least was comfortable. Molly always knew how to make a nest for herself, with a thick mattress, a pillow filled with duck feathers, good sheets, and fringed shawls and painted screens for decoration. She took baths often, and kept out of the rain and harsh sun. She also had a knack for doing as little as possible without seeming lazy, getting others to help her with a smile or a tease. Robert doubted she had ever lifted anything heavier than a five-pound sack of cornmeal. She managed to get the seat closest to the fire without seeming greedy or ashamed to take it. Nor did she walk far, but wheedled lifts, either on horseback or, preferably, in a wagon, where she sat back and surveyed the land around her with the entitled air of a queen. It made the miners' ill treatment of her all the harder to bear. While he was there he brought her coffee in bed each morning, as if to make up for the other men's cruelty. He knew how to make only a crude version with burnt beans he'd hammered and boiled, but Molly acted gladder than she need be for this small gesture.

After breakfast on the third day, Robert saddled up the gray, Molly watching. 'I've packed you food for the road, honey,' she said, 'but you don't have to go.' She did not plead, but Robert sensed the rising panic in her and struggled not to be infected by it. He did not let himself tighten the stirrups any faster. He respected Molly enough to hide his desire to get away. 'I have seeds to collect,' he said.

'When are you coming back?'

She did not give him the opportunity not to return, extracting his promise to visit again within three months. Which is how Robert Goodenough became Molly's backup plan in case a respectable miner did not emerge from the jackals she lived among. Every few months he stayed with her at French Creek for two nights – never more – pumped her until he was sore, then escaped back to his trees. He felt guilty for not falling back in love with her, but though he tried, he could not recreate that week in Texas when all the world led back to her. That feeling belonged to other people.

Robert was at the stables near Mrs Bienenstock's, checking on his horse. It was early December and he had just come back to San Francisco after another visit to Molly, leaving as the snow came, which would mean no visiting for months unless he wanted to risk getting caught in a snowdrift and freezing to death. Seeing Molly was still new enough that he thought he might risk it, though the gray was not fond of snow. The horse had stepped on a sharp rock on the final stretch of road. Robert had taken care of it as soon as they arrived, removing the gray's shoe and scraping out the pus before applying a poultice. Now he wanted to make sure there was no infection. The horse seemed all right, though he was not the sort to communicate much. Perhaps he sensed Robert's own lack of commitment, for he showed little affection for his owner. Robert had been around men who loved their horses more than their wives, and cried when they died or were stolen. Some swore they could feel their horses laughing under their thighs. Robert suspected that if the gray had a sense of humor, it was a dry one.

He sat back on a barrel, watching his horse and eating an apple – a Gravenstein, one of the few apples available in California. Newly picked, they were juicy and tasted of berries, but they didn't keep well and by December were mushy and tasteless, with a disagreeably waxy skin. Robert grimaced, wondered why he was bothering, and fed it to the gray, who was not picky about the taste or feel of an apple.

'I got one you'll like better.'

William Lobb stood in the doorway. Pulling an apple from his pocket, he tossed it to Robert. It was small and yellow and wrinkled, and Robert turned it over and over in his hand.

'Try it. I've brought it all this way for you, lad. Go on, bite into it.'

Robert bit, and though old and soft from its long journey, the apple still contained a trace of the distinctive honey and pineapple taste of a Golden Pippin.

'Thought that would make you smile. Pitmaston Pineapples have become quite the thing in England. Even Veitch is selling 'em, and he's not much bothered about apple trees.'

Robert thought about shaking William Lobb's hand, but such formality didn't seem appropriate with him. They had only ever shaken hands once, when they first met. 'Did the shipments I sent arrive?' he asked instead. 'There were three of them, but I didn't hear anything.'

'They did indeed. Didn't I write to tell you? No? My apologies. Yes, they all arrived, and mostly intact. The Ward's cases were fine, the seedlings fresh as the day they were dug up. You lost three cases of cones to damp, but that's not bad out of a few dozen. It's what you'd expect.' Lobb stepped over to the stall that housed his buckskin mare. Others had used her while he was away, but she had begun whinnying the moment she heard his voice. Lobb patted her and fed her an apple – not a Pitmaston Pineapple, Robert hoped, for it would be wasted on a horse.

'Did I collect what you wanted?'

'Yes. You mixed up the Noble Fir and the Red Fir cones – but that's easily done, and easily made right,' William Lobb added when he caught sight of Robert's face, perhaps understanding that after over a year away, what his assistant needed was reassurance rather than a list of things he'd done wrong.

'How are the sequoias doing in England? Did they believe you about the size?'

'Oh, they did, they did! The English love the idea of these huge trees. In fact, I've rather done Billie Lapham a disservice. His publicity of Calaveras Grove reached as far as Europe, and once they'd read about the Mammoth Tree grove, everyone wanted one. My timing was perfect.' Lobb continued stroking the buckskin mare. 'Of course, at first customers were put out that there were no giant trees ready for them to plant – as if they expected us to dig up mature sequoias and send them by ship! But we grew seedlings quick enough, and that seems to satisfy them. It tickles them to imagine their great-great-grandchildren enjoying a tree whose size they can only dream of.'

'What about the seedlings?'

'Of the four I brought back, two are still growing; the other two perished after being transplanted into English soil, the like of which probably shocked them to death after the Californian soil they were accustomed to. I myself felt rather similarly.'

Indeed, William Lobb did not look quite himself. He seemed tired, the T of his face more prominent because of his sunken cheeks and hollowed eye sockets. Of course it was not surprising – three months on ships would likely carve out any man's face. But there was something deeper than surface fatigue and illness. He moved stiffly, as if he didn't have his legs entirely in control. His black hair was much grayer, and lank rather than glossy. His talk was also less modulated: his laughter seemed louder, and he swore more. Later when they went to an eating house – a place where rough talk was more common than kind words – his tone made customers glance over, though they were careful not to meet Lobb's eye.

His anger at James Veitch made a vein bulge in his temple. 'He's milking me dry, like an old cow with withered dugs!' he exclaimed, shoveling ham into his mouth. 'All he wants is for me to collect plants till my balls fall off, the cheating bastard. Makes his money from my knowledge with no respect for it!'

'How much is he selling the sequoias for?'

'Two guineas a seedling.' When Robert didn't respond to the figure, Lobb added, 'That's eight dollars a tree!'

Robert widened his eyes. 'We could buy a hundred and fifty apple seedlings for that price back in Ohio.'

'Yes, and do I see any of that money? Only a pittance!'

Robert let him continue to rant, hoping he would eventually empty himself of his bile and they could talk more sensibly about work. He did not really care about how much the trees cost, or even how Veitch was treating his employer. He just wanted to know if he would still be working for Lobb.

When there was a pause, Robert ventured to ask, 'What will we be collecting next?'

William Lobb exploded. 'Goddammit, lad, can't a man rest without being pestered and bullied? I'm just off the boat, my legs hurt, my head hurts, I just want to sleep without your badgering!' He stood up from his unfinished plate and stormed off, leaving Robert to pay.

Lobb remained in his room for several days. If he hadn't been there Robert would have made his own plans, but now that his sometime employer was back he felt obliged to wait for instructions from him. He hated being idle, though, and took to helping Mrs Bienenstock when he could. He tidied up the backyard for her, and one afternoon they cleared mud from the road in front of the house – a futile effort since it would reappear with the next rain, but Mrs B. insisted. 'Standards,' she replied when he pointed this out.

As they worked, he asked her what was wrong with William Lobb. Mrs B. paused, leaning on her shovel. 'Spanish disease, of course. What do you think he got up to down in South America? It wasn't all plants.' She gestured at his crotch. 'Mind you don't get it yourself, with your trips up to French Creek. It's called the French disease too, you know!' Mrs B. enjoyed teasing him about Molly.

She stopped chuckling, however, when she noted Robert's stricken expression. 'Don't worry about him, man – he'll be up in a day or two. I've seen some suffer much worse than him.'

She was right – William Lobb was up the next day. He said nothing about his outburst at the eating house; nor did he repay Robert for his meal. Instead he announced that they would go south to collect flowering plants. 'Yellow flowers, that's what Veitch says the English want now. Poppies, violets, primroses. They've already got 'em in purple, but now they want yellow Californian poppies and violets to plant near their Californian conifers. You know about trees – now it's time I taught you about flowers.'

They spent the next eighteen months collecting a wide variety of flowers, shrubs and trees for Veitch to sell to English gardeners hungry for novelty, traveling as far south as Santa Barbara and as far north as the Oregon mountains. Or rather, Robert went north: William Lobb was less willing to go to more remote areas. Physically he suffered from joint pains and numbness and blinding head-aches. Mentally he was at times confused and forgetful. Emotionally he was temperamental, sometimes shouting at Robert but most often directing his anger at Veitch, who he complained didn't appreciate his skills as a collector. 'Without me Veitch Nurseries would be *nothing*,' he ranted. 'They'd be selling only roses and daffodil bulbs and box hedges. The most exotic plant they'd offer would be a subspecies of *Sambucus nigra*! I have brought them rhododendrons and ceanothus. I have brought them the fuchsias you see in every decent British garden. I have brought the monkey puzzle and the redwood. And what do I get for my trouble? Complaints and demands!' Yet he also fretted when he didn't receive letters from Veitch asking for more seeds and specimens. 'He's found someone else,' he declared. 'Bridges or Beardsley or some other biddable lackey who will work for him for less money.'

Robert learned not to listen, and to offer to go alone on the more strenuous trips. Sometimes Lobb agreed. Other times, though, his paranoia extended to his assistant and he became convinced Robert was trying to take over his business. Then he would insist on coming along, though he rode more slowly now, sometimes hiring a wagon instead of riding the buckskin mare. Though he learned a great deal from his employer, Robert was disappointed that they never rediscovered the charmed magic of that first trip they had taken together from Calaveras Grove to San Francisco, when Robert was the sponge and Lobb the river of knowledge he soaked in.

After a year of increasingly slow and difficult travels, William Lobb decided to remain in San Francisco at Mrs Bienenstock's and focus on the packing and shipping while Robert did the collecting. It was Mrs B. who suggested the arrangement. 'Jesus H. Christ,' she interrupted Lobb one day as he sat in her kitchen complaining of the aches and pains he'd suffered from their latest trip to Monterey. 'Stay here and do the packing and let the young one run all over California for you! Don't you always say the success of collecting is in the packing? You're the boss – take the most important role and stop moaning!'

Lobb was silent for a moment. He still showed Mrs B. more respect than he did anyone else, his mania miraculously abating whenever she gave him a look or made a sharp remark. 'Maybe you're right,' he agreed at last.

Mrs B. raised her eyebrows. 'Maybe?'

The arrangement suited Robert too. He could travel alone, visit Molly now and then, and enjoy small doses of William Lobb, tempered by Mrs Bienenstock. He was, almost, happy.

The British mania for giant sequoias showed no signs of dying down, and Robert made regular trips up to Calaveras Grove to collect seeds. Whenever he had the chance, he took a few days to explore the surrounding area. He never told anyone – not William Lobb, or Billie Lapham, or Mrs Bienenstock, or Molly – but he was looking for more sequoias. Lobb himself had suggested early on that there could be more growing somewhere along the mountain range at a similar elevation, but now his illness had eroded his adventurous spirit and he preferred to collect at known places.

It took three years of searching, but in the late summer of 1856 Robert at last stumbled upon more giant trees. He was picking his way through thick woods only five miles southeast of Calaveras Grove when the gray began to snort and whinny, then kick out with his hooves. Robert assumed he had seen a snake, but the horse was looking ahead rather than down. He dismounted and held tight to the reins, his heart beating faster. Though he couldn't see anything – no telltale auburn presence in the distance – Robert sensed a difference in the woods ahead. It was quieter, with fewer birds and less rustling of leaves.

He dragged the gray through the trees until he saw the first sequoia, then tied up his horse with its back to the grove and its nose in a bag full of oats, and went to explore. Here were dozens of giant sequoias, more spread out than at Calaveras Grove, and even bigger and more beautiful. There were no raked paths or signs or laughing tourists spilling out of saloons or standing on giant stumps. He was amazed that no one had found the grove before him, though he had learned in his travels that people tended to stick to well-worn paths rather than push into new places.

Robert was the trees' only witness, and he planned to keep it that way. He would not collect cones here: the grove would remain untouched, as trees should be. James Goodenough would have

174

approved. It was even worth paying Billie Lapham for the privilege of continuing to collect at Cally Grove if that would keep these sequoias secret. Robert had come to like Billie Lapham, but he knew the businessman would want to lay claim to the new grove and expand his business if he could.

The next day he continued on to Calaveras Grove. As he arrived, passing the Two Sentinels that marked the beginning of the grove, he saw that there was dancing on the Great Stump. Indeed, there had been dancing on it every time Robert visited, and he had grown used to the sight, though he still refused to set foot on the stump himself. Californians loved to dance more than any other people he had met. This was the case both of gold rush miners and of Californios up from Mexico. It seemed once they arrived they caught two fevers: gold and dance. There was dancing everywhere, even when there were no women to dance with. At the mining camps he'd lived in, after a long day bent over pans, the men danced with each other or did a solo jig to a fiddle and a guitar.

Today there were just two couples, dancing a fast polka to the whistling of one of the men. They danced with their partners; then, after a signal known only to themselves, switched. Robert was always surprised by this unspoken fluidity. He was not a dancer. Despite Molly's attempts to teach him a few simple steps, he had never been able to join dances after supper when the tables and chairs were pushed back, or outside by the fire. Instead he had stood or squatted on his heels and watched.

Now his eyes followed the women first, as they always did. One was round and buxom, and once she realized that Robert was watching her, she began exaggerating her movements so that her hips swayed and the arcs of her turns followed the curves of her body, drawing them in the air. He didn't know if she intended to embarrass him or if she liked the attention, but he shifted his eyes to the other woman. Small, slight, with wisps of hair escaping her bun, she did not look at Robert, or the men who held her, or anyone, but danced as if she were not in the arms of a gold miner on top of a giant sequoia stump, but somewhere far away.

At least today there were only four of them. Robert had witnessed a Fourth of July cotillion where thirty-two people had danced on the Great Stump, with enough space for the musicians as well. The cotillion had made the newspapers in Stockton and Sacramento and even San Francisco, with a drawing of the dance published alongside the articles. They were more like advertisements than news, orchestrated by Billie Lapham to publicize Calaveras Grove.

His eyes moved from the women on to the dancing men. Both had the weathered skin of miners, their obsession with gold putting them outside in all weathers and giving them a reason to ignore the hail, the heat, the ice, the wind that chapped their cheeks and lips. It was not just skin that marked them as gold miners, though, for Robert also had the scoured face of a life lived outdoors. These two still had that trace of gold obsession haunting their eyes, eight years after gold had first been discovered in California, and six years since the peak of the gold rush. Their dreams were still full of those minute glittering flashes. It was a dream common to many, wherever they came from. Robert had met French and Spanish and German and Dutch and Chinese chasing that dream. He had met men and a few women from Maine and Florida, Indiana and Missouri, Wisconsin and Connecticut. He had met people from Ohio. He had even once met a man from the Black Swamp, who had lived there only briefly, long after Robert's time. Robert almost asked him about the Goodenough farm, but stopped himself: the man was drunk, and besides, Robert was not sure what he wanted to hear. From their clothes and the fact that they were drinking French brandy – a flamboyant expense when so much cheap Cuban rum or local whiskey was available – it seemed these two had done well out of gold, had managed not to gamble away all of their earnings. This was rare; no wonder the women, with their pale indoor skin and well-cut dresses, were willing to dance with them. These were the kind of men Molly was looking for to take her away from French Creek. These were the tourists Billie Lapham had been trying to attract with his ads and his well-kept road and his hotel and bowling alley.

And here he was. 'Goodenough! Ain't you the man of the moment. There's a gal been lookin' for you.'

Robert turned around. Billie Lapham's top hat was pushed back as usual, its brim partly detached from the crown, and he was stroking his moustache with one hand and reaching out to shake Robert's hand with the other.

'Nancy wants to see me?' Robert said.

Billie Lapham's face fell. 'Nance is a little poorly – though of course she'll want to see you, sick or not. Put your head around the door, make her smile again.'

Lapham's wife Nancy was soft and sickly, with faded hair and a face wide at the cheeks and narrowed to a point at the chin like a cat's. The first time he heard her cough, Robert had known what it meant: eventually consumption would take her. Every time he came to Cally Grove, he braced himself for Nancy's absence, and was relieved to find her still greeting visitors on the front porch of the Big Trees Hotel, or sweeping the floor in the saloon, or washing glasses out back. She always smiled at Robert and seemed pleased to see him.

It also pleased Billie Lapham to see his wife happy. He was not the jealous type, but hospitable, inviting Robert to supper or for a whiskey, both of which Robert always accepted. Or he told him he could dance on the Great Stump for free rather

than pay fifty cents like the others. This offer
Robert never took up. But he was happy to estab-
lish with Lapham an easy business relationship
that tipped over into friendliness, helped along by
the five dollars he handed over as a fee each time
he collected seeds there.

Billie Lapham fingered his moustache and
watched the couples dancing their polka. 'Just
between us, Goodenough, I'm selling my share of
Cally Grove and taking Nancy to live at Murphys.
More people there who can look after her, rather'n
her lookin' after people.'

'Who are you selling to?'

Billie Lapham made a face. 'Haynes bought me
out.'

Dr Smith Haynes had been Billie Lapham's business partner for almost two years, and Robert had
never taken to him. He was a harder man than
Lapham, with a full beard, a long stare, a snug
waistcoat and his hands always in his pockets. He
insisted on being called 'Doctor,' though Robert
had never heard of him doing any doctoring. He
treated Billie Lapham with unwarranted disdain.

What bothered Robert even more was his dismiss-
iveness of Nancy's role as hostess of the Big Trees
Hotel. Haynes wanted a hostess to be everything
Nancy wasn't: loud, bosomy, funny and assertive.
He wanted her to ply visitors with drinks, tell them
jokes, flirt with the men and commiserate with the
women. Nancy did none of these things, though
she had a quiet charm that worked if given a chance.

Haynes never gave her a chance, though. As she grew sicker and weaker, he glared as if she had deliberately contracted TB to provoke him. Of course he couldn't fire her since she was his business partner's wife, and Billie Lapham defended her robustly, if anxiously. 'She's improving, looking better, don't you think?' he'd say to Robert in front of Haynes, and Robert would agree even when Nancy was clearly worse. 'The customers like her,' Lapham would remind Haynes. It was true that visitors liked Nancy, despite her flat chest and lack of jokes. She was gentle, and she listened when they complained about fog obscuring good views of the sequoias, or fleas in the beds, or their losses at the card tables, or the blisters they got from dancing on the Great Stump's rough surface. When she could she did something to help: stuffed mattresses with pennyroyal and rosemary to drive away the fleas, suggested excursions to escape the fog, appealed to her husband to install a sprung floor on the stump. Otherwise she sympathized with a smile and a cough. But Haynes felt it wasn't enough. He would be delighted the Laphams were going.

'In fact,' Billie Lapham continued, 'you'll need to make a new deal with Haynes about the seed collecting. He always thought five dollars a time wasn't enough for what you're takin' from the property. Me, I don't mind. I know how much Nancy likes to see you. My wife's smile is worth a lot more than the five extra dollars Haynes wants to charge you.'

'Thanks for the warning. I'll come see you and Nancy at Murphys when you move.'

Billie Lapham nodded. 'We'd like that. Now, this other gal . . .'

'What other gal?'

'The one I just mentioned was looking for you.'

'I thought you meant Nancy.'

'Naw, this was a visitor. She came yesterday and asked for you.' Billie Lapham grinned. 'Looked urgent to me so I sent her to Nance. Women know the right questions to ask, you see. Best to find out from her. I'll take you to her now – I want to check on her anyway.'

Robert followed him to the hotel, a sinking feeling in his belly. The last time he'd seen Molly, four months before, she'd talked about visiting Calaveras Grove to see the trees. So, as she had with her threats to come to California, she had actually done what she'd said she would do. While she was at French Creek Robert felt he could keep her separate from the rest of his life. If she came here, though, she would stay. Haynes would love her, and with Nancy going, Molly could be the hostess he wanted, with her laugh and her bosom and her big open bed.

Nancy and Billie Lapham slept in a small room at the top of the hotel where you would expect the maid to live rather than the proprietor. But that was how businessmen made their money – by renting out the good rooms and ignoring their own comfort until they could afford to think about it.

181

Nancy lay in a bed that took up most of the space yet was hardly big enough for both of them. Though the window was open, the room smelled of milk someone had left to sour in the glass, of the chamber pot that was not emptied often enough, of a body confined. Robert wished he could carry her downstairs and put her in one of the rocking chairs on the hotel porch, but he suspected Haynes wouldn't want her there, advertising illness to the visitors.

He stood in the doorway, hat in hand, while Billie Lapham woke his wife. Nancy whimpered, but when Billie whispered Robert's name to her, she struggled to sit up. Her pointed face was white apart from two bright dots of red on her cheeks, as if she had been leaning on her hands. And she smiled. 'Robert,' she croaked, 'I'm so glad you've come.'

'Yes, ma'am, I am too.' Whenever Robert was with her he became formal.

'Don't you "ma'am" me. I'm your friend, not a minister's wife. Come and sit with me.' Nancy patted the edge of the bed.

Robert glanced at Billie Lapham, who nodded. 'I brought you a pitcher of fresh water, Nance,' her husband said. 'Straight from the well, nice and cold. I drew it myself.' Throwing the sour milk out of the window, he rinsed the glass and filled it with water. 'You want anything else?'

'No, thank you, honey. I'll just visit awhile here with Robert. We got things to discuss.'

Billie Lapham chuckled. 'You sure do.' His laughter puzzled Robert, as did Nancy's widening smile. They seemed to be sharing a joke at his expense.

When Billie Lapham had clattered down the stairs, Nancy's smile dimmed a little, and Robert frowned. He was often surprised at himself for caring so much about her. 'How are you keeping, Nancy?' he asked, making sure to use her name.

Nancy raised her free hand and gestured to her bed-bound body, then let it drop. 'Well, it's obvious, ain't it? I just get worse 'n' worse. Did Billie tell you we're moving to Murphys?'

Robert nodded.

'I'm doin' it to humor him, really. Bein' in bed there or here won't make no difference to me. Might make him feel better, though – rest easier about me. And he won't have to deal with Haynes any more. That man: I wish a sugar-pine cone would fall right on his head.' Seeing Robert smile, Nancy became more elaborate in her revenge. 'A big one, a foot long like they come, nice and green and heavy. And with the sap on it that's so sticky you can't get it off you, and the dirt gets in it and you can't get that off either, so you go round lookin' unwashed. That's what I would like to have happen to that man.'

'Want me to shoot some cones off a tree when he's passing under it?'

'You do that.' Nancy closed her eyes and leaned back into the pillows. 'I'll miss the big trees. That I do regret.'

Robert waited. After a few minutes he thought she must be asleep, the glass of water tipping in her hand. He took it gently from her and set it on the small table by her bed, where there was a Bible, a candle and a stack of handkerchiefs freshly laundered. One of them was crumpled; Robert could see specks of blood on it.

Then he froze. Behind the handkerchiefs was a small brown glass pot with a label that read: 'Jonah Parks' Respiratory Balm – for efficacious breathing.' Next to the words was a crude sketch of a woman holding a bouquet of flowers that Robert himself might well have drawn fifteen years ago, for the pot looked that old.

He reached over and picked it up, and Nancy opened her eyes. 'Nancy, where'd you get this?'

'Oh, a visitor gave it to me last week, said it would help me to breathe easier. And it has! Why, have you ever used it?'

'No.'

Nancy looked at him more closely. 'What is it?' When he didn't answer, she sighed. 'Robert Goodenough, you never tell me anything!'

'It's nothing, really – just that I once worked for Mr Parks.'

'Did you? That's funny! Where was this?'

'Indiana.' Robert did not add that the balm was simply a mixture of beeswax, camphor and sassafras root cooked in a pot over a campfire – as was the snake oil, brain salt, cure for baldness, and all the other medicines Jonah Parks made up. Nancy wanted to believe it helped her breathe, and for that reason, maybe it did. He sat now looking at this piece of his past, and marveled that it had found its way to Nancy's bedside table. Indiana was a long way from California, and Ohio ever further. And yet, what a small world this was.

Nancy's eyes had drooped again and Robert thought he would slip out and let her sleep. When he got up, though, she grabbed his arm with more strength than he'd expected. 'Where do you think you're goin'?' she demanded, her eyes still shut.

'I thought you were asleep.'

'You think I'm gonna sleep when we got a woman to talk about? I was just restin' my eyes, is all.' She opened her eyes and Robert sat back down.

'You know,' Nancy said, 'when I first met you a few years ago, I couldn't believe you weren't married, or at least have a gal. "Somebody oughta snap him up," I told Billie. You're a handsome fella – don't duck your head, you are! You got the brightest brown eyes, would make any gal happy just to have you look at her. You keep clean, you don't drink or gamble, and you listen to people. If you'd had any money to invest, Billie would've asked you to partner him running Cally Grove. We knew you'd look after these trees.'

Robert had never heard of this idea, and wondered how he would have responded if they had asked.

'Anyway, it's too late now – we're stuck with Haynes, and Billie and I are gettin' out of here.' Nancy closed her eyes again. Talking clearly tired her, and Robert would have to wait and let her catch up with herself. He didn't mind: he was in no rush to hear about Molly.

Nancy opened her eyes again. 'So wasn't I blown over to find out you *did* have a woman. Why didn't you tell us, Robert? All this time I been worryin' over you when I didn't have to!'

'Well . . .' Robert couldn't think how to describe his relationship with Molly in a way that would satisfy Nancy. 'I didn't think you minded one way or another.'

'Course I mind! I like to know you're happy. 'Cause you don't always seem happy, you know, except out in the trees. With people – with Billie and me, even – you don't say much. Like I never knew till just now that you were in Indiana once. I always hoped you'd feel you could tell me things, if you wanted.'

'I – I know.' Robert felt his chest tightening, as it had whenever Molly asked him too many questions. 'I just don't think about the past much.'

Nancy could have asked why that was, but she seemed to know that she had pushed far enough. Instead she said, 'So all those times you say you're off collecting trees you're actually with her?'

'No,' Robert protested. 'Mostly I *am* collecting trees. It's just now and again I visit her.'

186

'Sure.' Nancy was smiling again. Clearly she didn't believe him.

'When did you see her?'

'Yesterday. We had a little visit. She sat right where you are now.'

Robert blushed and rubbed his head. It was hard to imagine Molly here with her curves and her laugh and her desperation. The room was too small. He was embarrassed too: Molly was not the kind of woman Nancy would expect him to be with. He was embarrassed, and he was ashamed that he was embarrassed, for it was disrespectful of Molly. He wished he could leave this hot, stale room, but he couldn't walk away from Nancy.

'What did she say?' he asked.

'Not much – didn't need to. She wants to see you, of course. It's lucky you turned up when you did!'

'Where is she now?'

'I told her I didn't know when you'd be passin' through next, and that she should get herself a room and wait, and we'd try to get word out to you since it's urgent. She said she couldn't afford it, so I told her to rest herself here a day or two, then get a lift back to Murphys where the rooms are cheaper and more plentiful.'

Robert's mind rested on the one word both Billie and Nancy Lapham had used: urgent. He could only think of one reason why it might be urgent. 'Where is she – resting?'

'In the barn. Billie knows. I told her to keep out

of Haynes' way. That man would happily throw out a woman in her state, just like the innkeeper in Bethlehem. So she's stayin' out of sight.' Nancy's speech was getting slower and more garbled as she grew tired, and Robert wasn't sure he understood. Or he did, and didn't want to.

'What do you mean? Nancy?'

Nancy's eyes were closed. He waited with increasing impatience for her to rouse herself, but this time she slept. If he wanted to confirm why Molly was here, he would have to find her himself.

She wasn't in the barn. Robert wasn't surprised – it was stifling inside. Molly wasn't in the stables looking at the horses as she liked to do sometimes at French Creek. She wasn't on the porch, pretending to be a visitor having coffee. She wasn't in the saloon, or the bowling alley, or at the Great Stump, or in the kitchen chatting to the cooks.

He returned to the barn again to make sure she hadn't gone back while he was looking for her elsewhere. There he ran into a young hand, forking hay into a wheelbarrow to take to the horses. 'You lookin' for the lady?' the boy said. 'The one like this?' And he made the gesture Robert had feared since Billie and Nancy Lapham had both smiled at him: the unmistakable curve of a belly carrying a child.

'You know where she is?'

'She *was* here, but she went to see the trees.'

The boy grinned as Robert turned and stumbled out into the fresh air.

He had never asked Molly about babies. He'd never asked her much about herself since their first few nights together. As far as he knew she'd not had any. But nor had she made him withdraw early or wear something on his cock. He knew there were things women did to prevent babies involving hot baths and mustard or vinegar, or visits to doctors. They were women's things he did not ask about, or feel he needed to know about.

If she was as big as the stable hand had indicated, she must have already been pregnant the last time he'd seen her four months before. She'd said nothing, though Robert tried to think back to how she'd been. Had her stomach swelled and tightened like a drum? Had her already substantial breasts gotten bigger? He couldn't recall. His visits to Molly's bed blended into one long session of sweaty flesh and rumpled sheets, of a release that only ever scratched the surface of his itch, no matter how often he entered her. That a child would emerge from that chaotic pleasure seemed improbable. But then, his parents had had ten children that way. He shook his head, standing in the sun, the sequoias flashing red in the distance.

He headed out to them. A trail wound among the big trees for the ease of visitors, but Robert ignored it, for walking through undergrowth did not bother him. Apart from making the path, Billie Lapham and his various partners had also named some of the trees, hanging signs on them. Visitors liked that, for they wanted a way to differentiate between the sequoias and make sense of them. So there were the Two Sentinels at the entrance to Calaveras Grove. Nearby was the Discovery Tree, which the hunter from Murphys first saw when he was chasing a grizzly bear; it was the sequoia that had been felled and now had the bowling alley built on it. Then there were the Three Graces, a trio of beautiful trees standing side by side. The Old Bachelor, a rough tree. The Hermit, a tree that stood alone. The Siamese Twins, with two trees growing out of one trunk. The Burnt Tree, which had fallen and been burnt hollow by lightning so a person could ride through it on horseback. Robert hated the signs; he hated the names. Occasionally he thought about stealing all the signs and burning them, but he knew they would just be replaced.

Another fallen sequoia had broken in two when it came down, and parts of it were half buried. Billie Lapham had measured these parts and esti-mated that the tree was the largest in the grove, at over four hundred feet long. Robert thought the length exaggerated, but Billie Lapham stood by his measurements, and named the tree Father of the Forest. Whenever Robert saw it he thought of his father, and so he avoided it.

He also stayed away from Mother of the Forest, which made him even sadder, for its bark had been stripped over a hundred feet up the tree, to be shipped to New York and exhibited for those skeptics who thought the sequoias were a tall tale. The trunk was naked except for the scaffolding it was still clad in. Robert assumed this was to show visitors how it had been done; otherwise he could not imagine why Billie Lapham would leave up something so ugly. For a couple of years Mother of the Forest seemed to suffer no ill effects from this stripping, but Robert had noticed recently that its foliage was thinning. He suspected it would eventually die, after hundreds, maybe even thousands of years free from human touch. Robert liked Billie Lapham, but hated what he and his partners had done in the name of promoting the Calaveras Grove trees.

There were other family groups: Mother and Son, with a larger and smaller tree, their foliage touching. Husband and Wife, leaning towards each other. The Three Sisters. He did not find Molly by any of these trees, though. Instead she had chosen to sit under the Orphans, two sequoias on the eastern edge of the grove, which stood so close to each other they seemed to have grown from the same root, with their branches entwined. She looked very small sitting under those giant trees, though when she saw him and struggled to her feet, already starting to cry, Robert saw that Nancy and Billie Lapham had been right about her condition. She was very close to having a baby.

They were wrong, though, about the other important thing. Very wrong. It was not Molly. It was Martha.

When he recognized his sister, eighteen years

BLACK SWAMP, OHIO

FALL 1838

'Robert, bring me some cold water.'

'Martha, git me another quilt!'

James and Sadie Goodenough spoke at the same time, and had to repeat themselves before their words could be untangled and understood. They were lying side by side in their bed, flat on their backs. James held himself as rigid as possible to counter the shakes that racked his body. This was how he had always dealt with swamp fever – fighting it by not succumbing to its demands. If he felt cold he refused to wrap himself in quilts. If his teeth were chattering he gripped his jaw tight. His only concession was water: if he was thirsty, he drank, demanding cold water freshly drawn rather than taking it from the pitcher left on the floor by the bed.

As expected, Sadie had a different response to illness: she indulged in it. If she was thirsty she drank the whole pitcher dry. When she shook she rattled the bed so much James thought he would fall off. During a spike in her fever she would talk all sorts of gibberish, laughing and swearing and holding imaginary conversations, sometimes with other men in a way that embarrassed him. Now she was cold, and rubbed her arms more vigorously than she needed to. Rolling around in the bed, she pulled the quilt off James, then called again for another.

Martha appeared with the nine-patch quilt in her arms, hesitating by the bed, her small face wary, as it always was around her mother. 'It's still damp from your sweat, Ma,' she said. 'I been airing it but there hasn't been enough sun today to dry it.'

'Give it to me!' Sadie snatched the quilt. Someone was calling out upstairs and Martha went to climb the ladder and see what they wanted.

James was less demonstrative, taking the mug Robert held out to him and managing a mild, 'Thank you, son,' to contrast with Sadie. Robert watched while he gulped down the water, then took the mug from him, refilled it, and set it down on the floor within James' reach. 'You want anything else, Pa?'

'No. You fed the animals?'

'Yes, Pa.'

'How's the corn? You brought any of it in yet?'

'Tomorrow. Mr Day's gonna help me now the hay's in.'

'What are you doing today? You been working with Martha in the garden?'

'Yup. We're gonna pickle cucumbers and stew tomatoes. Mrs Day said she'd be along to help.'

'The Days are helping too much.'

196

Robert shrugged. There was nothing they could do about that: Nathan and Caleb and Sal were all sick too. One of them was going through the shakes now in the attic, rattling the floor above them. It was one of the ironies of swamp fever that it normally struck at the height of harvest when everyone was most needed. The crops were ready; the people weren't, except for Robert, who had to be counted on to do the work of a grown man, though he was just nine. And Martha, unexpectedly: usually she was the first to go down with the fever and the last to get up again.

'You checked the apples?' James couldn't help asking. He asked every day. 'You sure they aren't ready? Some of the spitters could be ready by now.'

'They don't look ready, Pa.'

'Bring me one. No, bring me two. Bring me the reddest of the spitters and a Golden Pippin.'

Robert sighed, and James understood he was being a nuisance. His son would have to pull up some of the deer fence poles to get to one of the Golden Pippin trees. He knew the apples were not ripe, but he could not help fretting.

Sadie poked her face out from beneath the folds of the quilt. 'Stop talkin' 'bout those goddamn apples,' she growled. 'If I wasn't abed I'd chop down those trees!'

'Shut up. You're even more of an idiot when you're sick than when you're drunk.'

Sadie kicked at her husband, but she was so weak that it did not have much effect. James inched himself to the edge of the bed, though he was still within kicking reach. Hearing the racket one of his children was making above him – the crack of teeth battering uncontrollably against each other – almost caused him to start shaking as well.

James and Sadie had not spent so much time together in months. Since returning from the camp meeting in May, she had avoided being alone with him, and kept quiet, throwing herself into cleaning the house, working in the garden, and even trying to clear a strip of land to plant with winter potatoes, something she had nagged James to do for years. James had watched her go at the trees – mostly elm and ash and oak – with an axe, chopping them down and cutting up the trunks and branches to stack and dry out for firewood. She had managed that much on her own. But the stumps defeated her. She hacked and dug at one, pulling off pieces of wood and making what was left even harder to get a hold on, until she collapsed and lay on her back next to the stump, sweating and swearing. James said nothing. Still bruised from her behavior at the camp meeting, he offered no help or advice. Sadie left the rest of the stumps, now an ugly strip alongside the garden covered with creepers and brambles.

Her new activeness coincided with a new sobriety as well, for the applejack had run out. She could only drink cider, and it was hard to get drunk on that. When she came to bed at night – the only time they were alone together – he no longer reached for her. They slept side by side, as far apart as possible, chaste as children.

Swamp fever brought back the meanness in her, though it left her too weak to act, so she had to resort to speech. James had to listen to endless complaints, accompanied by a torrent of swearing, and strange talk and sounds when the fever spiked each day in the late afternoon. Most of it made no sense, but she often spilled out names: of their children, of John Chapman, of family back in Connecticut. Never of him, though. Never James. He was not sure if he wanted her to say his name, for other names were often accompanied by mutterings and curses, and he did not want to hear what she thought of him in her delirium. He already knew anyway.

While he waited for Robert to bring him the apples, he lay as still as he could and studied the planks of the ceiling above him, with its distinctive oak grain festooned with cobwebs – a familiar sight from yearly bouts of fever. When James had built the cabin nine years before he'd used pine logs for the walls and oak he'd had planked in Perrysburg for the floors and ceilings. His father had used oak back in Connecticut, and James liked the familiarity of its whorls and knots and dense grain. Later he discovered he would have been better off using maple for the floors as it was lighter and more flexible. Only the English used oak for building, and James was made fun of for it. 'English Goodenough,' he was called for a time by neighbors, a nickname taken up by Sadie, though she'd added to it, calling him 'English Ain't Goodenough.' Now, though, he was glad to have the close oak grain above him.

He closed his eyes for a moment, and then Robert was back, holding out a small yellow and brown Golden Pippin and a red and green spitter – more green than red. James took the apples and bit into the spitter. 'Not ready.' He handed it back to Robert. 'Give it to the pig.'

The Golden Pippin was clearly not ripe either, or it would have been yellower. James bit into it anyway. It was still sour. They would need another week, probably two, before they could be picked. By then he would be well enough to oversee their harvest.

James lay back and let the apple drop onto the bed. Sadie promptly kicked it, and it thudded into a corner. Then she began throwing herself back and forth and calling out – though it was still morning and she didn't usually have a high fever then. She started to moan and rant, and James heard her cry out 'Charlie!' and make unmistakable rutting sounds and moves. After it became clear what she was doing, he blocked his ears with his pillow.

I punished him with his brother Charlie. I didnt have no fever, I jest wanted to tug his chain. I seen him watchin me try to clear that tater patch full of stumps, not liftin a hand or gettin Caleb or Nathan to help me or even jest tell me what I was doin wrong.

I so badly wanted to make things better. Everyone was silent with me after the camp meeting. Wouldnt meet my eye or ask me how I did or fill my plate without askin. Not even Sal, who I could usually count on for the little things that showed she respected her Ma. It was like I had a disease and everybody took a step back from me.

I cleaned that cabin better than Id ever done before, scrubbed and swept every speck of dirt, brought down every cobweb, washed away the mold, aired everything that could be aired then aired it again. Washed all the clothes to get out the mud, scrubbed all the boots ready for winter. I weeded every inch of that garden, picked slugs off the lettuce, shooed away the birds and rabbits. Boiled the jars ready for puttin up the vegetables, and put up the beans soon as they was ready.

Then I had the idea to make me that winter tater patch. If you planted em in the fall in a trench full of manure and dead leaves, they grew even during winter and were ready earlier in the spring, when we usually ran out of food. My Pa did it back in Connecticut. I told James – one of the few things I said direct to him – and all he said was, Good luck. Caleb and Nathan and Robert looked on while I was choppin down the trees but their father must of said something cause none of them come over to help – though when Robert passed by he did whisper to me to sharpen the axe and it would go easier.

When I wanted to do something nothing stopped me doin it. That was how Id always been. Determined. My Ma called it ornery but she was jest jealous. Those stumps, though – they were one of the few things that ever defeated me. Id no idea trees got such strong roots clingin to the earth like that. Clearly they had no interest in ever movin. I spent a whole day trying to pry out a stump and couldnt get but half of it out. And this was jest one of twenty stumps. Sweated half myself away on that stump, got the worst head-ache I ever had, worse than a jack headache even. Had to sit down every few minutes cause I was so faint I had black spots in front of my eyes. Next morning I woke and knew I couldnt go back to those stumps or theyd kill me surer than any fever or rattler bite. There had to be a way to get em out but nobody was gonna tell me and I was too proud to ask. Maybe if John Chapman came along then he could of told me, but he didnt usually visit in the middle of the summer. So I left the stumps settin there like a whole line of rotten teeth I had to look at every day I was out in the garden.

Now in bed with James, both of us with the shakes, I got back at him. There werent many ways to wage a war when you got the fever, but I thought of one. I pretended the fever was worse and I started to call out names – any old names mostly but then I fastened on to Charlie Goodenough and kept repeatin it. I bunched up the quilt and stuck it tween my legs and started to hump it and called out Charlie, Charlie, give it to me good. And the thing was, it felt good, fever and all. I could of thrust for a long time. James muttered and shoved the pillow round his ears and I jest laughed. Thats for the stumps, I thought. Thats for carin more about your apples than about your wife.

James was thankful Sadie had finished with her rutting and was asleep when Hattie Day came by to help the children put up the vegetables. The first thing their neighbor did when she arrived was to string a rope across the room and hang the quilts Sadie had tossed off the bed over it so that he and Sadie were curtained off from the kitchen. 'Tush,' she answered when James feebly protested. 'You don't need to see us and we don't need to see you while we're working.' She was so firm that he didn't try to argue. He knew Sadie would have if she'd been awake, and he was tempted to nudge her. Instead he lay in bed listening to Mrs Day's efficiency on the other side of the quilt.

They got to work stewing tomatoes and pickling eggs. Normally the Goodenoughs didn't need to pickle their eggs, as they ate and baked with what the chickens produced each day. But now with all but two of the family ill for over a week and consuming nothing but water, the eggs were rotting. Hattie Day declared they mustn't go to waste and they'd pickle them before they did the cucumbers. She set the eggs to boil on the range as well as a pot of salted water and vinegar, and soon the house was filled with its tang. Then she had the children peel the hard-boiled eggs while she chopped the tomatoes and put them on to stew, and boiled and dried the jars.

For the most part Robert and Martha were quiet, with just the sound of eggshells cracking and sliding off to indicate they were there, and Mrs Day clanking the jars and knocking the spoon against the side of the pot. James had a sudden desire to see his children bent over their work at the table, but he didn't dare pull back the quilt for fear of the look Hattie Day would give him. Instead he traced a finger around the patchwork squares in blue and yellow and brown. Closest to his head was a square of green silk from an old dress of his mother's that caught the eye more than any of the other patchwork squares.

'Brine's ready,' he heard Hattie Day say. 'You finished peeling the eggs?'

'Yes, ma'am,' Robert answered.

'You dipped 'em in water like I showed you to get all the shell off before we put 'em in the jars?'

'Yes, ma'am.'

'All right, then. What flavorings you like to add? Mr Day and me just like salt and pepper, but maybe your family does different.'

'Salt and pepper's good.'

'Bring me the peppercorns, Martha. Put a little handful in each jar. That's right. Now, sometimes I put in a little beet to color the water pink, just for show – it don't make the eggs taste different. Want me to do that with these?'

'Hell, no!'

James started. He'd thought Sadie was asleep. Her voice was cracked and croaky, so she wasn't as loud as she intended. Hattie Day must not have heard her, but she did hear Martha's soft words. 'We usually just leave the water plain.'

'Bitch is takin' over my kitchen,' Sadie muttered.

'Leave her be – she's just trying to help. God knows we need it.' But James shared Sadie's sentiment. There was something too cozy about Hattie Day in their house, telling their children what to do. Worst of all, she said something he didn't catch, and he heard a sound he hadn't for a long time: Martha and Robert's laughter. They never laugh around me, he thought.

That was it. The colored water was bad enough, but I couldnt stand it any more when that woman made my children laugh.

It took every bit of gumption I had left but I sprang from the bed and pushed right through the hanging quilt. Get the hell out of my kitchen! I shouted. That was all I could say before the quilt got tangled in my legs and brought me down and I knocked myself out.

When I come to I was back in bed with James next to me. The quilt was hung up again but it had a big rip down the middle where Id pulled it and the wool for the batting was comin out worse than before. Id have to get Martha to mend it, her stitches was more even than mine or Sals.

Stupid woman, he muttered when he saw my eyes open. Why did you do that? But he was smilin as he said it. You should of seen Hattie Days face, he added all quiet so the others couldnt hear. Look like a cat had crawled up under her skirt.

I chuckled. Whens she gonna go? I said, not loud but not quiet either. I didnt care if she heard me or not.

Hush now. Shes just being neighborly. Once were up and about we wont need the help.

Jest then Martha come in with a mug of cool water, helped me to drink it. I looked up into her face so pinched and felt a pain in my chest. But I couldnt think of a thing to say except, Them tomaters aint catchin are they? I think I smell em burnin. That made her run off to check. I could feel James lookin at me and I didnt want him to anymore so I turned on my side and pretended to sleep. It was murder havin to listen to that bitch bossin my children and busyin herself in my kitchen but I shut myself up and let her.

James was the first of the Goodenoughs to improve enough to get up. To start with he could only stagger around the kitchen to get Sadie water or sit at the table for a little while. Soon he was fetching wood, a log at a time, from the stack outside the door. Eventually he was able to stop using the chamber pot and go out to the outhouse, though the barn and the orchard seemed impossibly far away when each step tired him. He was glad to take in the fresh air and feel the sun on his skin, but it was jarring too, for all of his senses were heightened on first stepping outside. The sun was brighter, the breeze stronger, the rattle of the leaves and branches louder, the surrounding buildings and trees in crisper outlines.

Though warm enough in the afternoons, the sun was at a slant now, radiating a golden rather than a white heat. September always felt like a turning point to James, when the ease of the summer must be replaced by hard work and a gearing up to survive the winter. It was a matter of measurement. Were there enough oats and corn and hay to feed the animals for a year? Was the pig fat enough to slaughter soon? Had the garden produced enough to see the Goodenoughs through to the next growing season? He was always anxious until the barn was full, the pantry was full, the cellar was full. And they were not always full at the end of the harvest. The Black Swamp was fickle land: too wet, or too dry, or too rotten, or too dead. It was too unpredictable to guarantee a good crop.

Once he was able to walk further, there was a

lot for him to catch up on. He needed to go to the barn to look in on the animals and see that John Day had brought in the hay all right, and check on the kitchen garden. The last of the corn needed bringing in: he should at least inspect the field even if he couldn't help yet.

James should have concerned himself with his corn, his vegetables, his pigs. They were where he should have focused what little energy he had. Instead he went to see his apple trees – stopping twice to rest and joined midway by his youngest son shadowing him again.

To James an orchard in September was at its climax. The whole cycle of an apple tree – the sap and leaves and blossoms – peaked in its fruit. As he stood with Robert on the edge of the orchard and looked at the Goodenough trees, he saw a field full of laden trees that could feed his family for months. He knew you could not eat fruit and nothing else, but if it were possible he would be content to eat only apples every day.

Most of the apples were not quite ready. They had grown to full size but were still green, with red creeping across here and there. James preferred them now, before they could be eaten, when they hung on the trees and promised much. It was like finding a wife but not yet marrying her – lusting after her and not knowing about her temper or her laziness or her roving eye. These apples might end up mushy and full of worm holes or as bruised windfalls only good for cooking – but they were not yet. On the trees, they were perfect.

The three Golden Pippin trees were particularly heavy with apples, and of the fifteen trees he and Robert had grafted in the spring, twelve had leaves on them and were thriving. The deer fences with their spikes had held up all summer and kept out the deer, and Sadie. In two or three years they would produce sweet apples.

The fifteen seedlings from John Chapman that spring were all growing in their own small nursery, and could be transplanted the following year when James had cleared land for them. After the harvest and before the ground froze he would make a start on it.

'Looks like we'll reach fifty trees producing in a couple of years,' he said, aware that he had said this before but for once truly meaning it.

Robert nodded. 'That's good, Pa.'

'Yes. Then we'll really be settled. All right, let's give these a week, then we'll pick them.'

The next day James felt well enough to work again, though he had to rest often. Sometimes his heart beat fast like a bird's and he went to sit in the shade of an elm next to the field where he and Robert were bringing in the corn. Soon Caleb was able to join them, then Nathan. Sadie and Sal were the last to get up from their beds, leaving Martha the bulk of the cooking and cleaning. Her face was becoming more and more gaunt, with blue rings hooking under her eyes and a vertical frown line growing between her eyebrows that should not be seen on a young girl's face.

One evening James came back from the barn to find Sadie sitting on the bench outside the door, smoking a pipe in the late sun. She looked peaceful and rested and entirely clear of fever. There were no rings under her eyes, no frown line.

'Why aren't you helping Martha?' he said. 'She's had enough to do looking after us all.'

Sadie leaned back against the house with her pipe between her teeth. 'Ain't that why we have children – to do our work for us?'

He did not even hesitate before slapping his wife. The pipe flew from her mouth and landed in a patch of dried grass, and James went to stamp it out to be sure it didn't catch fire. When he turned back, Sadie was gone.

Inside she was not helping Martha. He could hear her up in the attic, getting into bed there. Martha did not look up from frying johnnycakes on the range. James was glad, for he did not want to see her frown line appear.

It suited me when he slapped me. I never felt easy when James and I was gettin along. Havin a common enemy like Hattie Day jest messed things up, put us on the same side and that didnt feel right. James hadnt been on my side since back in Connecticut. Maybe not even then.

Eventually I got bored pretendin to be sick. I

made Sal get up too so I wouldnt have to face the little mouse in the kitchen alone. Cause I hated how without even sayin a word Martha made me feel like I was the worst mother ever in the world. Which I probably was.

At first I was weak as a rag doll so I did my work sittin at the table, let Martha do the fetchin and the stirrin. Thats why I didnt see the jar of pickled eggs for a few days. Then one day I went back in the pantry lookin for some cucumbers to set out with the bread and cheese and lettuce and tomaters. There were three jars of pickled eggs on the shelf, and one of them was colored pink. I brought the jar back with me and set it on the table. Whats this, I said to the little mouse.

She was mendin the nine-patch quilt and looked up all fearful the way she always did. Pickled eggs, Ma.

I know what they are. Whyre they pink?

Martha cleared her throat like maybe that would make a different answer come out. That was from the beet Mrs Day put in to make it colored that way, she said.

I told you I didnt want colored water. I know you heard me say that.

Martha didnt make even the tiniest squeak. She tried to go back to her sewin but her hands were trembling so much she couldnt hold the needle. So she set it down and went to tuck her hair behind her ears.

Dont you touch your goddamn hair. Whyd you go against what I said?

Sorry, Ma, she said so quiet it was like she was hummin.

Sorry nothin. You like Mrs Day better than me. Is that it?

No, Ma.

You want Hattie Day for your mother?

No, Ma.

I think you do. Maybe I should jest send you over there right now and be done with it. Let her dress you in one of them straw hats. Youd like that, wouldnt you.

No, Ma. The look on her face was a sight to see.

Then why did you do it when you know I didnt want my eggs sittin in pink water?

She didnt answer for a while. Then when she did I couldnt hear her. Whatd you say? I said.

I thought itd look pretty, she whispered. She was cryin by now.

Pretty? I laughed at that. You dont think its pretty enough around here? You dont think thats pretty? I pointed at the quilt in her lap. Martha had been fixin the tear down the middle but it still didnt look so good. What about my face? I added. Aint that pretty enough for you? Or Sal? Shes the good lookin one in the family.

Martha was fumbling with the quilt corner to dry her tears.

I didnt say anymore but kept gettin supper on the

table. But as I was passin I let my elbow nudge the jar of eggs and it fell and smashed.

Oh dear, you better clean up that pretty mess, I said. Cause I sure as hell aint.

Once the corn was in, the apples were ready, apart from the three Golden Pippins, which needed a few more days. James had Robert and Martha and Sal to help pick them, while Caleb was digging up the garden and planting onions and cabbage. Nathan had gone back to bed with fever.

Illness had taken the bite out of Sal, subduing her enough that they were able to have a peaceful time in the orchard. Wearing a sack tucked into a belt, Robert climbed the trees and picked the hard-to-reach spitters while Martha gathered those closer to the ground. Sal picked up the windfalls – they were already bruised and would be used for cider, so it didn't matter how rough she was with them. James reminded Robert and Martha to twist the apples so that they came off at the stem rather than taking part of the branch with them, and also to keep the stems on – otherwise a hole where the stem should be might turn mushy and rot. They must also place the apples gently into their sacks so they didn't bruise. Though most of the spitters would be immediately cooked or dried or pressed for cider and so could be bruised without consequences, James remained a perfectionist, determined to keep his apples unblemished. He kept the windfalls separate from the rest, and he had the children empty their sacks slowly into the wheelbarrow to avoid knocks, taking them back to the house himself. Those that would be eaten he placed one at a time in boxes in the cellar; the windfalls went into barrels outside, to be pressed for cider in Port Clinton.

He brought a wheelbarrow full of spitters in to Sadie. She was busy making bread while the last of the tomatoes from the garden stewed on the range. 'There's good strong sun today,' James pointed out. 'You can get a start on drying apple rings. You want me to send Sal back to help? She's only collecting windfalls, and they'll be all right for a day or two more on the ground.'

'Don't tell me how to keep house,' Sadie muttered. She was kneading dough, punching and slapping it hard. Its surface reminded James of the smooth soft flesh of her buttocks back when they were first married. To his surprise the memory made him hard, and he had to turn away to hide it while he was unloading the apples.

He sent Sal back to help Sadie anyway, while he and Martha and Robert remained in the orchard to finish picking and storing the apples. As he trundled to the house each time with a laden wheelbarrow, he watched Sadie and Sal's progress; by mid-afternoon they had cut up dozens of apples and laid the rings out on the nine-patch quilt to dry in the sun. He noticed, though, that the apples had not been cored – they were not rings so much as slices, with the seeds

214

and tough membrane left in, forming stars in the centers.

When they finished picking the apples from a row, Robert celebrated by climbing the tallest tree in the orchard – a spitter James had planted next to the Golden Pippins the first year that was now twelve feet high. Martha watched, and James felt sorry for her. Though long past his tree-climbing days, he still remembered the freedom of being up in the branches, swaying with the sun on his face.

'Come up.'

For a moment James thought Robert was speaking to him.

'I don't know how,' Martha said, standing at the base of the tree, her face turned up towards her brother.

'Put your right foot onto that low branch, and your left hand onto the branch above you, then pull yourself up and put your left foot up onto the next branch.' When Martha hesitated, Robert said, 'You're stronger than you think.'

That seemed to spur her on. As James watched, his daughter put her foot and hand into position, remained like that as if assessing her folly, then gritted her teeth and pulled herself a foot off the ground.

'All right, now, reach with your right hand and grab the branch, then put your left foot up as high as it will go.' Robert steadily talked Martha through the moves that brought her higher and higher off the ground. James resisted the temptation to go and stand under the tree, for that would just scare her into letting go. Besides, this was their game; it did not include him.

Eventually she was sitting in a fork in the tree, Robert a little above her. Both were smiling, and Martha was swinging her legs and humming 'Blest Be the Tie That Binds.'

James did not want to break up their pleasure, and sought his own, moving aside part of the deer fence and picking a Golden Pippin. 'Come down and try this,' he said.

Robert coached Martha down, then they shared the apple between the three of them, James nodding at the taste. The Golden Pippins were almost ready.

When they came in at the end of the day, their cheeks were flushed and their eyes bright as if they had fevers. They were not sick, however, but happy. The house smelled of apple butter Sadie was making from more of the spitters. The apple rings had been brought inside to dry overnight. James should have kept his mouth shut about them not being cored, kept the peace, protected that rare happiness he shared with his children. But he couldn't help it: Sadie had a way of stamping her mark on everything, even on apple rings. 'Couldn't you find the corer?' he said.

Sadie was ladling apple butter into jars and ignored him.

'Sadie,' James said.

She didn't look up. 'What.' Her arm jiggled so that a ladle full of hot apple butter hit the table and splattered. James jumped back to avoid being burned.

'Why didn't you core the apples before you cut them into rings? With those seeds in, the rings won't go sweet but will taste bitter.'

'I did it for Martha.' Sadie glanced sideways at her daughter. 'She's got such a taste for pretty things now Hattie Day's been here turnin' her head that I thought she'd care more about the stars in the rings than the sweetness. You like them stars, don't you, gal?'

Martha ducked her head as if trying to dodge her mother's sudden attention. 'Core the next batch,' James said, knowing as he spoke that telling Sadie would make no difference. Indeed, it might encourage her to do the opposite, and then he would have to respond to her deliberately disobeying him, which was what she wanted. And so their feud would continue, probably for the rest of their lives. The thought exhausted him.

There was no time to find out how she might have responded, however, for at that moment they heard John Chapman's unique whistle. 'John Appleseed!' Sadie dropped the ladle into the pan of apple butter and ran to the door. She was never so eager to see any of the family as she was John Chapman. James knew he should not care – it was understandable that someone you saw only two or three times a year would be more exciting than the people you were with every day. Still, he gritted his teeth and had to force a cheerful greeting when John Chapman followed Sadie in. She was clutching two bottles of applejack.

'Sit yourself down, John!' she cried. 'Take the rocker by the fire. It ain't that cold yet but you don't get much time inside, so you need to warm up proper. Here, have a dish of apple butter. I jest made it. Must've known you were comin'.' Sadie set down the applejack with the sort of care James reserved for sweet apples, then ladled apple butter into a bowl. In her eagerness to serve him she handed him the bowl so quickly that hot apple slid over the edge and spilled onto the floor. 'Don't worry about that!' Sadie knelt to wipe it up with her apron. 'There. Will you take some cream on it? Martha, git Mr Chapman some cream!'

'No need,' John Chapman reminded her. 'You remember I don't eat animals or anything that comes from them.'

'Leave it be, Martha, you silly fool! Didn't you hear the man?'

Martha stood stricken at the sideboard, pitcher of cream in hand, looking as if she might drop it. Then Robert was at her side, taking the pitcher and setting it back down.

Was it only five minutes ago, James thought, that we were happy with apples?

But John Chapman smiled at Martha and she gave a weak smile back. He looked as ragged as ever with his bare feet and his long hair and his coffee sack for a shirt. 'I'm glad to see you've got your apples in.' He nodded at the drying slices. 'Good crop this year?'

James opened his mouth to answer, but Sadie jumped in first. 'Oh, it's been the best season. More apples than ever. We'll have plenty for cider and jack, besides the butter and the stewed and the dried.'

'How are your Golden Pippins?' John Chapman directed this at James.

James sat up, pleased to be asked. 'A heavy crop. They're never big apples, but there's a good number. I'm giving them a few more days before picking. But there's one or two ripe at the top of the tree. Do you want a taste?'

'I'd like that.' John Chapman sat back and rocked.

'Robert, run and pick Mr Chapman a good ripe Golden Pippin. Get two if you can find them.' Because Golden Pippins were abundant at the moment, he could afford to feel generous.

The whole family watched while John Chapman bit into the Golden Pippin Robert brought him – even Nathan, who had come to sit at the top of the attic ladder when he heard the visitor come in. Though his expression didn't change, John Chapman nodded. 'There is that surprising taste. Pineapple, did you say it was?'

'That's how my father described it,' James replied. 'Though I never tasted pineapple myself. There's a pine needle flavor to it too. It's still a little tart just off the tree. They mellow over time. Here, take this.' He handed John Chapman another Golden Pippin. 'Save it till Christmas, then eat it. It'll be sweet as honey then.'

'Enough apples!' Sadie cried, clearly put out that she'd not had John Chapman's full attention for a few minutes. 'Have a bite of applejack. It's too late to be medicinal – we're over the fever already – but it's surely welcome.' She pulled the cork from the bottle and poured a slug each into two mugs.

John Chapman pocketed the Golden Pippin. 'Thank you, Sadie, but just a drink of water for now. I want to savor the taste of that apple.'

Sadie shrugged and drank the shot from one mug, then the other. 'Martha, git the man some fresh water.' She shoved one of the mugs across the table at her daughter. Martha fumbled with the mug and it clattered to the floor.

After supper John Chapman told me the news fresh from Heaven. Everybody else disappeared to their beds or out to the barn, which was rude of em but that was all right with me as it meant I had him all to myself. Him and James had spent most of supper talkin apples, which jest about killed me. You would think after all these years theyd have nothing left to say about apple trees. Thank God the jack took the edge off. It was good and fiery. I was careful with drinkin it, as itd be a couple months before itd be cold enough to make more.

I let John Chapman go on with his God talk till real late and the fire was low and the candles burned out and everybody was asleep. He kept talkin about the need to take a moral inventory of our lives lived so far. I didnt know what that meant. I liked hearin him talk but it never moved me the way the preachers did at camp meetings. I tried not to think of the last camp meeting but of course once it was in my head I did.

John Chapman stopped talkin then and gave me a funny look. You all right, Sadie? Youre looking red. The applejack too strong for you?

No no, I said. Its not that. I didnt want to tell him about bein abandoned by my family at the camp meeting. Do you ever wish you was somewhere else? I said.

What do you mean?

Do you ever jest want to jump in your canoe and go?

John Chapman smiled. That *is* what I do. All the time.

Thats what I want to do too. Maybe I could go with you.

There is no room for more than me and my trees, Sadie. You know I go alone.

There was space – he had a whole canoe jest for his trees. There was space for me there. Goddamn trees, I muttered.

What is it that bothers you about trees?

I thought a second. It only took a second cause Id thought about this before. Ill tell you what it is, I said. When we come from Connecticut James brought his sticks from his damned Golden Pippins and planted em here. Stuck em right in the trees you sold him and they were like magic cause three of em grew up and are doin as well as any tree around. Its like theyve always been here.

Why does that upset you?

I aint upset, I said. But I was and John Chapman knew it. Its jest – well, those trees are doin better in the Black Swamp than I ever will. Theyve got used to it here. And theyre jest trees!

John Chapman didnt say anything, but looked at me with his flinty eyes.

Trees aint supposed to move, and then thrive when they do, I added.

Sadie, trees move all the time! My business is about moving trees. I go to Pennsylvania in the winter, get sacks of seeds from the cider mill there. Then I take them and hand them out to some, plant others in my nurseries. A year or two later I dig up those seedlings and sell them to people all over Ohio and heading into Indiana too. And they do fine. Most of this countrys finest apples have come from somewhere else – usually from Europe. When you think about it, trees always move at the start. A seed has to land a ways from its mother to grow, otherwise its in the shade and wont thrive. Birds can take seeds for miles in their bellies, hundreds of miles even, then shit them out and the tree grows where it falls just fine. Now you know Im not a believer in the grafting your husband does. But I have to admit its impressive that the branch of an apple tree in Connecticut has been turned into a tree out in Ohio. And that tree came from a branch back in England.

Well. Aint trees jest the best thing ever, I said. Guess theyre better than people. I jumped up and started rakin ashes over the coals to bank the fire for the night.

John Chapman chuckled. Actually trees are ruthless. They fight each other for light, for water, for all the good things that are in the ground. They survive only when they have enough space between them. You ever notice how your husband spaces his apple trees far apart? The closer you put them to each other, the less fruit they produce. You see all the saplings around in the woods? Most of them wont grow up. Just one will, and kill off all the others. Its a battleground out there.

I looked at him. In here too.

Im only talking about trees. I am no expert in people.

Time to sleep. Heres your beddin. I grabbed the nine-patch quilt that was layin on the floor with the apple rings on it and thrust it at him, letting the rings rain down all over without pickin em up.

In the morning John Chapman was gone and the apple rings were layin out on a sheet all tidy in rows. I never asked who did that.

*   *   *

Every day James checked the Golden Pippins, feeling the flesh for the slight springiness that would indicate they were ripe. Robert often came with him to inspect the fruit, and Martha sometimes too. Now that she could climb, she liked to go up the largest spitter tree and sit in the fork, smiling down at them.

During the last few days as they waited for the Golden Pippins to be ready, Sadie grew drunker. She'd had no applejack since May, and took up drinking it again as if it were water or coffee. The applejack John Chapman had brought was particularly strong, and it took only two mugs full to take her legs out from under her. At least the bottle would be empty soon. John Chapman had carried off three barrels of windfalls in his double canoe to Port Clinton for them, and James would make sure when he returned with cider in a few days that he wasn't bringing more jack as well. Once Sadie had made her own, James would secretly water it down, as he usually did.

The applejack ran out the day the Golden Pippins were ready for picking. Though he didn't really need them just to pick the apples from three trees, James had Robert and Martha help him anyway. First they pulled up the sharpened sticks that made up the deer fences around the trees and stacked them to one side. Then they started with the smallest Golden Pippin – James on a ladder reaching for the highest apples while the children picked the rest. When they'd filled the wheelbarrow, they took it back to the house, lifted the

224

cellar door and transferred the apples to the wooden boxes, James crouching in the dark cellar while Robert handed them down to him. Sal was in the kitchen, churning cream into butter while Sadie lay still on their bed, sleeping off her hangover – or so James thought. When he climbed back out of the cellar, he glanced over and saw that his wife had her eyes open and was watching them, though she did not move.

'You all right, Sadie?' James said, surprising himself, as he never asked her such a thing – for he knew the answer.

Sadie just looked at him, the corners of her mouth pulled tight as a drawstring bag. James said nothing more, but picked up the handles of the wheelbarrow and trundled it out, Robert at his heels, the thump-thump-thump of the churn following them.

Back in the orchard, they were almost done picking from the second tree when Sadie appeared, heading towards them in a swift hobble, as if coming down a hill and unable to stop herself. The sight made James' stomach tighten: hers was the gait of someone ready to cause trouble. She stopped at the bottom of the ladder he had climbed. 'Where's my bottle?' she said, running her hands up and down her thighs.

'It's empty – you finished it last night.'

'You poured it out, is more likely!'

'No, you did the damage to that bottle all by yourself. But don't worry – John Chapman will be back in a day or two with cider, and when it's cold enough you can make your own jack.' James turned away from her fury and back to his apples. He could feel her eyes on his back almost as a physical presence. Then, suddenly, the press of them was gone, and he dared to look down. Sadie had fixed her gaze on the third Golden Pippin tree, still laden with fruit. It was the largest of the three – Robert would need to climb it to pick the topmost apples. James studied his wife as she studied the tree, every part of her lean frame alert now. 'Leave it alone, Sadie,' he warned, knowing the moment he spoke that he'd made things worse by sparking the idea in her.

Robert and Martha paused from their picking and stared at their mother. Sadie saw them all watching her and snorted. 'Git your Goodenough eyes off me.' Then she turned and strode back towards the house with the same jerky gait.

James let out his breath. 'All right, now. Almost done.'

They were loading the last of the second tree's apples into the wheelbarrow when she returned. 'Pa,' Robert warned in a low voice.

James looked up. Sadie held an axe. He just had time to stumble after her, knocking apples from the heaped barrow, before managing to grab her arm as she swung wildly at the third Golden Pippin tree.

'Git your goddamn hands off me!' Sadie whirled around, brandishing the axe. 'I'll kill the whole lot of you!'

James took a step back. 'What's gotten into you, woman? Put that axe down, you'll hurt yourself!' Out of the corner of his eye he saw Martha dart over to the large spitter and scramble up it. Behind him he heard rustling but didn't dare to take his eyes off his wife. He guessed it must be Robert picking up the spilled Golden Pippins. Then he couldn't resist, and turned. 'Don't put those back with the others, they might be bruised. Set them aside for eating now.' He needn't have said it – Robert knew about apples.

It was the mistake Sadie had been waiting for. She turned back around, stepped up to the Golden Pippin tree, swung the axe hard and sunk it into the trunk with a thud. It bit deeply, but did not cut all the way through.

'No!' James cried. He ran to the tree and grabbed Sadie as she was wresting the axe from the trunk. They struggled together, then fell against the trunk, sending a blow through the tree that caused apples to rain down around them. Hugging each other, the axe between them, they stumbled and crashed into the neatly stacked pile of poles, scattering them into a pile of spikes that stuck out like a porcupine's quills.

At last Sadie managed to butt her head against James' forehead with a crack that sent him reeling away with a blinding pain. Shaking his head to clear it, he saw three flashes of his children: Sal striding down from the house, arms folded across her chest, looking just like Sadie; Robert, apple in hand, frozen by the wheelbarrow full of fruit; and Martha's pale leg with a muddy boot on the end dangling from the spitter tree. Then he saw Sadie spinning with the axe to give the Golden Pippin what he knew would be a mortal blow, and all he could do was throw himself in between.

The axe sank into his side, cracking his ribs and collapsing a lung and filling his chest with blood. James fell to his knees, the shock of the blow blunting the pain. 'Pa!' he heard over the roaring in his ears, but he did not know which of his children was shouting. Sadie was staring at him, her eyes as blue as her dress.

'Damn,' she said. 'I guess I won.'

It wasnt what I meant to do. I meant to take the axe to every one of them apple trees and cut em all down. Without em we wouldnt have to stay in the Black Swamp. We could go anywhere we wanted. We could go west to the prairie where there werent any trees. Or we could go back east, back to Connecticut even. Anywhere but here, was what I wanted. We could move, like those seeds in the belly of a bird. But I made the mistake of startin with the Golden Pippin. Stupid of me. James would never let me touch the tree he loved best.

I went up to him and reached out for the axe in his side. There was blood everywhere and he was makin a terrible rattlin noise. I wasnt thinkin straight. Maybe I was thinkin if I jest pulled it out, his flesh would close over the hole in his side and he would be all right. Maybe I was thinkin I would continue cuttin down the trees. Whatever it was I was thinkin to do, thats not what happened. James saw me comin and kicked my ankles so I lost my balance and tumbled backwards, flappin with my hands and fallin right into the pile of fence poles. One of em was stickin up and went straight through me.

Funny, it didnt hurt more than a bee sting at first. I lay on the pile of poles under the tree lookin up. I could see Marthas leg hangin down but it wasnt close enough for me to reach up and touch it. It was real quiet. Then all of a sudden it got hard to breathe.

After a little while I heard the sound of a bob white out in the woods and wondered was that John Appleseed come back with the cider. I sure could do with some nice fresh cider.

Then Robert was standin over me. Ma, he said.

I looked up at him and though I was hurtin – in fact I was dyin – I knew it was time to tell him what he ought to know. Your uncle Charlie is your father, I said. Not him. I looked over at James. His eyes were open so I guessed he heard me. My last blow.

Somethin happened to Roberts face, like a jar that got broke, like a cracked mirror where I could see myself cut in two. It hurt too much to hurt him, my changeling son, the one I loved best out of all of em. Hes probably your father, I added, to soften the blow. Cant know for sure. At least you know youre your mothers son.

He stood there at the edge of the orchard, lookin like he would never be whole again, the way I wasnt whole either. You go now, I said. Get out of this swamp. Go out to the prairie where there aint no trees.

He looked up at Martha sittin above us in her tree, her foot swingin back and forth.

Leave her, I said. Shell jest hold you up.

Marthas foot stopped swingin.

You got to save yourself, I said. Go on out there now. Go.

So he went. And so did I.

BLACK SWAMP, OHIO

1844–1856

June 25, 1844

Gilbert Hotel
Racine
Wisconsin Territory

Dear Robert,
Today Mrs Day brought me a letter you wrote
from Wisconsin. It is 6 months old. She got
it when she was at the general store in
Perrysburg and Mr Fuller had it sitting there
waiting for a Goodenough to come along. It
has been there months because Caleb doesn't
use the store much, and no one thought of
me, until Mrs Day happened to see the letter.

I was so happy to hear from you that I cried.
It has been almost 6 years since you left home,
and I am very glad to know that you are alive.

You will want to know what has become of
your brothers and sisters after what happened.
Caleb and Nathan ran the farm as best they
could, but could not manage it the way Pa
had. We were all right that first winter,

because we had what you and Mr Day and Pa had brought in from the summer, and you and I had put up the garden, and all of the apples. The boys hunted, and we got through the winter, though the house was always cold and not as clean as it should be. The Days looked in on us and brought us sacks of flour and some wild turkeys. Other neighbors helped us out too. Mr Chapman came by with the barrels of cider, and when he heard what had happened he left and has not been back to the Black Swamp since.

The next summer the oats were poor, and they stored the hay damp so it rotted. Sal and I kept the garden but it was hard to remember everything we had to do and how to keep the rabbits and deer out. I did remember to prune the apple trees, and they were all right. Our clothes were too small and we had no money for anything, and barely enough to eat. Then Nathan took the fever and died, and then Sal ran off. She lives in Toledo now. I am ashamed to say what she is doing, so I will not write it.

After that Mrs Day asked me did I want to live with her and her husband. She and Mr Day never did have any children and she needed the help. I was glad to leave, for I did not like being alone with Caleb as he has taken to drink. I became a kind of daughter to the Days, except they worked me harder, more like a servant, except unpaid. It was

Mrs Day who taught me my letters well enough that I can write this to you. Do you recall her straw hat? She still wears it to town and it makes me smile to see it.

So that is how we all are. Caleb is still on the farm, though he does not grow crops except a bit of corn for the horse and the cow. He sold the team of oxen. Mostly he hunts and trades furs. I do not go by the farm much, but once in October when I was with the Days I did, and I am sorry to tell you the apple crop was poor, very small what there was and Caleb had not bothered to pick them so there were many windfalls. Mrs Day said it was a waste of God's bounty.

Now I can be happy, for I know where you are and that you are remembering your family. When are you coming back? Please write to me at the Days, for I do not think Caleb will give me a letter from you. Or send for me and I will come, as though the Days are kind enough they are not Family.

I am your sister
Martha

Days' Farm
Black Swamp
Near Perrysburg
Ohio

January 1, 1845

Gilbert Hotel
Racine
Wisconsin Territory

Dear Robert,
I have been waiting for a letter from you. I know it takes time for letters to get to their destination. I do not know how far Wisconsin is from here but Mr Day told me it is a long way west. So I thought my letter might take 2–3 months to reach you, maybe until September. And then when you wrote back it would take 3 months again to reach me. So I did not expect to hear from you until December, though of course I could not help myself: even just after I sent you a letter I would get excited when Mrs Day went to Perrysburg because there might be a letter waiting for me.

But there has been no letter all these months and so I am writing again – on New

Year's Day, the way you did. It is night, for I could not take the time during the day – Mrs Day kept me ironing during much of it, to dry the clothes we washed yesterday and that were frozen. It is hard as my hands are little and the iron heavy, and I burn my arms. But at least it is warming work, and that is something in this cold. We were snowed in before Christmas for a week. But you said in your letter that it was even colder in Wisconsin than the Black Swamp. I hope you are keeping warm with all the horses.

I remember all the lines of your letter, from reading it over and over – though I no longer have the letter itself. Mrs Day felt Caleb ought to see it since it was addressed to all of the Goodenoughs. When we gave it to him, he said he would read it later as he was busy – though all he was doing at the time was sitting in the doorway and whittling – this when there was plenty to do. Also I do not think Caleb can read, and I would have read it to him but he did not want that. A few days later I went back to get the letter but he said it had dropped in the fire and burned up. I cried a little then – not in front of Caleb, but when I was alone.

I may not have the letter but I remember your words and the hotel name. Every day I wait to hear from you and hope that you will

237

write with money so that I may take a stage-coach – or many stages – to reach Racine.

Sal came by for a visit this summer – the first she has made since she run off, though Toledo is not very far away. She has a child now, a boy she calls Paul. So you are Uncle Robert and I am Aunt Martha. She did not say who the father is. Paul was naughty. He pulled the dog's tail and threw cinders from the fire onto the floor. Then Sal beat him though he is only little. I told Sal about your letter. Though she did not say anything, I am sure she would want me to say hello from her.

You will be pleased to hear that I found the Golden Pippin tree you planted on the Injun Trail. It is doing all right even with no one to prune it. I was able to pick some apples from it to carry back to the Days. We ate them and they tasted so sharp and sweet, do you remember?

I am going to go out to the road to Perrysburg tomorrow with this letter and hope to find someone to take it for me. I hope you are keeping well and that you will write to me soonest.

I am your sister
Martha

238

Days' Farm
Black Swamp
Near Perrysburg
Ohio

August 15, 1845

Gilbert Hotel
Racine
Wisconsin Territory

Dear Robert,
It has taken me a while to write because I did not have any paper and did not want to ask Mrs Day for some as I do not want her to know that I am writing to you. I have stopped asking her about letters from you when she comes back from the general store because she began to act funny about it. I suspect she worries one day I will leave to join you and she will not have anyone to work for her. Still I am hoping for that letter. I am wondering if you are still in Racine or if you have gone somewhere else. People move around so much now. Every day we see people passing through on their way west. The road is better now than when we were young. Remember the mud and how we got

stuck. Since it was macadamized it is not too bad.

It is very hot here and the mosquitoes have come early. The Days are both in bed with fever and I am looking after them, and also putting up the garden and looking after the animals. The hay is not in and if Mr Day isn't better soon I will have to ask Caleb to help. He is still at the farm and has a woman living there now, so he is a little nicer to me. I do not know her name.

I think maybe you have gone west and I will write on the outside of the letter for the hotel owner to send it on if he knows where you are. But maybe you are still there. I have been thinking that I would try to get there to you. I have begun saving so that I can take myself on the stage, though it is hard as the Days give me no money. I earned a little finishing off a quilt for a woman who had fever in the eyes that made her blind for a time, and looking after the baby of neighbors nearby. I have 31 cents so far. I will have to give some to the neighbors who mail letters for me. But I will keep saving and then one day I will find a way to get to you.

I am your sister
Martha

Days' Farm
Black Swamp
Near Perrysburg
Ohio

January 1, 1846

Gilbert Hotel
Racine
Wisconsin Territory

Dear Robert,
I am writing to wish you a very happy and prosperous New Year. I hope you are keeping well.

I am doing all right. I have now saved 75 cents towards a stagecoach trip to Racine. I talked to some settlers passing through about the route and I now know I will need to go to Fort Wayne and Valparaiso Indiana and to Chicago, then on to Racine. I was glad to get this information and wrote it down, to ready myself for the journey. But I need at least 5 dollars, and a letter from you to say you are there and would like me to come.

I miss family.

I am your sister
Martha

Days' Farm
Black Swamp
Near Perrysburg
Ohio

May 2, 1846

Gilbert Hotel
Racine
Wisconsin Territory

Dear Sir,
I am looking for my brother, Robert Goodenough, age 17. I once had a letter from him saying he worked at your hotel, in the stables. Please can you tell me is he still there, and if not where he has gone. If he is still there, could you give him the message that his sister Martha would like to hear from him.

I am sincerely
Martha Goodenough

Days' Farm
Black Swamp
Near Perrysburg
Ohio

May 15, 1847

Fort Leavenworth
Near the Missouri River
Missouri Territory

Dear Robert,
I was full of the best kind of joy when I
received your letter from Fort Leavenworth.
Though it has been 3 years since your last
letter, I never gave up hope that I would
hear from you again – even after the hotel
owner in Racine wrote and said you had left
2 years before and sent me back all the
letters I had written to you. He said you
had gone west but he did not know more.
The west is very big, the word covers a lot
of territory. That was a great blow to me
but I still believed you would write again
one day, even though you never got my
letters.
I was not expecting a letter when I went
to Perrysburg with Mrs Day. She took me

with her to carry the heavy sacks of flour and cornmeal she was buying, as her back troubled her. I know you must remember me as small and weak but I am stronger than you think. Remember you told me that once. I have never forgotten, and those words have seen me through some hard times. So there was your letter at the general store, sitting on the shelf behind the new owner, Mr Malone. I saw it while he was talking to Mrs Day, and I nearly screamed. But instead I held my breath and read 'Goodenough' and knew it was your writing even though I have only seen that writing once before.

I didn't want to ask for it in front of Mrs Day because she is funny about the Goodenoughs and wants to pretend I am a Day. I have been with her and Mr Day almost 8 years now but I am still a Goodenough. So when we left I dropped my handkerchief and went back for it. Then I asked Mr Malone for the letter. He looked surprised and I reminded him I'm a Goodenough, not a Day. At first he said no, to wait for Caleb or his woman. But I said that could take a long time and that I'd take it to Caleb, and so Mr Malone gave it to me.

I will not spend ink and paper on describing all that has gone on these 9 years since you left. I will just say: Nathan died of fever. Sal lives in Toledo and has 2 children. She works in a hotel, I guess you could say. Caleb is on the farm and a woman lives with him and they have a baby. So you are Uncle Robert and I am Aunt Martha. I live with Mr and Mrs Day who still live 2 miles from the Goodenough farm. I work hard for them, to take the place of the children they never had and the help they can't afford to hire.

I have been saving the little money I earn here and there to pay for a stagecoach to take me west to you. I now have $4.86 but I do not think it is anywhere near enough to get to you now you are even further away than Racine. I do not even know where the Missouri River is but I am going to find out. Please write and tell me where you are going and I will meet you there, if you can send me money for some of the fare. Or I will ask Sal, she might lend me some, though I never see her.

I am thinking of you and hoping that before long we will meet again.

I am your sister
Martha

Days' Farm
Black Swamp
Near Perrysburg
Ohio

July 7, 1848

Fort Leavenworth
Near the Missouri River
Missouri Territory

Dear Mr General,
I am writing to ask about my brother, Robert Goodenough. He worked in the stables at Fort Leavenworth, and I had a letter from him dated January 1, 1847. Since then I have not heard from him and I am trying to find him. Please, Sir, can you tell me if he is still working there, or do you know where he has gone? He is the person who means the most to me in this world, and I would like to find him.

I am sincerely
Martha Goodenough

Days' Farm
Black Swamp
Near Perrysburg
Ohio

January 1, 1850

Fort Leavenworth
Near the Missouri River
Missouri Territory

Dear Robert,
I am writing to wish you a very happy
New Year. I am sending this letter to Fort
Leavenworth even though I suspect you are
not there. I wrote to the General there about
you but never heard back. But I want to write
anyway and I don't know where else to send
it except the place where I know you've been.

I have sad news to tell you of the Goodenoughs. Our sister Sal died in the summer,
leaving 2 children. I should take them as I
am their aunt but the Days are not willing
to have them. Too many mouths to feed and
too much trouble, Mrs Day said. She did not
suggest they go to Caleb, though, as she
understands that would not be good for them.
His woman and child left him and he is back

to his old ways. So they have gone to an orphanage in Toledo. I am real sorry about that. It makes me grateful that the Days took me in. Though they can be a trial at times, it would have been much worse in an orphanage.

I wish I knew where you were. America is such a big country, you could be anywhere. If I could find you we could take the children and make a new Goodenough family, and give them a better life than they are destined for.

I will keep hoping to hear from you, though it is hard. I am still saving my money ($7.31 now!) and can pack and leave the moment I get your letter.

I am your sister
Martha

Goodenough Farm
Black Swamp
Near Perrysburg
Ohio

March 11, 1855

Fort Leavenworth
Near the Missouri River
Missouri Territory

Dear Robert,
It has been almost 8 years since I received a
letter from you. I do not know where you
are, or if you are alive. All of the letters I sent
to Fort Leavenworth were returned to me in
one bundle. It made me cry to get them back.
But I wanted you to know where I am, so I
am writing anyway, because maybe you will
come back one day to the fort, and if so, this
letter will be there for you.

I am back living on the farm with Caleb.
Mrs Day died of a tumor last summer, and
after that it was difficult living with Mr Day.
I am sorry to say that I was going to have a
child, though it came much too early and was
dead. After that I hoped Mr Day would leave
me be, but it became clear he intended to be

unkind again, and so I had no choice but to come back home.

It has been many years since I lived here. The house is drafty and very dirty, for Caleb lives like an animal. I am trying to clean it. I am going to dig the old garden too, and I even pruned the apple trees to see if I can get them to produce better. I remember what Pa taught you, because I was listening too. I am looking forward to seeing the blossoms in May. Two of the Golden Pippin trees are still alive and seem to be all right. I look forward to that sweet fruit.

It feels better to write, even if you never see this letter. I hope beyond hope that some-where out in the world it reaches you yet.

I am your sister
Martha

Water Street Guest House
Water Street
New York City
New York

February 2, 1856

Mrs Bienenstock's Guest House
Montgomery and California Streets
San Francisco
California

Dear Robert,
I have wanted to write to you since November but I have not had a moment to do so until now. I am in New York City, waiting for the river to unfreeze so that I can get on a steamship that will take me to you. For at last I know where you are! I am sending this letter in case it arrives before I do to let you know that I am coming.

There are many things I would like to tell you but they can wait until I see you in California. I will just say that these past months have been a trial almost beyond what a Goodenough can bear. But I am still alive. And you are alive too. I have been able to read all of your letters, for Caleb had them.

It was strange that he kept them, though he could not even read and he had no feeling for the family. I was living back at the farm with him after Mrs Day's death and Mr Day was unkind. Caleb was also unkind, but he is family and I had nowhere else to go. Of course you do not know: Sal and Nathan are both long dead.

One day in November when I was at the general store, Mr Malone said there was a letter for me. It turned out to be the last letter I sent to you in Fort Leavenworth, returned to me. I was so disappointed I shed a tear or two right there. Then Mr Malone said something about a letter for the Goodenoughs some months back, and that he had given it to Caleb. When I got back to the farm I asked Caleb, who denied it, but when he was passed out – for he has taken to applejack same as Ma – I searched and finally found that letter, and all of your letters, under a loose stone in the chimney. I was so angry that Caleb had kept them from me all these years that I did something foolish – I woke him up and shouted at him. I know I should have 'let sleeping dogs lie,' but I was so angry I couldn't help it. When Caleb realized I'd found the letters he got mad too and was unkind. That made me do something else foolish, and then I had to leave the Black Swamp in a hurry.

I walked to Toledo, where I thought I would try to get a stage going west. I would just keep going west, changing stages wherever I could, to get to California. But in Toledo a man who had been out to California himself for the gold explained to me about America, how it is huge with many long rolling plains and a big mountain range in the middle. And he told me there weren't stages much past Chicago, but wagons across all those plains and mountains, and that I would be better off going by water: Lake Erie, then the canal to New York City, and finally a ship that will go all the way around South America to San Francisco. He drew a map for me so that I would understand where I was going. It seemed strange to go east and south in order to go west, but my life has been strange for so long that I knew I had to do it.

It has been frightening because I have never been out of the Black Swamp since I was a little girl, but at times it has been exciting, and for the most part people have been helpful. Now I am waiting for the ship that will take me to California. It is a very long journey but I trust in God to bring me safely to you. For a while there in the Black Swamp I lost sight of Him, but now I have faith again.

I am always your sister
Martha

CALIFORNIA

1856

Martha could not stop holding on to Robert. His sister kept her hand on his arm all the while they sat under the Orphans sequoias and he read the packet of letters she handed to him. He did not really want to read them – his reading was slow even when he wasn't distracted – but Martha insisted. 'They explain better than I can now what happened to me, when it happened,' she said. 'Besides, it tickles me to see you read them at last.'

'But how?' he kept repeating even after he'd skimmed the letters, not fully taking them in. 'How did you find me?' He'd known – or had thought he'd known – exactly where she was, but he'd never imagined his sister could find him in such a vast country.

'It wasn't so hard,' she explained patiently. 'I had the address of Mrs Bienenstock's boarding-house from your letter, so I knew where I was aiming for. There are two ways you can do it: overland or by sea. It was winter and I didn't want to travel through all that snow, so I knew I'd have to go by sea. So I got up to Lake Erie and took a boat over to Buffalo, then got a barge along the Erie Canal to New York. I was lucky, 'cause it wasn't cold enough yet to freeze the canal, otherwise I would've been stuck in Buffalo all winter waiting for the thaw.'

'You went east?'

'Yes, first I had to go east so I could then go west to find you. I know it is strange,' she added as Robert shook his head, 'but sometimes that's what you have to do – go back to go forward. Then I went by ship all the way around South America and up again to San Francisco. It took six months.' Martha tucked stray hairs behind her ears, pulling out her bonnet to reach them; Robert recognized the gesture from childhood and it almost made him cry. She seemed so fragile, and yet she spoke confidently of America and how to navigate its tricky expanse.

'When did you leave Ohio?'

'Middle of November. I had to wait in New York City for some weeks 'cause I was ill with—' Martha gestured at her belly. 'Once I was better I got on a ship, but it all took such a long time. You know I even wrote to you from New York, but the letter ended up on the same ship as me! It arrived at Mrs Bienenstock's just an hour after I did.'

'How did you pay for the passage on the ship? It's not cheap.'

'There was some money at home.'

'Caleb know you used it?'

His sister's hand tightened around his arm in a

fierce grip and she fixed her gray eyes on him. 'Don't you ever say his name again.'

Robert looked away and took a deep breath, then ran his eyes up and down a ponderosa pine, following the deep cracks in its yellow-gray bark. What he really wanted to ask was the most obvious question: who was the father? But it seemed she had given him the answer. Suddenly he understood how a man might feel able to kill another man.

'How'd you know I was up here?' he asked when he was calmer.

'Mrs Bienenstock told me you'd gone to Calaveras Grove. She's real efficient – found me a steamboat to Stockton and even paid for the ticket, saying she'd get it back from you. I hope you don't mind.'

'Of course not!'

'Then I got a stage to Murphys, and there I asked around and they all knew you. The Tree Man, they call you. They were nice too – for a mining town.' Again Martha seemed to have unexpected knowledge of the world. 'Put me on a horse this way.'

'You rode a horse like that?' Robert nodded at her belly.

Martha shrugged. 'I just wanted to find you, Robert. You're my family. I traveled all these months, and I wasn't going to wait around when you were only fifteen miles away.'

'How come you didn't tell Nancy you were my sister?'

'I didn't want you to find out from someone

259

else that I was here – I wanted to surprise you, see your reaction myself.'

'You sure did surprise me. I thought . . .' Robert's throat became tight with what he'd thought.

'What?'

'I thought you were dead of the swamp fever. I'm sorry.' He choked on the last words, and his eyes filled with tears.

Martha let him swallow a sob, then squeezed his arm. 'I don't believe you. You know why?'

Robert shook his head.

''Cause when you wrote all those letters, you wrote "Brothers and Sisters" – not "Sister" like you'd have done if you thought only Sal was left. No, you thought I was alive, or you *hoped* I was alive – and that's the same thing in my book.'

Robert stopped trying to hold back sobs, for Martha's words made them dry up, except for a tear that got away down his cheek before he could catch it. 'Maybe you're right,' he said after a while. 'How come you know me better than I know myself?'

Martha smiled. 'It's easy to know other people. Not so easy to know ourselves.'

It was then that Robert really saw her, saw that she might be small but she was not frail as he had remembered; she was huge of heart. It almost made him cry again, and so he focused on the practical. 'You tired?'

Martha shook her head. 'Hungry. I could eat a whole pot of beans!'

'Let's go back to the hotel, get you something to eat.'

As they walked along the path that wound through the grove, still talking, Martha kept her hand tucked in Robert's elbow. At first she didn't seem to notice the giant trees they walked past, and he did not point out Father of the Forest or Mother of the Forest or any of the others. But eventually as they were passing the Three Graces, she seemed to take them in for the first time. 'They're so big, aren't they? How come they're so big and other trees aren't?'

'I don't know,' Robert replied, wondering why he had never asked this question himself. 'There's another grove of these trees a few miles away where there's one that's even bigger, and more beautiful. Nobody knows about it but me. I'll show you sometime if you want.' Already he was giving his sister his most precious gift – his secret grove of trees.

'I'd like that.'

'We could go now – it's only a few miles. You could manage that on a horse, couldn't you?' Suddenly the idea of taking his sister to see the secret trees was all Robert could think of.

His eagerness made Martha smile. 'Maybe tomorrow. I've got some pain now and then.'

'That doesn't sound good. Do you know when the baby's coming?'

'Soon. Real soon. It's moved down.' Martha shook her head at his alarmed look. 'You haven't been around women having babies, have you? Mrs

Day and I helped out with neighbors in the Black Swamp. The labor starts a long time before it gets going for real. It's just getting itself ready. I've got time.'

They walked for a bit in silence before Robert said, 'What are we going to do?'

'I already know,' Martha replied firmly. 'Mrs Lapham talked to me about it. She's real nice, Mrs Lapham.'

'Nancy? What did she say?'

'That we should go with them to Murphys. They're leaving tomorrow. I can have the baby there.'

Robert nodded. Though he had been thinking further ahead, her answer made him realize it would be best to concentrate on the next few days for now, and leave the future to sort itself out.

Nancy Lapham was delighted to discover that Martha was Robert's sister rather than his lover. The knowledge seemed to rally her. 'A sister! Of course!' she cried, sitting up in bed and reaching out to pat Martha's arm. '*That* makes sense. You got a Goodenough look about you, now I see you two side by side. Oh, how wonderful that you've found each other! Tell me how it happened,' and she made Martha tell the story all over again, of lost letters and her journey by boat and barge and ship and steamboat and stage and horse. Already Martha was repeating phrases, leaving out unnecessary details, hurrying over questionable moments, shaping her journey into a story ready for retelling.

Nancy asked her many more questions than Robert had – not about the baby or its father, but about the months on board the ship going down and up the South American coastlines and around Cape Horn. 'Did you see penguins?' she asked. 'Natives with spears? Dolphins? Were the men respectful? Respectable? How many other women were on board? Could you wash? How much fresh water did you get? Was the passage rough? Were there rats? Fleas? What did you eat? Were there weevils in the flour? What kind of fruit did they bring on board? Coconuts? Pineapples?'

At the mention of pineapples, Martha started. 'Oh! Robert, will you get my bag? I hid it in the last stall in the stables. Please.'

By the time he'd brought it back, the women had come down to the front porch, aided by Billie Lapham, and were sitting side by side in rocking chairs. 'I am truly honored to meet you, ma'am,' Lapham was saying to Martha, his top hat in his hands. 'Really and truly. Any sister of Robert's is a sister to me.'

'Where'd you get this?' Robert asked as he handed his sister a battered carpetbag.

'New York.' As Martha rummaged around in the bag, Robert marveled at the thought of his timid sister navigating the streets of America's biggest city. She didn't seem capable of it. But then, she had gotten herself all the way across the country to him. He was going to have to change his idea of her from the shy, defenseless girl he'd known when they were young, the last sight of her a muddy boot dangling from an apple tree.

Martha pulled out a handkerchief. As she unfolded it, something scattered into her lap and rolled off her belly onto the porch floorboards. 'Oh!' she cried. 'Don't move!'

'What is that?' Robert stepped carefully over.

'Seeds. They're for you. I brought them all this way, and now—'

'It's all right, I see them.' Robert picked at the floor till he held a dozen small brown seeds shaped like tears. He recognized them but asked anyway, 'What are these?'

'From one of the Golden Pippin trees back home, the one that tasted of pineapple. They're from the tree you grafted on the Injun trail that you mentioned in your letter. I thought you could plant one out here.'

Robert rolled the hard seeds between his fingers. 'I know they'll mostly turn out to be spitters,' Martha added, 'but isn't one in ten trees usually an eater if you plant them from seed?'

Robert nodded. 'You remember.'

'Course I do. You've got more than ten seeds there, so if you plant them all you'll likely get at least one sweet Golden Pippin.'

'Yes.'

Nancy was staring at them. 'What are you two talking about?'

'Apples,' Martha said. 'Family apples.'

*   *   *

After a while Nancy sent the men away. 'Get me my shawl, Billie. Me and Martha are gonna sit here and get to know each other.' She held out her hand and Martha took it.

Billie Lapham glanced at Robert, who shrugged. This would give him a little time to collect the sequoia cones he had come to Calaveras Grove for – though now that he was free for a moment he found he didn't want to leave his sister, fearful that she was a dream he would suddenly wake from.

He forced himself to head for the stables to get sacks and his shotgun, but he kept turning back around to look at Martha. Seeing the two women together, he understood at last why he'd always been drawn to Nancy Lapham, even in her illness: she and Martha were alike enough that they could be sisters. Nancy's face was wide where Martha's was narrow, and her hair was darker to Martha's fair, but both were delicate and shy and loving.

Each time Robert looked back, Martha laughed and waved. Her laughter was tinkly, tinged with a hint of hysteria, or perhaps merely fatigue, as the nine-month journey caught up with her. Or maybe she worried that, after her coming thousands of miles to find him, Robert might walk into the giant sequoia grove and disappear. After all, he had walked away from her before. He hated to do so now.

He collected his equipment and hurried into the woods. At the nearest giant sequoia, he shot down

265

a few branches and threw the green cones into a sack, not bothering to inspect each for signs of rot or chickaree damage.

Deeper in the woods, though, out of sight of the hotel, he slowed down. In fact he was glad to have the time alone as he tried to put what had just happened into some kind of order. In the space of an hour, his life had changed completely. Seeing Martha was a dream he had never dared to think would become real. All of those letters he'd sent had been a hook thrown out into the wilderness to snag her, or the memory of her; he had not actually expected her to come and find him. Now she had, with a Goodenough baby on the way, and that brought him a stack of new responsibilities and expectations. Since the age of nine Robert had lived his life more or less alone: he could walk away from work, from people, move on, go west. No one had been gripping his arm. When someone did – when Molly did – he had ducked from her. But he could not duck from Martha. Nor did he want to: he was thrilled to feel her holding on to his arm. Only a sliver of him wanted to pry her hand loose and say, 'I don't know how to be a brother anymore.'

While he pondered this sudden change, his collecting instincts took over and he began to gather cones more methodically, even finding three seedlings to bring back. He had just dug up the third one when the stable boy appeared to tell him he was needed back at the hotel.

Though he had only been gone an hour, Martha was in tears on the porch, with Nancy rocking in time beside her, squeezing her hand. Robert set down the sack and the seedlings and took his sister's other hand. 'Martha, Martha, I'm here, I haven't gone away. I was just collecting seeds. It's my job. I won't leave you. I promise.'

'Your brother is a good man,' Nancy added. 'Billie and me always said so. Anybody here will tell you that too: Robert Goodenough is a good man.'

Martha nodded and pulled free the hand Nancy held to wipe her eyes. 'I know. Course I know.'

But Robert was not sure she did know.

They made a stately procession down the mountain from Calaveras Grove the next day. Robert was used to traveling on his own, just him and the gray, or with William Lobb before his employer's illness kept him close to San Francisco. And he was not used to traveling with women – one ill, one close to giving birth. They rode together in a wagon bed, Nancy lying down on a mattress, Martha preferring to lean beside her on one of Robert's sacks of cones. A second wagon carried the Laphams' possessions: a bed frame, a chest of drawers, a table and chairs, quilts, dishes, trunks of clothes. Wedged among them were the sequoia seedlings and Martha's bag. Two of Haynes' men drove the wagons while Robert and Billie Lapham rode behind. Robert had never ridden so slowly. Though it was a reasonable road, they were being careful because of Martha, who winced occasionally, though whether from the jolts from the road or the pain of the baby preparing to come out, he was not sure.

Billie Lapham was full of plans. 'It'll be better being based at Murphys,' he explained. 'I can drum up business there, and bring tourists up to Cally Grove, act as their guide, without having to worry about running the place. Leave that to Haynes. I bet there are plenty of miners at Murphys and the surrounding camps – Angels, Columbia, Jamestown – who'd like a day or two out to see the trees. Maybe even the French and the Chinese.'

Robert smiled to himself. Clearly Billie Lapham didn't know miners if he thought they would willingly take time off from their search for gold to look at some trees, no matter how big they were. But he did not say so. It was heartening to hear of Lapham's dreams – ever the optimist, even when his business was failing and his wife dying. Also, he was clearly attached to the sequoias, and that love of trees endeared him to Robert. For a moment he considered telling him about the second sequoia grove; it could change the business-man's fortunes.

Before he could, though, Lapham continued, 'This state is made up of people from other places, but they don't know California at all, except for the little bit where they are. The mining's dying down and people want to move around, see what there is here before they take their earnings back home. Some of them might even look around for a place to settle. It's the best time to be in the tourism business. Not just these big trees, but the mountains all around. I hear there are rock formations and waterfalls south of here in Yosemite Valley that'll knock you over with how big and bold they are. Lots of potential there. Then you got the shoreline with whales and seals, and canyons full of redwoods. Me, though, I'm settin' my sights on a lake north of here they call Bigler. You seen it? They says it's the most beautiful lake in the world, huge, with sandy beaches and green bays. Perfect for steamboats and saloons.'

That was never how Robert would envisage a lake, but he was not in the tourist trade. Perhaps Billie Lapham's enthusiasm could inspire even hard-bitten gold miners to lay down their pans and sluice boxes to look at giant trees and whales and waterfalls, and paddle in an emerald lake. Who was he to say? He was glad he'd just kept his mouth shut about the secret sequoias; otherwise he could have seen them ruined with saloons and bowling alleys. Let Lapham take his tourist attractions to the emerald lake instead. 'What about Nancy?' he asked. 'Is she going to come with you to this lake?'

'Oh, of course I won't go anywhere till Nance is better. Give her some time to convalesce at Murphys, then we'll see.'

They were quiet for a bit, riding down through

the pines and cedars lining the road, the sky an intense blue backdrop. Other times Robert had relished this ride from Calaveras Grove, admiring the trees, and the jays and finches and flycatchers flying back and forth, and the layered hills in the distance. Now, though, he was distracted by his companions, noticing, for instance, how closely Billie Lapham was studying the women in the wagon ahead of them. 'Your sister gonna be all right?' Lapham murmured under the sound of the wagon wheels and horse hooves.

The question was like a punch to Robert's stomach. 'What do you mean?'

Billie Lapham pulled up his horse and let the wagons move away. Taking a handkerchief from his pocket, he wiped his brow. 'Well, now, she's a little thing, ain't she, a lot like Nancy. Doctors always warned Nance she was too small to have a baby easily. Said it was a risk she shouldn't chance. Course, maybe we would've tried anyway,' he added quickly when he saw the look on Robert's face, 'but she got sick and that was the end of that. But I tell you what – I could ride ahead and find a doctor in Murphys who can be waitin' at the hotel, ready to check on Martha as soon as you get there.'

Robert stared at his sister, measuring her swollen belly against her slight frame, and knew Lapham was right. Some women were built to give birth easily; others struggled. Martha was likely to be a struggler. She was pale, too, and a film of sweat glistened on her forehead. Though she was smiling now at something Nancy said, she was also gripping the side of the wagon so hard that her knuckles were white. 'You don't mind going ahead?'

'Not at all. My horse could do with a run anyway after goin' so slow all morning. You look after the girls. Nance,' he called to his wife, 'I'm just gonna ride ahead, take care of a little business at Murphys, get things ready for you. Want to make sure we get rooms out back, away from the saloon. Robert will stay with you. I'll see you down there, all right?'

His wife nodded; she knew her husband.

Billie Lapham was about to spur on his horse when a wagon appeared in the distance on the road below, climbing towards them. All Robert could see from where he sat was a bright red and yellow parasol, twirling slowly.

'What kind of fancy tourist is that?' Billie Lapham said.

They pulled up and watched the wagon draw closer. After a few minutes it became clear the parasol was made of Chinese silk brocade, and was being spun by Molly Jones, who sat in the wagon bed while a bemused old man drove. There was just enough room for the wagon to stop alongside the one carrying Nancy and Martha.

'Halloo there!' Molly cried. 'Well, now, Robert Goodenough, ain't you a sight for sore eyes – or sore thighs, I oughta say. You never told me the big trees were so damned out of the way!'

Nancy and Martha sat up and stared at Molly, then turned their heads to look up at Robert. Billie Lapham gazed from Molly to Robert and back again, then chuckled. Robert sat frozen on the gray, unable to move for all the sets of eyes on him – even those of the wagon drivers, who had felt invisible up to now.

'Ain't you gonna come down here and kiss me hello?'

It was only when Robert dismounted and stepped up to the wagon, hesitating with his hand on the edge of one side, that he took in the full enormity of Molly, understanding long after the others had worked it out that she was carrying a child. Carrying his child. Carrying his child he'd thought the day before he had managed to dodge when it turned out to be Martha's.

Molly leaned over and kissed him full on the lips. 'Surprise, honey!'

No one spoke, but the gray whinnied and it sounded like a laugh.

'You ain't runnin' away from me now, are you?' Molly looked over at the women in the other wagon across from her – a direct, assessing gaze that said, 'Explain yourselves.'

Nancy at least knew how to respond. 'I'm Nancy Lapham.' She held out her small, pale hand. 'And that's my husband, Billie.'

Billie Lapham removed his top hat and nodded at Molly. 'Ma'am.'

Molly turned her attention to Martha, eyes

fastened on her stomach. 'Well, now, who've we got here?'

Robert was too stunned to speak. Martha, in the midst of a contraction, clutched the side of the wagon again and could say nothing. Their silence brought on the expression Robert had seen in Molly when he was leaving her at French Creek: that desperation, the desire to be in control when it was clear she was not in control. It was almost unbearable, and he did not want the others to see it. 'That's my sister, Martha,' he managed to mutter. 'She's only just come out here from Ohio.'

Immediately Molly's face cleared and she was able to laugh. 'Of course, I should've guessed! Ain't you two the spits of each other. You never told me you had a sister. And look at that, a baby, jest like me. When you due, honey?'

'Soon – now,' Martha gasped.

'I've still got a couple of months to go, I think, but I'm as big as you now. Wonder if it's twins?' Molly pulled the skirts of her yellow dress – already let out in most places – tight over her belly.

'We're headed down to Murphys,' Robert explained. 'Billie and Nancy are moving there, and Martha and I . . .' He didn't finish, though several pairs of curious eyes watched him to see how he would finish that sentence.

'What, you're not leavin' the big trees when I ain't even seen 'em yet, are you? I come all this way!'

Robert shrugged, not knowing how to answer her question.

'You gonna stay at the new hotel at Murphys?'

'We are indeed, ma'am,' Billie Lapham replied, clearly sensing that Robert needed help.

'I loved it there. It's got two floors, with balconies running around three sides. There are basins in every room, and mahogany everywhere! I didn't like the first room they gave me, so I had them show me all the others and I chose the one in the front, above the street. You can sit out on the balcony and watch all the comings and goings – of which there are plenty 'cause there's a saloon *and* a restaurant. And they let me store my mattress in the barn.'

Robert pictured the big feather mattress he had spent so much time in, and began to understand. 'Have you left French Creek?'

Molly wrinkled her nose. 'Of course! You don't think I'm gonna bring up a child *there*, do you? Not with all those rascally miners around, I'm not. No, this baby's gonna have a better life than that.' She smiled at him expectantly.

'Why don't you go on up to Cally Grove and stay at the hotel there?' Robert suggested. 'I'll come back up in a day or two.'

'Why would I want to stay there on my own?' Molly spun her parasol again as if trying to mesmerize Robert with it. 'Ain't you gonna come back with me and show me the trees?'

Martha stared at Robert with big eyes, one hand still clutching the side of the wagon as if it had jolted her. The look on her face decided him. 'No,' he said to Molly. 'Martha's having her baby now, and I'm taking her to Murphys to see her through it. I'm her brother. That's what a brother does.'

Molly stopped spinning the parasol. 'You hurtin', honey?' she said to Martha, who nodded.

'Poor thing. You should be in bed, not out here in a wagon! Of course, you all go on. I'll settle myself up at Calaveras, see what there is to see. Isn't there a bowling alley up there?'

Billie Lapham sat straighter in his saddle. 'There sure is, ma'am!' He was proud of the bowling alley.

'Maybe I'll try it, if this don't get in the way.' Molly patted her belly. 'Give me another kiss, Robert, then I'll head on up, and see you soon as you're ready to come find me.' She seemed somehow to pull out of the awkward situation with her dignity intact.

'Nice to meet you, ma'am,' Billie Lapham said, raising his top hat again, and Nancy murmured in agreement.

'You too. And good luck, honey!' Molly nodded at Martha, then tapped her driver with the top of her parasol and they moved on.

They were all silent for a moment. Once Molly was out of earshot, Billie Lapham started to laugh. 'Well, I'll be damned, Goodenough! You sure keep us guessin', don't you?'

Once Billie Lapham had ridden ahead to Murphys, the wagon continued slowly down the mountain. Robert remained riding behind it until Nancy

called out, 'Don't stay back there, Robert Goodenough. You come up alongside us so you can
answer some questions!'

Robert sighed. He would prefer not to talk, and
to be alone, so that he could take in the reality of
Molly and another baby. His life was rapidly filling
with other people, without the time to figure out
how that was going to change things. No one else
seemed bothered by this, though. It wasn't their
life that was being tumbled around.

He brought the gray forward so that he was level
with the women. Even looking at them made him
blush: though Martha was clearly in pain, she was
also smiling, and Nancy was openly grinning. 'All
right, now,' she said, 'tell us all about her!'

Robert reluctantly explained about meeting
Molly in Texas and again in Sacramento, and his
subsequent visits to French Creek. He mentioned
her cooking but not the other side of her job, and
hoped they would not speculate too much. He
found it embarrassing to have to reveal this side
of his life, but at least it distracted Martha from
her contractions. She let Nancy ask the questions,
but she listened as closely as she could.

When Nancy had finally finished interrogating
him, Martha nodded at her belly and said, 'This
baby will have a cousin.' Put that way, with her
simple words making the lines between her and
Robert and Molly clear, Robert felt a whole lot
better.

Billie Lapham had two back bedrooms ready for

them at Murphys Hotel when they arrived mid-afternoon, and had found a doctor and even a rare woman to help with the birth. The room was as nice as Molly had said – nicer than any room Robert had stayed in, with carpet on the floor and striped wallpaper and solid mahogany bedboards and washstands and good glass in the windows. He could not imagine sleeping well in it.

He hovered in the doorway as the woman got Martha into bed, but she waved him away. 'Out – you're no use,' she muttered. 'Don't need a doctor either – this ain't no illness.'

'I'll be nearby,' Robert called to his sister, but by then she had moved into the kind of pain that blocked out everything around her, and he doubted she heard. For a while he waited out in the hallway, but when she began to scream he went out and walked up and down Main Street.

Murphys was like other mining towns, full of supplies and alcohol, but it had a heft to it – like a building with a proper foundation laid – that made it likely to survive gold fever and become something more. Robert saw none of this, however, too shaken by his sister's screams to notice the sturdy planks laid out for walking along the streets, the brick buildings, the gutters that had been dug. For a while he sat in one of the saloons with a glass of whiskey before him, but he was not a drinking man, and eventually he left, the glass untouched.

He preferred the outskirts of Murphys, where a

few miners were camped. A creek – a tributary of the Stanislaus River – ran back behind the hotel, and he sat for a long time on its bank, watching a family dig up the mud from the bed and sluice it through a rocking box – one of the few who were still mining using the early methods Robert was familiar with. It was unusual to see a woman and children mining. He wanted to stop the woman and ask her what was happening to Martha, how a woman could survive so much pain. But he didn't: she'd had the two children he could see with her and clearly survived that, and she would probably say as much about his sister. So Robert sat in the sun and watched them find their meager flakes of gold and tried not to think.

That was where Billie Lapham found him. Lapham was a man who wore his emotions physically, and Robert knew from the moment he saw his friend hurrying down the path that Martha was all right. He let out a breath he hadn't even realized he was holding.

'Goodenough, you got yourself a nephew!' Billie Lapham pumped Robert's hand and wiped his forehead. He clearly liked being the bearer of good news.

'How's Martha?'

'Oh, she's fine. Tired, of course. It's incredible what women have to go through, ain't it?' He shook his head in wonder. 'She's asking for you, and I said I'd find you. Looked everywhere except back here. C'mon, I'll take you to her.'

She was lying in bed with the baby in her arms, oblivious to the activity around her: Nancy Lapham bringing her a cup of tea, the doctor putting away bottles and metal instruments Robert didn't want to look at too closely, and the woman bundling sheets into buckets of water. Before he joined his sister he paid the doctor and gave something to the woman too. Then he sat on the chair next to the bed. 'Martha,' he said.

'Oh, Robert,' she rasped, her throat raw from yelling. 'You're here.' Martha's hair was clumped together with sweat, and she had new lines around her eyes and mouth. The pain she had just been through had pressed its heavy mark on her. But when she held out her hand to take his, her grip was firm.

'You all right?' Robert asked. Despite the woman taking the sheets away, the room was metallic with the smell of blood.

'Sure I am. I'm just glad he's out. Look at him.' She pointed a tiny, wrinkled red face at him with the radiance only a mother can have for her baby. Robert couldn't take in his nephew for the moment; it was his sister he was concerned with.

'What shall we call him?' Martha said.

Robert shook his head. 'You decide.'

'I want to call him after our father. James.'

Robert flinched. 'Your father, you mean,' he said after a moment, though immediately he regretted bringing up the subject at such a time.

But Martha looked at him steadily. 'I meant what

I said. *Our* father. I never paid attention to what Ma said about Uncle Charlie. She was just – well. She was being Ma. Fighting to the last.'

Robert wasn't so sure. He had put his mother's last words to him up on a high shelf that he never visited. But maybe he would let Martha do the visiting for him.

'Let's call him Jimmy to start with,' she said. 'James is awful serious for a boy.'

Robert had another, dim memory of the name Jimmy carved on one of the wooden crosses that marked the graves of his dead brothers and sisters in the Black Swamp. When his mother was drunk she had shouted at God and the swamp fever for taking her oldest boy. Maybe a new Jimmy was some kind of an answer to that loss.

The red face let out a sudden cry. Robert reared back like the gray would when it saw a snake, but Martha pulled open her dress and put him on her breast. Robert looked away. 'You want anything?'

'Some bread soaked in a little milk would be nice – I'm starving! And a towel to wrap around Jimmy for a diaper.'

Robert went down to the restaurant and ordered food for Martha and himself, and asked about towels. These were unfamiliar domestic arrangements to him, and he found himself thinking about his bedroll, about the gray in the stables, about the camps surrounding Murphys and the fires the miners would soon be sitting around, eating tack and hard biscuits and smoking cigars. Would he ever join such campfires again? He could not imagine Martha sitting by one with a baby in her arms or, later, a child playing at her feet. But then, he had never imagined her coping with the rough life on board a ship going around South America.

While they ate together in the hotel room, the baby asleep on the bed beside Martha, he asked her more about that trip, about New York City and, tentatively, about the Black Swamp. Martha was in the middle of telling him something funny about Hattie Day when she stopped. 'You know I can't ever go back there,' she said, interrupting her own story. ''Cause of what I did to Caleb.'

Robert swallowed. 'Is he . . .'

'I don't know. I run off. But there was a lot of blood.' Martha fixed her eyes on the candle by her bed. 'I thought they might be looking for me in New York so I kept real quiet there, and slipped onto the ship at the last minute. But there's a whole country between me and the Black Swamp. They won't come looking for me all the way out here, will they?'

'Of course not. I'll keep you safe.' Robert tried to sound reassuring, hiding his shock over her mention of blood. 'We can live somewhere out of the way. There's plenty of land out here. California is where you get to start over.'

Martha turned her eyes back to him from the candle. 'What about Molly?'

'What about her?' Robert's reply was cockier than he actually felt.

'She's family now. Her baby will be a Goodenough too, and so will she once you marry her.'

'Marry Molly?'

'She seems real nice. Spirited. And it'd be good to live with someone else having a baby at the same time – makes it easier.' Martha chuckled at the look on his face. 'You haven't thought about it much, have you?'

Robert shook his head. 'There hasn't been any time.'

'Well, now you can start to plan. Tomorrow you go up to Calaveras Grove and talk to her about the future, make sure she doesn't mind if I live with you all.'

'Of course she won't mind!' Robert didn't add, 'No one has talked about living together.' Martha was making assumptions, and he suspected Molly was too. That was how women had to be, he supposed: pragmatic, looking out for their children.

To his relief, they didn't have to talk about the future anymore, for exhaustion had caught up with her and Martha's eyes were closing. Robert quietly unrolled his bedding and spread it on the floor. He pretended to be asleep each time his nephew woke for a feeding.

In the morning, despite the night's interruptions, Martha was clear-eyed and smooth-faced, and insistent that he go back to Calaveras Grove to see Molly. 'Please,' she added as Robert hesitated. 'It'll set me at ease to know where Jimmy and me fit in to the future. And besides, she's carrying your child. You got to see she's all right.'

The Laphams were with them by then, Nancy sitting with Martha and Billie walking up and down with the baby in his arms. 'Go on, Goodenough, we'll take good care of your family,' he said, jiggling his bundle.

'Course we will,' Nancy added. 'I'll get my knitting and sit here all day for company. This little boy needs some warm clothes for the winter!'

'All right,' Robert agreed finally. 'I'll be back tonight.' Part of him was relieved to get away from his nephew. He had only held him once, briefly, and his red skin and his eyes squeezed shut and his grasping mouth were alien to Robert. Secretly he couldn't understand why the others were praising the baby so much when he resembled an animal rather than a human.

He leaned down and kissed his sister's forehead. She smiled up at him. 'Say hello to Molly for me. Tell her I'm looking forward to the cousins playing together.'

Robert nodded. As he left, Nancy Lapham was making arrangements for a tin bath to be brought up so that Martha could wash away the sweat and blood of the previous day.

At Calaveras Grove he found Molly leaning against the Chip Of the Old Block, chatting to other visitors and looking as if she lived there. As he dismounted and headed towards her she was saying, 'Myself, I like a waltz, especially when I'm so big. Imagine trying to polka with this belly!' The group with her laughed.

Molly brightened when she saw him, and went to put her arm through his. 'Robert Goodenough, you were right about this place. It's wonderful!'

'You walked through the trees yet?'

'Naw, just saw those.' She waved at the Two Sentinels. 'I've been waitin' for you to come and show me. How's your sister?'

'Good. She had the baby. She's calling him James – Jimmy. She – she sends her regards.' Robert could not bring himself to repeat the part about the cousins playing together, and about living together: it was too much too soon. 'Let me stable the gray, then I'll show you the trees. I can only stay for the day.'

Molly frowned. 'Ain't you even gonna stay the night? The food is good here – I had a long talk with the cook. And I love the bowling! Have you tried it?'

Robert shook his head, remembering how scathing William Lobb had been about the game. 'I promised Martha I'd come back tonight. She's still pretty tired, and I want to make sure she's all right, and knows I'm there.' Thinking of his sister gave him a pang, and he began to regret having left her to come to Cally Grove.

Molly looked as if she were going to say something, but stopped herself. 'All right, then, Robert Goodenough, let's enjoy the day while we got it.'

She accompanied him to the stables to put up the gray. After only a day she clearly knew her way around, and she hallooed everyone in sight, for it seemed she had introduced herself to those who worked at the Grove and all the visitors too. In fact, Molly seemed much more interested in the human element of Calaveras Grove than she was in the sequoias themselves – which to Robert was missing the point. However, it did mean he didn't have to take her all the way around the mile-and-a-half circuit to see every tree. She was content to look at the trees that were only a little way into the woods, insisting as they went around on leaning on Robert's arm, as Martha had two days before. This time he felt the weight of her expectation even more heavily than Martha's. She held herself like a ship steering a slow, proud passage through calm waters. The visitors who encountered them smiled to see such a large woman among large trees – a response Molly accepted as if it were her due, like a queen or a president.

When they neared one of the named trees, Molly stopped and squinted. 'The Old Bachelor,' she read aloud from a plaque that had been hung on it. 'Huh!' She glanced sideways at Robert. 'Let's set here awhile.' Without waiting for him to agree, she settled onto a nearby bench placed so that there was a good view of the tree. Robert perched beside her.

'Sit back!' she said, pulling at his shoulder. 'You're tense as a cat in a thunderstorm.'

He knew he was sitting as if he were about to stand again, run back to the stables and gallop off on the gray. He leaned back and tried not to think about his sister.

Molly arranged her yellow skirts around her bump. 'Now, we got to have a little talk.'

Robert studied the Old Bachelor. It was a huge, grizzled old tree, set off from the others a bit up the hill. It would have been even bigger but the top had died and come down, leaving it with the rounded crown you saw on the older giant trees. He was beginning to understand its name better.

'Look at you. Can't even look at me.'

Midway up the trunk of the tree was a line of woodpecker holes. Robert counted them in his head, then asked what he needed to ask. 'Is the baby mine?'

He could feel her flinch next to him. Though in his head it seemed a logical question, spoken aloud Robert understood how hurtful it was.

But Molly did not shout at him. 'I'm sure as I'm ever gonna be that it's yours,' she replied evenly.

He knew that was the most honest answer he would get. 'Do you want . . .' Robert could not finish his sentence.

'How do you know I actually want something from you?'

Robert noticed that Molly had at last dropped her cheerfulness. It was a relief.

'I'll do right by you,' he said.

'What does that mean? You know, you ain't even said you're glad to see me. Are you glad?'

'I—'

'I think you ain't glad. That's what I think.' Molly was getting that look again that he hated, that made him feel a metal band was strapped around his chest and tightening. But she was also angry.

'I *am* glad. But—'

'You don't want me here, do you?'

'Molly! Stop. Just—' Robert held up his hand. 'Just let me speak.' He held Molly's eye, and she became still, her hands folded over her belly.

'My sister Martha only just arrived two days ago. I haven't seen her in eighteen years. In fact, I didn't even know if she was alive or not.'

'You didn't?'

'No.'

'What about the rest of your family? Your parents?'

'They're dead.'

'You never told me that. When did they die?'

'Eighteen years ago.'

Molly raised her eyebrows.

Robert hesitated. Then, because she was waiting for more, he finally spoke aloud the words he had never said before. 'They – they killed each other when I was a boy.' The words cut through the air like a knife through meat – resistant, and then gliding effortlessly.

Molly stared at him. 'Say that again so I'll know I'm hearin' right.'

'They killed each other.'

'How can two people kill each other?'

Robert sighed, then told her in as few words as he could what had happened in the orchard. He could feel the splinter of sadness poking at his heart. 'I ran off afterwards. Never went back.'

'Good Lord.' Molly sat still, twisting her hands in her lap. She was not easily shocked, but Robert saw that the Goodenough family had managed to stun her.

'I left Martha behind,' Robert added. 'I can never forgive myself for leaving her. In fact, I shouldn't have left her today.'

But Molly was already beginning to recover, and anger was overtaking her surprise. 'Why in hell's name didn't you ever tell me this, Robert Goodenough? I told you about my Ma and Pa and my brother and sister, but you never said a thing about yours – jest told me silly stories about your medicine man and the wooden leg when you had all this in your past!'

'I'm sorry, Molly, but I don't talk about it to anyone. It's easier that way.'

She was glaring at him, and he knew he owed her more than that. 'If I don't tell people about it, I don't have to think about it, and it can be like it never happened.'

'But it did happen.'

'Yes.'

'Then don't you know that anyway? Underneath all your silence, you know it's still there.'

288

'Yes.'

'Ain't it better to be open about it? Then at least you're honest, so you don't have it diggin' at you, deep inside.'

'Maybe. We're just different, I guess.'

'I guess.' Molly's anger had burnt out as quickly as it flared. She took his hand. 'Lord, I feel real bad for you, Robert. This world's full of sorrows, ain't it?'

They sat for a while, and Robert let her hold his hand.

'The Bible's never brought me a whole lotta comfort,' Molly said presently, 'but I can see how these trees might. They been around a lot longer than any of us with our foolishness, and they'll still be laughin' at us in a few hundred years, don't you think?'

'Yes.' It was easier to agree than to explain what he really thought. Back when he'd first seen the giant trees, Robert too had marveled at their age and what they had witnessed. Now, though, he did not see them as witnesses at all. Trees lived in a different world from people. However much he pruned their branches, picked their fruit, collected their cones, dug up their seedlings, they did not respond to him. Even his horse responded to him more than trees did. They were not made to. They were not selves. It bothered him when people gave them human qualities when they were so clearly not human. That was why he did not like the sequoias' being given names; the Old Bachelor was a tree, not a man. Yet he knew he still slipped into that trap too. For instance, he had been stupidly pleased that Martha had chosen the Orphans to sit under, though the trees were not orphans.

But he let Molly turn the trees into witnesses of human folly, and then he said, 'Molly, I need to go back to Murphys. It don't feel right leaving Martha.' It was easier now to say these simple words.

Molly accepted them with more ease too. 'Go back to her,' she said. 'Make that flea-biter gallop faster than he ever has before.'

'You can come down with me if I can find you a wagon.'

'Naw, I'll jest hold you back. I'll be down in a day or two.' Molly stretched her legs out before her and pointed her toes. 'Right now I'm gonna set here a bit and look at the trees.'

The gray was not an eager horse, but he had a sense from his rider that now was the time to gallop. They flew down the mountain in an hour and a half.

But Robert too had a sense, and it was of a dread that grew faster than he could ride.

He stood in the doorway of the hotel bedroom, looking at the bed soaked with blood, at Martha's head turned towards the door as if expecting him, at her open eyes like two candles blown out, at Billie Lapham next to her with his handkerchief over his face, crying, and he thought, There is a

God and He is a very harsh one, giving with one hand and taking more with the other so that I am even emptier than when I started.

He removed his hat and went up to the bed and took Martha's hand. It was only just starting to cool. 'If you are still in this room,' he said, 'I want to tell you that I never should've left you in the Black Swamp. I did it because I was scared and I was only thinking of myself when I should have been thinking of you too. I was just a boy, but I should've looked after you and I didn't, and I will be sorry for that for the rest of my days.'

There was a wailing sound behind him, and when he turned, Nancy was standing in the doorway with Jimmy in her arms, wrapped in Martha's shawl. 'I'm real sorry, Robert. I truly am.'

'What happened?'

'Hemorrhage. The doctor said it happens some-times when something's left inside the mother that should've come out. She was fine, chattin' away with me while the baby slept, then suddenly there was blood everywhere. Billie ran for the doctor, but it was too late.'

Jimmy cried louder. 'I know I shouldn't be holdin' him 'cause of my illness,' Nancy said, 'but Billie ain't in a fit state to. He always was soft.' She gazed fondly at her weeping husband. 'Here.' She walked over and held out the baby. 'Go on, take him,' Nancy chided when Robert hesitated. 'You're all he's got now.'

291

Robert took Jimmy, propping him in the crook of his arm as he'd seen Nancy do. The transfer made the baby go quiet for a moment and open his eyes. It was the first time Robert had seen them open. They were not brown or blue yet but a muddy mix of the two, and they could not focus, but Robert could see they were Goodenough eyes. He stared at Jimmy and it was like looking at his family all pressed into one face, young and old, man and woman, boy and girl.

After the baby found this new holder was not giving him any food, he began to cry again, voicing his displeasure.

'You got to get him something to eat,' Nancy said. 'Problem is, there's only twenty-five women in this town, and none who got babies.'

Robert was finding Jimmy's crying almost unbearable.

'Jiggle him, and walk him up and down,' Nancy suggested. 'That's what I been doing.'

Robert took his nephew out to the hallway, for walking with him in front of the mother he would never know seemed heartless. As he passed along the carpeted corridor, two men were coming the other way: the hotel owner and another who introduced himself as the sheriff. They were brisk, talking over the baby's cries. 'Just come to check,' the sheriff said. 'You got the money to bury her?'

Robert nodded.

'Then someone'll be along to measure for a coffin. That'll cost you six dollars. You want to have a wake or a service? We'd have to send to Stockton for the minister who comes up to the church here. Could take a day or two.'

'No, no need to wait.'

The hotel owner looked relieved: a death in the hotel was bad enough, but a body remaining for any length of time was not good for business. He nodded at Jimmy, who by now was screaming. 'Looks like you got your hands full. I'll get two boys to dig a grave for you. Cost you a dollar. All right?'

Robert could only nod again. All of these practical questions, accompanied by Jimmy's urgent cries, made it hard for him to hold on to the fact that Martha was dead.

'You know what my wife used to do to quiet a baby?' the sheriff said. 'She stuck her little finger in its mouth, gave it something to suck on. Sometimes that's all they want – to suck. Try it.'

Robert frowned, then put his pinkie up to the baby's mouth, tickling his lips. Jimmy dived at the finger and began to suck, surprisingly hard.

'There you go. Course, once it finds out there's no milk in that teat it'll yell louder'n ever.' The sheriff chuckled.

'Now, you gonna stay in that room tonight?' the hotel owner asked.

'I guess so.'

'You'll need to pay a night's charge up front, and pay for the sheets and the mattress – they're ruined.'

Robert nodded. His nephew's pull on his finger was beginning to hurt.

'I'll tell you another trick,' the sheriff interjected, sensing that Robert was out of his depth. 'Pull out the bottom drawer of the dresser and line it with a quilt, and the baby can sleep in that.' He clapped Robert on the back and went into the room where Martha lay.

Robert had been around deaths before. He had seen men die from fever or a snakebite or a fall from a horse or, once, a goring from an angry bull. Sometimes it wasn't clear why they died; it seemed they just gave up. He had dug graves and moved bodies and stood at gravesides, hat in hand. Some of the dead were strangers, others he knew and had been friendly with. But never had he had to deal with the aftermath of the death of someone he loved, with its uncomfortable mix of the practical with the emotional. He had not seen his parents' final moments – their eyes were both still open when he left, and they were staring at each other. It must have been Nathan and Caleb who took charge, building coffins and digging graves, Sal who ran for the neighbors, she and Martha and Mrs Day who washed and dressed Sadie and James for their laying out. During that time he would have been following the Portage River down to Lake Erie, already losing himself in America.

Now as he began to thaw from that icy moment of finding Martha on a bed soaked with her own blood, Robert feared he might sit down on the hallway carpet and not get up again. The only thing keeping him from doing so was the hard, persistent tug on his little finger. Angry now that he'd been duped into sucking something so dry all he swallowed was his own spit, Jimmy was letting little squawks erupt from the sides of his mouth. In a minute he would start to yell again. Robert had to think of something.

He hurried along the hallway with the baby tucked in the crook of his elbow and went into the restaurant kitchen, where a man with a bulge of tobacco in his cheek was frying steaks on the range. Around his feet were gobs of tobacco and spit.

'You got any milk?' Robert asked.

With a glance the man took in man and baby, then jerked his head towards the back door. 'Out in the creek.'

'You mind if I take some for—' Robert waved his arm with Jimmy in it, which caused him to start up his kittenish wail.

The cook winced. 'Ten cents a cup. We'll add it to your bill. Which room you in? Never mind, I remember. Now, get it out of here. Cryin' babies—' He shook his head and spat.

Upstream from where the mining family worked, a silver milk can sat in the creek, the water being the most effective way of keeping things cold. Robert awkwardly fished it out with one hand. Would he ever be able to put this baby down? How did women manage? He thought of the women he'd seen with babies. Indian women tied them in slings to their backs or chests, leaving their arms free for work. White women swaddled them tight and left them with girls or old women. But newborns generally stayed with their mothers in bed for a few weeks till both were stronger.

Robert set Jimmy on the ground. Squinting and crying, every part of his face tightened with misery, he flung his arms out, his tiny hands making a pair of stars in the air. Robert paused between milk can and baby, then decided Jimmy might squirm and wave but he could not actually move himself.

Unscrewing the lid, Robert poured milk into a tin mug he'd brought, took out a handkerchief – not very clean, but it was all he had – and dipped a corner of it in the milk, soaking up as much as he could. Then he sat down, took the baby in his lap, and rewrapped the shawl around him to stop him from flailing. When he brushed the milk-soaked cloth across his mouth, Jimmy ignored it and kept screaming. Robert tried a few more times, but his nephew seemed to have screamed himself beyond thinking about feeding. In desperation, Robert stuck his little finger in the baby's mouth again, and he quieted and began sucking. Then Robert pulled his finger out, wrapped part of the handkerchief around it, and stuck it in Jimmy's mouth again. His nephew looked so indignant when his palate and tongue met the rough cloth that Robert smiled a little. But he kept sucking, with a resigned expression. After a minute Robert pulled his finger out and shifted the cloth to a new section where there was more milk. 'There you go, little fella. Work on that.' He stuck his finger back in and Jimmy sucked. It was not an ideal solution, for he wasn't getting milk fast enough, but it would have to do until Robert worked out a better way to feed him.

At last, more from the exhaustion of crying than from a full stomach, Jimmy fell asleep, and Robert sat with him across his knees by the stream, afraid to move lest he wake. He studied his nephew's face, which was less red now that he'd stopped crying. His eyelids were pale blue, his nose flat, and his bow-shaped mouth was still going through the quivering motions of sucking. Everything about him seemed delicate, fragile. But he was quiet, and he was alive.

'There you are. Got him to sleep?' Nancy Lapham had come up behind him. She looked stronger than Robert had seen her in months. Crises make even the sick pull themselves up. She leaned over to peer at Jimmy's face. 'Ain't he sweet. Martha tell you who the father is?'

Robert shook his head, his mouth tight around the knowledge he would never voice.

'I've been askin' around to see if there's any women in nearby towns or camps who have babies and can feed him. Haven't found any yet, but I'll keep askin'.'

'Thank you.'

'If you want you can give him to me and I'll put him to bed in our room for tonight,' she offered.

To Robert's great surprise, he was reluctant to hand over Jimmy, even to someone as sympathetic as Nancy. The bond with his nephew had already tightened around him. 'That's all right. I'll take him back to the – the—' He stopped.

'They moved her,' Nancy said, filling in for him. 'She's down in the barn, where they're makin' the coffin. They'll bury her later – Billie'll come get you when they're ready.'

Robert nodded and got up carefully so that Jimmy wouldn't wake. Back in the bedroom, all traces of Martha were gone except for her carpetbag, which sat in a corner like an abandoned dog. The mattress and bloody bedding had been removed and a new straw mattress put in its place, less comfortable than the feather bed, but Robert figured he would end up sleeping on the floor anyway.

He laid Jimmy in the middle of the bed and opened the bottom drawer of the bureau. Then he unbuckled Martha's bag to look for something to line the drawer with. In it were two dresses, some underclothes, a hairbrush, the letters, and the nine-patch quilt, rolled up. Robert pulled out the quilt and spread it over his knees. Seeing the different squares brought forth a rush of memories. He sat for a long time, touching a bright blue square, a brown one and a dark green silk piece that was now frayed and threadbare but still the most beautiful patch of the quilt. Only when

Billie Lapham knocked on the door did he rouse himself.

They went together to see Martha buried in the graveyard next to the town's church. Little was said, but at Robert's request Nancy sang 'Blest Be the Tie That Binds,' her voice quavering.

Robert spent the next two days trying out different ways to feed his nephew. He was astonished at how difficult it seemed to be to get milk inside him. When Jimmy rejected the milky handkerchief – and who could blame him – Robert tried dribbling milk into his wailing mouth with a spoon, but it just made him choke. He visited a ranch outside of Murphys and borrowed a cow's horn drilled with holes that they used for feeding calves when the mother died, but it was too big for Jimmy's mouth. He spent some time fashioning a teat out of leather shaped into a cone while Billie Lapham reluctantly held the baby – after Martha's burial, Nancy lost what little strength she'd briefly gained and had gone back to bed. The baby managed to suck on the leather teat but then promptly threw up all the milk he had taken in.

It was bad enough hearing Jimmy cry. Even worse was when his crying grew weaker and it was clear he was failing. In desperation Robert walked all over town, as well as through the nearby miners' camps, looking for women and asking them what to do. Wherever he went, he got amused looks, for it was unusual to see a man carrying a baby around, especially a newborn. The women he met had plenty of advice. The one who had helped with the birth tore a towel into triangles and showed Robert how to pin it around Jimmy for a diaper. Another showed him how to properly swaddle a baby; when she got through wrapping Jimmy in Martha's shawl he could move nothing but his mouth, and seemed stunned by this fact.

The most sensible woman was the one Robert had watched mining with her family a few days before. Now she was sitting alongside the creek, resting while her husband and sons worked. She had a smear of dirt across her nose and cheek, and she rubbed at it while contemplating Jimmy. 'He's spitting up cow's milk? You gotta find you some goat's milk, then, or sheep. And if you can't find that? Go find a woman with a baby. Go farther away to the other camps, or better yet, down to Stockton. More women there, more babies maybe.'

Robert frowned. Stockton was sixty miles away. Even if he could find a way to tie Jimmy on so they could ride the gray that far, it would take another day to get there. His nephew might be dead by then. And there was no guarantee that there were babies in Stockton.

'Course, you could always try the Indians,' the woman added. 'There's Miwoks camped up near Cally Grove.'

Robert recalled that there were definitely babies there – he'd seen them recently in their slings on their mothers' backs, so natural there it was easy to forget them. He frowned. 'Think they'd do it?'

The woman shrugged. 'Everybody's got a price.'

Robert wasn't so sure. Most Indians he'd seen maintained a distance from white people, as if taking a step back and watching to see what would happen. Why would an Indian woman agree to feed a white child who might grow up to push her family off the land?

By the next day, though, he had no choice. He could not find any goats or sheep nearby. Jimmy continued to spit up the cow's milk, and the sugar water Robert managed to get down him was not sustaining him. When he stopped crying altogether, Robert went to saddle the gray. He would have to go back up to Calaveras Grove.

Jimmy was too small and floppy to be tied in a sling to Robert's chest or back. Instead he swaddled him extra tight – already he was getting better at that – and had Billie Lapham hand the baby up to him once he was astride the gray. His arm ached from carrying the baby almost nonstop for two days, but he couldn't see a better way.

'Goodenough, I never thought I'd see you ridin' round with your saddlebags stuffed with diapers and sugar water,' Billie Lapham said as he stood at the gray's side. 'You want me to water the seedlings while you're gone?'

'Oh – yes.' Robert had forgotten about the sequoias he'd collected. These last few days he had thought of little other than keeping Jimmy alive.

'It's good to see you lookin' after your nephew. Your sister would have been glad.' Billie Lapham's eyes grew watery. 'Poor gal.' He took out a handkerchief and wiped his face and blew his nose. It occurred to Robert then that Lapham's grief for Martha was a dress rehearsal for his wife's death. Molly was right: the world was full of sorrows.

Robert wanted to gallop up the mountain but didn't dare; holding Jimmy in the crook of his arm, he had to ride one-handed, trying not to think about the gray rearing up at a snake or stumbling over a rut in the track. But the horse seemed to understand that Robert was riding differently, that there was a new, demanding passenger, and adjusted his gait to a gentler trot than usual.

He had been so swamped with the practicalities of looking after a baby that he'd not had time to consider anything else. Now that Jimmy was quiet, and Robert had a plan and was moving, he was able to think about Martha. And then he was not thinking, but crying, sobbing so hard that the gray actually stopped and swung his head around to look at the sight, and Robert had to kick him to get him started again.

At last, empty of tears, he grew as calm as his listless nephew, and they rode up the mountain towards the big trees.

When he caught sight of the red and yellow parasol in the distance once again, this time coming down towards them, Robert was so relieved he almost began to cry again. Only now did he realize that these last few days he had been waiting for Molly to come and make things right.

She was lying flat in the wagon bed as the same old man drove, spinning her parasol above her and singing:

> I came to the river
> And I couldn't get across
> So I paid five dollars
> For a big bay hoss.
> Well, he wouldn't go ahead
> And he wouldn't stand still
> So he went up and down
> Like an old saw mill.
>
> Turkey in the straw
> Turkey in the hay
> Turkey in the straw
> Turkey in the hay
> Roll 'em up and twist 'em up
> A high tuck a-haw
> And hit 'em up a tune called
> Turkey in the Straw!

The old man accompanied her by whistling the tune. Because of the singing and the whistling, she didn't hear the first time Robert called her. 'Molly!' he cried again. This time she rolled herself up and squinted towards him as the wagon came to a halt.

'Robert Goodenough, here you are again!' she

cried, waving the parasol at him. 'You come out to find me?' Then she caught sight of the baby and went silent. Perhaps because hers was one of the few female voices around, Jimmy roused himself from his semiconscious state in Robert's arm and let out a thin, piercing wail.

'Good Lord.' Molly clutched her substantial breasts and laughed. 'Don't that hit me right here. Makes 'em feel tingly. Watch out, little baby, you'll get me started too soon! That your nephew? What'd you bring him up with you for?'

'Martha . . .' Robert couldn't finish, but one look at his red eyes and crumpled face told Molly all she needed to know. Getting to her knees on the wagon bed, she held out her arms. 'Come down here, both of you.'

Robert handed her the baby, and by the time he'd dismounted she'd already pressed Jimmy to her chest. She reached out and put her arm around Robert and hugged him hard, the baby squashed between them. For a moment Robert tensed, fearing for Jimmy. But he was fast discovering the resilience of newborns, and after a moment he relaxed, even allowing himself to rest his head on Molly's shoulder. For the first time since Nancy put Jimmy into his arms, Robert did not feel like the only one responsible for him.

When they pulled apart, Molly gazed down at Jimmy, who was now nuzzling at her bosom, his mouth seeking something he sensed was close by.

'What are you feeding him?'

'Sugar water is all. He won't take cow's milk and there's no women back at Murphys could feed him. I thought . . .' Robert trailed off, for Molly was unbuttoning the top of her dress to reveal a huge, dark nipple. Cupping her breast in one hand, she lifted and held out the nipple to the baby, who lunged at it like a drowning man come up for air. Latching on, he began to suck as hard as his weak mouth could.

Molly chuckled. 'Tickles. Ow!' Desperation was making him suck harder, for he seemed to know he was where he was meant to be, doing what he was meant to do.

'Is that gonna work?' Robert asked.

'Dunno. I've heard of it happening, but never seen it myself.' Molly winced. 'He'll jest have to keep sucking, see if that brings on the milk.'

Half an hour later Molly's milk came in.

Robert could not get used to living in a hotel. He shared a big bed with Molly that gave him a back-ache because it was softer than he was used to. Sometimes when she was asleep he moved to the floor. But that didn't really help, for he also sensed others close by, hearing murmurs and laughter and moans from adjacent rooms, and music and shouts from downstairs, and people walking up and down the street outside. Jimmy lay in the drawer near the bed, waking every two hours to feed since his tiny stomach held little and emptied quickly. Robert was woken by plenty of sounds when he was sleeping in the woods – bears crashing through the bushes, wolves howling, other animals snuffling nearby. Yet somehow these noises disturbed him less than Jimmy's insistent cry – for it was demanding something of him in a way the animals never did.

Molly loved Murphys. She settled into her preferred room, with its mahogany bed and its balconies overlooking the street, like a miner laying claim to a choice piece of river. Within an hour her dresses and petticoats hung from the bedposts, her bonnets dangled by their ribbons from hooks by the door, her shoes were piled in a corner and her hairbrush and hand mirror and powder and tin of rouge and hairpins littered the top of the bureau. The room smelled distantly of cooking from the restaurant below, and up close of warm flesh and talcum powder and souring milk and baby shit. Robert did not complain. He was grateful just to see Jimmy sleeping in Molly's arms, cheeks fat and rosy after two days of being wan and gray. Grateful too that she patted the bed next to her and made it easy for him to join them.

Molly asked the hotel owner to find a cradle for Jimmy, or have one made right away. 'A baby needs to rock,' she said when Robert pointed out that his newfound trick of the bottom drawer bed seemed to work. Soon a rough cradle made of elm appeared in the room, and that was when Robert began to understand that she was settling in. He had assumed they would stay at Murphys a day or two and then . . . but what would they do? He had cones and seedlings to bring back to William Lobb in San Francisco, but it was hard to imagine Molly and Jimmy living at Mrs Bienenstock's. He was pretty sure no woman had ever entered the boardinghouse apart from Mrs B. herself, and a baby there would be like a yellow dress at a funeral. San Francisco itself was too rough and dirty for a child. On the other hand, he needed to go there more regularly than anywhere else, and Molly and Jimmy couldn't follow him around while he was collecting plants and seeds. It would slow him down, and anyway a baby was better off in one place.

What Robert did not question was that he and Molly were now linked – by his nephew more than the child he had fathered, admittedly, but Jimmy was a real, demanding baby whereas his own was still just a mound under Molly's dress.

Molly quickly got to know the hotel staff – the owner, the cook, the barman, the maid. Being pregnant seemed to give her even more of an appetite for food and company. She would often take Jimmy down to the saloon and nurse him while she sat with the customers, laughing and singing. Her size did not stop her in bed either, and she was loud with it, crying out whenever they coupled so that passersby on the street could hear.

She did not become friends with Nancy Lapham, however, the way you might think two women would who were surrounded by men. Robert kept expecting them to seek the other out, but apart from courteous nods and Nancy's inquiries after Jimmy, they kept out of each other's way. Robert mentioned this first to Billie Lapham while they were checking on their horses in the hotel stables one evening. Lapham was dazzled by Molly, her sensual solidity combined with her matter-of-fact manner. 'Well, now,' he said, wiping his forehead with his palm – he seemed to be missing his handkerchief – 'Nance is funny that way. She likes women her own size – like your sister. She knows where she is with a woman like Martha. Whereas Molly – she's so – well, so full of life, she makes Nance feel even sicker. Course she didn't *say* that,' he hastily added. 'And she admires how Molly's taken up Jimmy so natural. We both do. She's really somethin' else, your woman.' Billie Lapham spoke the last two words in an incredulous tone, as if he couldn't believe Robert's luck at landing such a catch.

Molly was blunter about Nancy. 'She's sickly,' she said when Robert asked her. 'I don't need to get friendly with someone who's dyin'. Maybe that's heartless, but I'd jest lose her, and who wants to get set up to be sad?'

After two weeks at Murphys, Robert began to feel as if he were wallowing in mud, unable to escape. His daily life had slowed down. He slept later and later, sunk deep in the feather bed and Molly's flesh. He no longer hunted for his own food, but ate greasy steaks at the restaurant.

Someone else looked after the gray and washed his clothes and lit his fires with wood they had chopped. He had never had such an easy life, and he hated it. Only Jimmy's cheeks filling out, his eyes beginning to focus, his clear contentedness made Robert feel it was worthwhile.

To break out of the feather bed comfort, one day he rode up to Calaveras Grove with Billie Lapham, who did business with Haynes while Robert collected more sequoia cones. He had thought it would be a relief to be among the giant trees, but they only reminded him of Martha's death and the last time he was here, and he worked with little pleasure, a sadness gnawing at him that even the trees could not assuage.

He had planned to stay overnight, camping out as he used to. But when he came back to the Big Trees Hotel towards the end of the afternoon to wash, there was a letter from William Lobb waiting for him that had followed him up the mountain. Lobb was as brief as ever.

Bienenstock's
California & Montgomery
San Francisco

August 20, 1856

Goodenough —
A man on the Welsh border wants to plant the biggest redwood grove in Britain on his

estate. He is keen to get a head start on his wealthy friends, so wants seedlings rather than seeds. Bring back 50 as quick as you can, and a few sequoia seedlings to impress his neighbours.

William Lobb

He rode straight back to Murphys, relieved to have a purpose but uncertain what to say to Molly. When he got to their room, she was walking around with Jimmy on her shoulder like a sack of flour, patting his back to burp him. She brightened. 'Robert Goodenough! I guess you couldn't stay away even for a night. Did you miss your little family?'

'Molly, I—'

'Rub my feet, won't you, honey? Carryin' two babies around is swellin' 'em right up.' She sank onto the bed and stuck out her feet.

As he took one in his hands, Robert looked around the room at the new cradle by the bed, the bucket full of soaking diapers, a line strung across the room where clean diapers were pegged to dry. On a small table were the remains of a steak Molly'd had sent up. The place had an air of permanence that made him uneasy. 'Molly, we got to talk about what to do next,' he said.

'Well, first thing to do is to take Jimmy and put him in his cradle.'

Once he was settled back rubbing her feet, he started again. 'Willam Lobb wrote to me. I've got

310

to go back to San Francisco, and collect redwoods on the way.'

He was expecting arguments and complaints. But Molly surprised him. 'How long we got to pack?' she said.

'Oh. I wasn't expecting you to—'

''Cause I've been wantin' to see that city for a long time now. You know I've been in California three years and not been to San Francisco yet? I ain't even seen the ocean! Now's as good a time as any. Easier to do it now than when the other baby comes.'

'But you don't have to come with me. I can come back to Murphys after. Aren't you settled here?'

Molly snorted and gestured at the room. 'You call this settled? You got a funny idea of settled. Settled is when I have a range to cook on and my own front door and a garden full of beans and tomatoes. Anyway, we'd better come with you. Otherwise who's to say if you'll come back to us? This William Lobb I hear so much about will jest give you somethin' else to collect, then somethin' after that, and we'll never see you.'

Robert stopped rubbing her feet, stung by her words. He wasn't sure he could argue with her, though. 'I'm going to have to leave tomorrow,' he said instead.

'I can be ready tomorrow.'

'Are you sure?'

'Watch me.' Molly got up and began pulling

clothes down from hooks and folding them. As she moved around the room, Jimmy's dark eyes followed her as he lay quiet in the cradle.

'What about Jimmy?'

'What about him? You think babies ain't traveled all over this country? He'll be fine as long as he's fed and swaddled to feel secure. Little ones don't need more than that. It's when they start to walk that it gets harder.'

'And you won't have – the other one – on the way?' They had not talked about the baby Molly was carrying. Until it cried and needed feeding, it did not take their attention. Robert no longer questioned whether or not it was his. There would never be a satisfying answer to that question.

Molly shook her head. 'It ain't due for a while yet. Git my trunk out from under the bed for me, will you, honey?'

Faster than he'd expected, she dismantled the room, then went to arrange for the rest of her things to be brought back from the stables, leaving Robert alone with his nephew. Jimmy did not cry when she was gone, but regarded Robert at the foot of the bed, his long lashes making a fringe on his cheeks.

'Well, now, Jimmy, looks like we're going on the road again.'

Maybe it was hearing his uncle's voice, soft and wistful, but it seemed to Robert that Jimmy smiled a little.

★ ★ ★

They left Murphys amid something like a fanfare. Robert had met many people when he was struggling to get Jimmy fed and was memorable as the desperate man with the hungry baby. Molly was equally memorable for her laughter that filled the hotel saloon, her waves and halloos from the front balconies and her strolls through town, Jimmy in one arm, her other arm cupping her ballooning belly to support it, her yellow dress let out to its fullest and sweeping the dust behind her. Robert had hired a wagon to take them to Stockton, where they would get the steamboat to San Francisco. There he would get Molly and Jimmy settled, then go back out to dig up redwood seedlings, for he didn't see how he could do that with them in tow.

A crowd began to form as he and Billie Lapham and a few other men loaded the wagon with Molly's things and Jimmy's cradle, as well as the sacks of sequoia cones and the seedlings. Even Nancy Lapham came out and sat in a chair on the front porch of the hotel. She had insisted on getting dressed, and she made a point of kissing Jimmy and hugging Molly goodbye, though she stepped out of Molly's mountainous embrace as soon as she could. Robert went and sat with her for a few moments.

Nancy took his hand. 'Everything's changing, ain't it?' She seemed sad.

'I'll still come up this way to collect sequoias,' Robert assured her. 'I'll stop in and see you.'

'You better!' Nancy squeezed his hand. 'If I hear

you've been to Cally Grove and not come here to Murphys, there'll be hell to pay, Robert Goodenough!'

Robert smiled. It was hard to imagine Nancy giving him hell. He made to get up but she gripped his hand tighter. 'But something tells me I ain't gonna see you again.'

'Don't talk like that, Nancy.'

'It's not that.' She dismissed her own decline with a shrug. 'It's – never mind. You go on with your family now. Look after that little boy.'

'I'll see you soon,' he said. 'Real soon.'

'Sure.' Nancy let go of his hand.

After many handshakes and claps on the back – with Billie Lapham throwing his arms around him twice, and Molly laughing and crying, and the proprietor telling her she had a job at Murphys Hotel any time she wanted, and Jimmy squalling because of the noise – what Robert remembered most about their departure was Nancy seated and still on the hotel porch, dressed in white, watching them and nodding once. It turned out she was right.

Robert had only taken the steamboat from Stockton to San Francisco once before, when he'd traveled with William Lobb. Usually he preferred the gray and a mule or two and his own company coming down out of the golden foothills of the Sierra Nevadas and across the flat plain of central California, where the mountains disappeared; and then after a day of mesmeric riding in the bright hot sun, a blue haze of new mountains began to shimmer ahead. There were no miners in the plains to dirty it up, and the Indians and Californios he met along the way were benign.

But he could not travel with Molly and Jimmy and the wagon full of her belongings that way; it would take too long. As they boarded the steamboat, Molly grinned. 'Ain't this grand?' she cried. 'I seen these steamers docked in Sacramento and always dreamed one day I'd take one. Now that day's come!'

He left her on deck by the large paddle and went with the gray to his temporary stall. This time Robert could not stay with his horse for long – he had others to look after. He stood for a moment with his arm around the gray's neck, feeling the rocking movement of the boat under his feet that he knew the horse hated. 'Sorry about this,' he whispered. As he left, the gray turned to look at him, then pissed a long, hot stream all over the deck.

Molly was at the stern, feeding Jimmy and watching the buildings of Stockton pass by. When she waved at people on the bank they always waved back. Robert was amazed that she was able to nurse the baby while standing. 'This is the way to travel,' she said, still grinning. 'I could glide along all week like this.'

'Molly, I'm gonna need to collect some redwoods,' Robert said, thinking ahead to what he would need to do to fulfill William Lobb's letter. 'When we get to San Francisco I'll have to take off again once you're settled.'

Molly's smile faded, her expression becoming one part annoyance, one part pity. 'Can't you jest enjoy this? How long have we got on board?'

'About ten hours to San Francisco.'

'Tell you what: for ten hours, let's not think about trees. Here, you take Jimmy.' Molly detached the drowsing baby from her nipple and handed him over. 'I'm gonna go and have some fun!'

Something was shifting between them: Molly had lost her desperation and was becoming impatient. Though she had been forced to leave Murphys because of Robert, somehow it no longer felt like she was chasing after him; instead she was sweeping ahead and making him decide if he would follow.

Robert sat down on a bench in the sun with Jimmy in his lap and let the scenery pass before him much as it had when he'd made the first trip with William Lobb. There were Indians strung along the bank on their horses, and even the same boys – or their younger brothers now – racing the steamboat. After these past weeks of rapid change, the familiarity of the trip was a comfort, as was the baby's solid weight. He felt he should be thinking about something, worrying at a problem and finding a solution, but it was so peaceful sitting there in the sun that after a while he closed his eyes and, as Molly had suggested, allowed himself simply to be. Soon he was sleeping as soundly as his nephew.

★   ★   ★

It seemed Mrs Bienenstock had seen everything before, for she showed no surprise when Robert arrived with a pregnant woman and baby just weeks after a different pregnant woman had come looking for him. California was like that. People had gone west leaving behind all sorts of trouble; what they found in California was the space and freedom to create new trouble. Though Mrs B. had never had women or children board with her, she stood aside and let Molly and Jimmy cross her doorway without comment, except to say, 'Soak the diapers out back – they can add to the smells out there rather than inside.'

Robert began to say something, to explain, but she cut him off. 'You'll need a bigger room. Take the one on the second floor at the back: two dollars a week more. You go on up,' she said to Molly. 'I'll bring up bedding – or you got your own you prefer?'

'We're fine, thanks.' Molly and Mrs Bienenstock eyed each other, then nodded at the same time, coming to a wordless understanding that left Robert to one side.

He watched Molly climb the stairs, then turned back to his landlady. 'Is Mr Lobb around?'

Mrs B. frowned. 'He's down at the docks when he should be in bed. Couldn't even walk down there – had to get a wagon to take him 'cause his legs are so bad. He's been fretting about you, wondering when you'd be bringing back the redwoods. Fifty, is it? Where are they?' She glanced at the wagon loaded with all they'd brought from Murphys, Jimmy's cradle turned upside down and anchoring the mountain of pillows and sheets and blankets and mattress that Molly always carted around with her. Sandwiched in somewhere with the others was the nine-patch Goodenough quilt.

'I haven't collected them yet – I've been busy with – other things.'

'So you have.' Mrs Bienenstock seemed amused.

William Lobb appeared an hour later, after Robert had unloaded their possessions and was in the yard, spreading out cones to dry. 'Goodenough!' he cried, hobbling out. 'Where are those damned redwoods I asked you for? I've just seen Beardsley nosing around down at the docks. He's bound to be sending redwoods to Wales too. We have to get a move on!'

Before Robert could answer, Molly popped her head out of the window to their room. 'Honey, bring up some towels if Mrs B.'s got any to spare? Well, halloo there!' she called to William Lobb. 'You must be the famous William Lobb. You ain't gonna work Robert to death, are you? He's got others need him now.'

Lobb stared up at her, with her curly black hair sticking out and the shelf of her breasts resting on the windowsill. Then Jimmy began to cry. 'Ah, there he goes. Don't forget the towels!' Molly pulled her head back inside.

William Lobb turned back to Robert. Unlike Mrs Bienenstock, he did not keep quiet. 'Who the hell is that? That's not your sister. I met her. Quiet little thing, light hair. Didn't have much—' Lobb gestured at his chest. 'Where is she?'

The stark stillness on Robert's face made Lobb stop. 'Oh, lad, I am sorry.'

Robert reached for a sequoia cone that had been partially chewed by a chickaree and tossed it aside.

'Who is that?' Lobb nodded at the upstairs window. This time he asked more gently.

Robert continued to paw through the sack of cones so that he would not have to look up. 'Molly. I knew her back in Texas. She's been up at French Creek a few years. I may have mentioned her before.'

'And the baby?'

'My nephew.'

William Lobb nodded. They were silent for a few minutes, Robert with his cones, Lobb inspecting the sequoia seedlings. Their needles were yellowing and they were inferior to what Robert normally brought back, but the Englishman did not comment. When he judged enough time had passed, he said, 'There's a ship leaves for Panama in three days. If you can collect fifty redwoods and bring them back by then, we can get them off to Wales quickly. No time to dry those cones.' He nodded at the cones spread at Robert's feet. 'We'll just have to pack them green.'

'Why are you in such a hurry?'

'The gentleman's not hired any collector in particular, just said the first to get a grove worth

319

of seedlings to him gets the commission. Of course Beardsley will be looking to get it. Maybe Bridges, and it wouldn't surprise me if the Murray brothers tried their hand too. The man's planning a pinetum as well, so there'll be plenty more work if he's happy. He'll want every kind of conifer we can send him – probably as seedlings or saplings. So we need those redwoods now to demonstrate our collecting ability. I thought you'd have brought them back with you rather than a woman and baby.'

'What does Veitch say?'

'This isn't a commission through Veitch. It's separate. We'll get the whole payment.'

'Aren't you collecting for Veitch anymore?'

Lobb frowned. 'I've had enough of Veitch. I'm ill, and I'm tired. I'm done with him. This will be my way of thumbing my nose at him, and still get paid better.'

'What about me?'

'You?' William Lobb shrugged. 'You, lad, can do what you like. The British will still want Californian trees. You can collect for Veitch if you want. I won't stand in your way. It looks like you've got people depending on you.' He raised his eyebrows towards the window where Molly had appeared.

'But . . .' Robert couldn't tell if he was being cut loose by his employer.

'You've got enough knowledge. Use it now: where are we going to find fifty redwood seedlings fast?'

At least Lobb had used 'we.' That was something. Robert thought for a moment. 'It has to be close by.'

'Yes. And?'

'There need to be a lot of seedlings germinating.'

'And where do you get that?'

'Someplace where there was a fire a year ago.' Rather than destroying the redwoods, fire cleared the forest floor of the thick duff around them and provided seeds with a new bed full of minerals. Robert had seen many more redwood seedlings in scorched earth than in a ground full of old needles.

'Yes. Fire. There was a fire above the Oakland hills a year ago. Good redwoods up there and it's just across the bay. Oakland will do. You can take the ferry across.'

'But I need your help.'

Lobb winced. 'Listen, lad, I can't do a thing. There are shooting pains in my legs and I've no energy. All my years of travel have caught up with me.' He paused. 'Don't let that happen to you. Mind you, looks like you're heading in the right direction.' He nodded again at Molly's window.

'You can show me where the redwoods are, organize the wagon. You won't have to do the digging. Just come with me. Please.' Robert didn't know why he was so insistent that Lobb accompany him. Nonetheless, he stared at his employer intently until Lobb relented.

'Damn your brown eyes, Goodenough! All right. Never mind the ferry: run down to the docks and

321

hire us a boat and a man willing to take us first thing tomorrow – as early as possible so we've got a full day. Now, wagons: I think we can manage with just one if we stack the pails right. And pails – we've got to get more. A whole lot more.' As he and Robert began discussing the logistics of collecting so many trees in one go, William Lobb seemed to brighten and regain his energy, pacing Mrs Bienenstock's yard without the stiff gait he had adopted over the past year.

Molly did not seem to mind Robert going off almost immediately after they had arrived in San Francisco. Like him, she was used to doing things herself without expecting much from others. When he went to tell her, she was busy in the bedroom, settling in with her blankets on the bed, dresses on pegs, bottles on the chest of drawers, and Jimmy popped into the cradle, with the Goodenough quilt as his bedding. Again she seemed to be able to quickly make a home out of a space, pressing down a tangible mark where Robert would have left no footprint.

He was relieved that she was cheerful and amenable. She was only disappointed not to see the ocean right away. 'You could get Mrs B. to take you out to Black Point,' Robert suggested. 'Or out by Seal Rocks where they're building a fort. You get a good view of it there.'

'Naw, I want to see it with *you*,' Molly insisted. 'Anyway, there's plenty for me to see around here.

All those houses we saw on the way! And the saloons! And the ships! I'm gonna have me a little holiday.'

Going to Oakland felt like a little holiday to Robert. There were no women or babies to consider, and only a few drunk miners around. He did not have to be careful about tracking mud into Mrs B.'s, or lie in bed at night with Molly too warm beside him, feeling the four walls closing him in. After crossing the bay in a boat large enough to hold fifty pails, two men, the boat's owner and Robert's horse, he saddled the gray so he could ride into the hills, while William Lobb stayed behind in the small town to hire a wagon he would bring up after Robert. It had been almost a year since the men had gone out collecting together. Lobb also seemed happy to be out and away from the responsibilities and debilitations of the city. He walked almost normally and his brow was clear of its usual furrows.

'Up there.' He pointed at a ridge above Oakland. 'Take the Indian trail up, and go right at the fork. About a mile up you'll find a beauty of a grove. I've been saving it. You should be able to find enough seedlings there. Take some pails to get started on – we'll bring along the rest.'

He was right about the redwood grove. It was full of tall trees with their distinctive auburn bark and needled branches getting bigger the higher up they grew. Robert knew he didn't have much time to collect fifty seedlings, yet when he had walked a little way into the grove he took a few minutes to sit on a log and look around him. Last year's fire had charred parts of many of the trunks, but redwood bark was thick and full of tannin that protected it from burning, and redwood branches grew starting halfway up the trunk, which meant that flames couldn't use them as a ladder to reach the top of the tree. The forest floor had been cleaned by the fire, and now tiny seedlings were sprouting everywhere, amid a carpet of emerald-green redwood sorrel.

Though not so big as the Calaveras sequoias he had been among weeks before, the redwoods gave him the familiar soothing sense of being insignificant. If only I could keep this feeling with me everywhere I am, Robert thought. Maybe then it wouldn't be so hard to adjust to all the things that have happened to me.

He spent a happy few hours finding seedlings and digging them up. As he worked, he wondered which trees would not survive the long journey across the ocean, and what the rest would look like planted in foreign soil. It was a relief to think only of the trees and of what he needed rather than of what others needed from him. Though it was not easy finding so many seedlings at one time, Robert did not hurry or worry, but worked steadily, ferrying what he had on the gray down to the larger road where William Lobb waited with the wagon. The gray was not happy about being hung again with pails, but Robert had brought along a supply of sugar lumps and early Gravenstein apples to keep him reasonably quiet.

By sunset he had dug up the fiftieth tree and tipped it into a pail. When he brought the last seedlings down to the wagon, William Lobb nodded, satisfied. 'They'll do, lad. Good work.'

Back in Oakland, the owner of the boat was missing, and Robert went to search for him among the saloons strung along the main street. He was passed out in one of them, and Robert couldn't bring him to. 'He's too drunk to sail,' he said to William Lobb back at the wagon, worried about his employer's response.

But Lobb was sanguine. 'We'll rouse him first thing tomorrow,' he said. 'There's no steamers leaving tomorrow, so Beardsley can't take off before us. *Star of the West* leaves the day after tomorrow. We've got time.'

Lobb was too stiff to sleep outside, and took a room at one of the basic hotels, but Robert stabled the gray, borrowed a blanket and walked a ways out of town to light a fire, wrap himself up and sleep under the stars. He hadn't slept outside since Molly's arrival. As he lay by the fire, he marveled at how quiet it was without Molly and Jimmy with him, and how much easier it was to live this kind of traveling life. The next minute, though, he was feeling guilty about being apart from them. He would not describe it as missing them, exactly, but he was very aware that he was alone. He was not sure what a family was meant to be like. Not James and Sadie Goodenough, that was clear. But what else was there? It felt like fumbling around in the dark, trying to light a candle, losing track of where he was, touching things he didn't mean to touch.

Despite these thoughts, Robert slept well. He woke at dawn feeling more like himself than he had in weeks.

Mrs Bienenstock was standing in the doorway of her house, smoking a cigar. She stubbed it out when the wagon pulled up. 'Jesus H. Christ,' she muttered. 'Jesus H. Christ.'

Robert assumed she was reacting to the army of pails double-stacked on the wagon bed. The boat full of seedlings had attracted much attention at the docks when they landed from Oakland, and William Lobb had not been willing to leave them there, even for a night, for fear they would be damaged or stolen – or worse, other tree agents would see them and know they were collecting redwoods for the Welsh estate. So they'd brought them back to the boardinghouse till they could take them onto the *Star of the West* the next morning.

But Mrs B. didn't even glance at the seedlings. 'I told you I don't like mess in my house. I told you that the first time I saw you, Robert Goodenough.'

'Sorry, ma'am, but we'll be careful putting these

in the back,' Robert reassured her. 'If we track in any dirt, I'll sweep it up afterwards, and mop too.'

She didn't seem to hear him. 'You know how hard it is to get blood out of a mattress?'

Robert stared at her. Then he pushed past Mrs Bienenstock, took the stairs three at a time and ran down the hall.

Molly was propped up in bed, her back against the headboard. On either side of her were a few pillows stacked up, and a baby on top of each, her arms around them. Both sucked at the nearest nipple. There was no blood in sight.

Molly gave him an exhausted smile. 'Hello, honey. Surprise!'

Robert was so stunned he remained in the doorway, looking from one baby to the other. Here was Jimmy. And here was – his son or daughter, it was impossible to say which. He had left for one day and come back a father.

'How?' he said.

Molly snorted. 'The usual way: a whole lotta pain and yellin' and pushin'. Actually, it wasn't so bad – happened so fast I'd hardly time to feel it. Thank God for Dody. If she hadn't been here to help, I'd have had it alone on the kitchen floor!'

'Dody?'

'Mrs Bienenstock. Your landlady. Don't you even know her Christian name?'

Mrs B. had come up the stairs behind Robert and was leaning against the wall in the hall. Now she grunted. 'I don't give out my first name to most. Keep it formal, I say. Course Molly here asked it straightaway, so she could yell it all the while she was giving birth. Whole damned street knows it now.'

'Dody, I owe you one big batch of biscuits to thank you – when these two let me up!' Molly cupped the babies' heads with her hands. 'Now, you think you could get me a cup of coffee?'

'This one – nothing but trouble.' Mrs B. chuckled. It seemed she liked a bit of trouble.

When she had gone, Robert perched on the side of the bed. He gestured at the new baby. 'Boy or a girl?'

'Girl. What are we gonna call her?'

Robert shook his head. 'You choose.'

'No. You name her. It's time you started naming things. Your poor horse still don't have a name. Least you can do is give one to your daughter.'

Robert stared at the whorl of dark hair on the baby's head, which was all he could see of her with her face buried in her mother's breast. 'I don't know what to name her.'

'Well, you called Jimmy after your Pa. Why not name her after your Ma?'

Robert shuddered. 'I can't do that.'

'Robert, your mother's still your mother, whatever she done. What was her name?'

'Sadie.' Even saying it filled Robert's mouth with a bitter taste, and he thought for a moment that, whatever Mrs Bienenstock's restrictions about her house, he might just be sick in it.

'Sadie's a nickname for Sarah, ain't it?' Molly persisted. 'Sarah's nice. Quieter. Less sassy than Sadie. More like you.'

'Sarah Goodenough.' When Robert said the name aloud, it did not sting, but felt like a balm.

'Goodenough! You gonna help me with these trees or not?' William Lobb was shouting up at their window.

Molly shook her head and laughed. 'That man. If I worked for him I'd have run off by now.'

'I'll give him a hand with the trees, then I'll come back.'

Molly waved him away. 'We're jest gonna sleep anyway. Look.' Both babies were lolling away from her breasts, sated. 'Put 'em in the cradle before you go, will you, honey? One at each end.'

Robert picked up his daughter carefully so that she would not wake. It felt no different holding her from holding Jimmy. He laid her carefully on the Goodenough quilt, her head next to the green silk square, and smiled.

The next morning he and William Lobb took the redwoods back down to the docks. The seedlings were still in pails, for they didn't have the materials or the time to build the eight Ward's cases they would have needed to ship the seedlings in. Nor had they had time to pack and seal more than four tin cases of sequoia cones. 'We'll send these to Veitch – keep him sweet for a bit,' Lobb said. 'Soon enough he'll hear about the redwoods and there'll be hell to pay.' He chuckled, anticipating the hell.

Molly was up now, sitting in the kitchen nursing the babies and instructing Mrs Bienenstock on how to make biscuits. 'Don't pound the dough, Dody!' Molly was crying with laughter. 'You want to end up crackin' your teeth on 'em? Pat it gentle like it's a baby. That's better.'

Robert had only ever seen his landlady make coffee and eggs, and he did not think she would take kindly to being taught. But Mrs B. seemed willing; she was smoothing out the biscuit dough into a round on the table. Neither woman even glanced over at him as he moved between the yard and the wagon with the pails.

'Now, take this cup,' Molly ordered, 'and cut out some circles. Don't twist it! Twistin' seals the dough and it don't rise so well. Jest press and bring the cup back out. There now, put that on your sheet for bakin'.'

'We're taking the trees down to the ship now,' Robert announced.

'Course you are, honey. We jest saw you traipsin' back and forth with 'em. All right – twelve minutes, Dody! Just enough time for a cup of coffee.'

'See you later, then.' Robert went out to the wagon where William Lobb was waiting, seated next to the driver. He was about to climb up to join him when Mrs Bienenstock appeared at his elbow, her hands covered in flour and a white smear on her forehead. 'You bring him back,' she spoke up to William Lobb. 'You leave him on that ship and I'll make a pile of your possessions and burn 'em – notebooks and maps and all – right here in the street. You won't be welcome back in this house. I can guarantee that.'

Robert had no idea what she was talking about, but William Lobb flinched. 'It's all right, Mrs B.,' Robert reassured her. 'I'll be back in a little while.'

His words seemed to make no impression on Mrs Bienenstock, who was glaring at William Lobb as he kept his eyes fixed on a point in the middle distance.

Normally when they shipped specimens to England they paid one or two of the sailors to look after them: make sure the tin cases of cones did not break open or get wet, take the Ward's cases outside into the sun. Over the years William Lobb had gotten to know many sailors whom he felt he could trust.

This time, however, they were in such a hurry to send the trees that they were using a ship they had never tried before, and they did not know any of the crew. William Lobb had spoken to the captain of the *Star of the West*, who swore he'd looked after plants on other ships, including those of Lobb's brother Thomas, collecting for Veitch in the Far East. The captain had introduced him briefly to a sailor he would entrust the trees to. Now, however, when they found the sailor hauling sacks of mail on board, he didn't seem to recognize Lobb. His eyes were bloodshot, he stank of whiskey, and his walk was unsteady; he would have been sampling San Francisco's saloons before the voyage. Looking over the trees crammed in their pails, he swore. It seemed that fragile, awkward freight bothered him more than the heavy trunks and boxes that would make anyone stagger under their weight.

'I did tell you there would be fifty trees – well, fifty plus three extra.' William Lobb was including in the shipment the three giant sequoia seedlings Robert had brought back from Calaveras Grove, as a sweetener to the owner of the Welsh estate. 'If he wants a redwood grove, he's bound to want sequoias as well,' Lobb had explained. 'I'm just thinking ahead for him.'

Now the sailor grabbed four pails in each hand by their handles and headed up the gangplank, bumping them against the side of the ship as he went aboard.

'Careful, man!' William Lobb shouted, but his words were lost in the hubbub of porters around him yelling and grunting as they carried cargo on board: more sacks of mail, barrels of Gravenstein apples, redwood planks, boxes of gold accompanied by agents and guards. Horses were led up the gangplank, and two cows, and crates of chickens.

Robert and Lobb picked up pails and followed the sailor aboard and then down into the hold. There he dumped his load in a corner; one of the pails tipped over and spilled some dirt. Until then Robert had not really understood how vulnerable the redwoods would be to the conditions on board. Always before, he and Lobb had sent smaller quantities, in Ward's cases where they were protected. Without someone carefully tending them, these were bound to perish. No wonder William Lobb had insisted they collect so many.

Robert reached over and righted the toppled seedling, scooping the dirt back into the pail. Then he hurried after Lobb and the sailor, who had headed back to the wagon. It took them several more trips to get them all into their dark corner.

Lobb made only one trip back to the wagon before he had to sit down from the pain in his legs. 'Hang on a minute, now,' he called to the sailor, who had dropped the last of the pails and was running off. 'I won't pay you a penny till you stand still and listen to me!'

The sailor stopped and swore as he turned to face Lobb.

'Let me explain about caring for the trees,' William Lobb began. He pulled a piece of paper from his pocket. 'I've written it down as well.'

The sailor snorted. 'Can't read. What care do they need, anyway? Trees look after themselves.'

'Not on a ship, they don't. They need fresh water, for one thing.'

'What's wrong with seawater?'

'Don't be an idiot, man. Salt water would kill them and you know it. So you must water them every other day, and when it's fair bring them up on deck, for the sun.'

'I'm not doin' that!'

'Your captain said he'd tell you what was expected.'

'He didn't say nothin' about movin' trees in and out. I got other things to do than hump pails.' Clearly the sailor was put out by the fiddly, sensitive nature of the work.

'Then I'll find someone else,' William Lobb declared. 'I'm sure there are plenty other sailors who would rather have the ten dollars.'

The sailor narrowed his eyes. 'Give me the money now.'

'No. I'll give it to the captain to give you when they've got safely to Panama City and you've secured them across the Isthmus to Aspinwall. He'll subtract fifty cents for each one that dies. More than twenty die and *you'll* start paying *me*.'

The sailor spat and swore again, then stomped off. William Lobb swore as well. 'Untrustworthy. The man has no love of trees. And he can't read.' He glanced down at the instructions he had written out. 'Even if the captain keeps after him – and there's no guarantee he will, no matter how much I offer to pay – he doesn't care about keeping them alive. We'll be lucky if any survive. Got to try, though. We've no choice if we want to get redwoods to Wales before Beardsley or Bridges do.'

Robert looked out over the instant miniature forest of trees that had sprung up in the hold. Grown redwoods and sequoias were the most solid-looking of trees: they belonged to the land they were rooted in. It was hard to bring them down; even fire only made them stronger, and shoots sprang up from dead trunks. But these seedlings in their pails looked so fragile and out of place; already they seemed to have wilted. They would be neglected, left in the dark, blown around in the salt spray and heavy winds, or kicked over by indifferent sailors. They made Robert think of John Chapman's seedlings carefully placed in their own canoe in Ohio so long ago, and the way his father looked after his trees as if they were his children.

'Can't you go with the trees?' he asked, already knowing the answer, and indeed, the question and answer beyond that. Mrs Bienenstock was smarter than any of them.

'My legs hurt too much,' Lobb said. 'I can hardly walk as it is, and wouldn't be able to take them above and below deck. Crossing Panama would be hell. It was bad enough riding in the wagon around Oakland. No, I'm stuck here.' William Lobb held Robert's gaze. Then he looked out over the bay, his eyes latching on to a ferry heading across it.

'You want me to go with them.' Robert kept his voice neutral.

'I can't ask you that, lad. You've got a family.' But he *was* asking it, even if his words didn't.

Until recently, Robert's life had been clean and empty. Now so many conflicting forces pulled at him that he could hardly think straight. Instead his mind was filled with a jumble of images and sensations: John Appleseed gliding down the river in his double canoe, the blasted top of the Old Bachelor sequoia, Billie Lapham's battered top hat, Jimmy's fingers making a star on Molly's breast as he sucked, Martha sitting so tiny under the giant sequoias. Nancy Lapham's cough. His mother's raucous laugh. The pineapple finish of a Pitmaston Pineapple. His father saying, 'One in ten trees comes up sweet.' Finally his thoughts settled on the handkerchief full of Golden Pippin seeds Martha had given him that lay in a drawer in the bureau in his and Molly's room. Where would he plant them now?

'I'd better go back to Mrs Bienenstock's,' he said at last, 'and get my things.'

Mrs Bienenstock was waiting for him on the doorstep – unusually for her, doing nothing, not even smoking a cigar. Waiting seemed to be her chosen task for that moment.

'Don't be stupid, Robert Goodenough,' she said, folding her arms and leaning against the doorway so that she blocked the entrance. 'I am real tired of men doin' stupid things in this town.'

'How did you know?'

Mrs Bienenstock grunted. 'Men are too easy to figure out. I need more of a challenge.'

Robert cleared his throat. 'I would be obliged if you could sell my horse and give the money to Molly.'

'Sell the gray? See, that is stupidity right there. Nobody will want that fickle flea-biter.'

Robert frowned. 'Never mind, I'll ask Mr Lobb to do it.'

'William Lobb knows an ass' ass about selling horses. He sells trees, not animals.'

'Well, if you won't do it, I don't have much choice.'

'I'm not gonna do anything that will make this easier for you.'

'Where's Molly?'

Mrs B. jerked her head. 'Kitchen.'

Robert stepped up to the door, close to his landlady, and waited. Mrs Bienenstock stared at him, their eyes level. She had brown eyes like his, he noticed for the first time, though hers had dark specks floating in them. At last she stepped aside, and spat into the street as he passed.

Molly was sitting at the table with a plate of Mrs B.'s biscuits. They looked nothing like the fluffy ones she normally made: these were rock-solid and functional. Molly had spread hers with honey and was biting into it. The two babies were asleep in the corner in a basket that Mrs B. usually used for hauling wood. Already they were taking over. Robert wondered how long his landlady would put up with it.

'I'd forgotten how good it is to sit and eat without someone hanging off me,' she commented with her mouth full. 'I might jest eat this whole plate of biscuits. You want one?' She held out the plate to him.

'Molly.'

'They ain't like mine, I'll admit that. Dody don't exactly have a light touch in most things, much less biscuit dough. But I don't mind. Things always taste better when someone else has made 'em for you, don't they? I always liked the coffee you made for me up at French Creek – even though it was miners' coffee.' She was running on the way she did when her desperation became more marked, except that she didn't seem desperate now, but calm, even a little indifferent. Of course she must have heard him talking to Mrs Bienenstock outside.

'Molly.'

'What is it this time, honey.' Molly said it as a statement rather than a question. She took another bite of the tough biscuit and left a smear of honey on her chin.

'William Lobb wants me to go with the trees to Wales, to make sure they survive.'

'Course he does.' Molly wiped her chin. 'The question is, do *you* want to go?'

'I don't know. I guess so.'

Molly breathed out hard through her nose. 'That's the problem with you, Robert Goodenough. You've been bouncin' all over this country for years – since you was a boy. But you don't *choose* to go somewhere, you jest end up there because others are goin' and you're expected to, rather than because you think, "Right, *this* is what I want to do."'

'I *did* know what I wanted.'

'Which was?'

'To go west.'

'To get away from your family.'

'Well. Yes.' Robert chewed on his lip. Time was passing and the ship would be leaving soon – if it hadn't already.

Molly picked up a biscuit and began to crumble it between her fingers. 'So you kept goin' west. And then what happened?'

'I reached the Pacific.' Robert pictured the whale's tail, flipping up in the ocean. 'I saw it, and I couldn't go any further, so I had to turn back.'

'Why?'

'What do you mean, why?'

'Why stop? Why not keep goin'?'

'Because – because I can't swim.' It was a foolish answer to what felt like a foolish question.

But Molly was not foolish. 'You can get on a ship. Get on a ship,' she repeated, and it became a command.

'You want me to go?'

'Who said anything about "me"? You know, I've done a lot of thinkin' these past weeks, even with one baby or another grabbin' at me. How long did you mine for gold?'

Robert frowned. 'A year or so. Why?'

'I been around a lot of miners. I've seen how they are. You ain't like them. You don't gamble, you don't drink, you don't spend your money on women – well, you don't on me, that's all I know. Same hat, same boots, same saddle, same rundown horse. No flashy watch on a chain. You don't own

339

land or a house or even a bed, far as I know. But I bet you were a good miner. You kept at it, didn't chase down rumors like the others. So I thought about all this, and finally I realized somethin', and it made me laugh out loud. You want to know what it was I realized?'

Robert nodded, though he was painfully aware that an entire ship was waiting for him.

'It's *you*, Robert Goodenough. *You're* the miner I've been lookin' for – the one who's saved his gold money, who I can put my feet up with. You got some money from all that mining?'

'A little. It cost a lot to *be* a miner, but I saved a little.'

'Good. You got enough to pay for a woman and two babies to go to England?'

Robert stared at the babies in their basket. 'Can they go on a ship?'

Molly laughed. 'Honey, babies are made and born and live on ships.'

'But – don't you want to stay here?'

'Here?' Molly looked around the kitchen. 'I could. Mrs B.'s the only woman I've met in California I like. But I was three years in French Creek. I wouldn't mind movin' around some, babies or not.' As if that were her cue, Sarah began to whimper in preparation for full-blown crying. 'The question ain't about me, though, it's about whether you want to be alone or with us. Now, we don't have to come with you. I got offers of work at Murphys and up at Cally Grove, or I could stay in San Francisco and work, find a gal to look after the babies. I could make a life in California, and have fun without even havin' a miner to look after me. So don't you say you want me to come because you feel you have to. You got to want to.'

'Molly, I'm not good at family.'

'You're doin' all right with Jimmy and Sarah.'

When he didn't speak, she added, 'You ain't like your parents, you know. If that's what you're worried about. You ain't violent. I don't have any worries on that front. Besides, the way you described it back in Cally Grove, it sounds like your parents didn't mean to kill each other. It was an accident – a double accident. You said your Ma was goin' to chop down the apple tree?'

'Yes.'

'That's real different from goin' out with an axe intendin' to kill someone. She was aimin' for the tree, not your Pa. And she fell into the stakes, you said, 'cause he pushed her. Well, that's jest pushin' away, it don't mean he meant to kill her.'

Robert was silent, playing through the scene in his head. 'Maybe you're right,' he said at last. 'Actually, I am like my father, a little.' If he *was* my father, he said to himself, then understood that he could choose to make him so, as there was no one to tell him otherwise. 'He was a tree man,' he added, because he could.

'Then your father must have been a good man

– 'cause you're a good man, Robert Goodenough. *Better* than your name. Don't you forget that. You can choose to be different from your past. You *have* chosen, haven't you?'

'I guess so.'

'Now you got another choice: do you want the babies and me to come with you or not?'

She waited for him to answer and he knew the pause was too long, even though at the end of it was a 'Yes,' and even though he meant it.

'All right, then. When does the ship sail?' If Molly was disappointed by his hesitation, she didn't show it. It was a moment, however, that he knew would always remain between them.

Robert cleared his throat. 'Now. We have to go right now.'

'Dody! We got some packin' to do!'

The next half hour was a blur of panic, of throwing things into trunks and running up and down the stairs to load a wagon commandeered by Mrs Bienenstock. Robert stopped thinking and simply did whatever Molly and Mrs B. ordered. Jimmy and Sarah cried all the way through the commotion, and Robert marveled at how easily Molly ignored them when she had to.

Robert himself had little to pack. He took a few clothes, the Goodenough quilt, notebooks full of tree notes, and the handkerchief of Golden Pippin seeds, selling Mrs B. his shotgun, saddle, and a few cook pans. She also bought the gray, very cheaply. Robert was surprised to find he regretted selling his horse, but he didn't know when he'd be back. He had no idea what was going to happen to him. To them. He would have to get better at thinking in the plural.

Though there was no time, Molly insisted he go to the stables where he kept the gray and say goodbye. When Robert protested, she just looked at him. 'It's your *horse*.' And so he went and stood with the gray for a few minutes while it chewed on oats and ignored him. When he moved to go, though, the gray stretched out and nipped Robert on the arm. 'Fair enough,' he said. 'Guess I deserved that.'

Back at the boardinghouse he told his landlady the gray's name was Pippin. 'No, it's not,' Mrs B. replied as she wrestled a trunk down the stairs. 'He's mine now, till I sell him on, so I get to name him. His name's West.'

As they pulled up to Pacific Wharf, the *Star of the West* was already under steam, and the deck lined with passengers taking their last look at San Francisco and the people they were leaving behind. William Lobb was among them, leaning on the rail and arguing with the captain. 'There he is!' he shouted when he spotted the wagon with its mountain of possessions. 'Goodenough, where the hell have you been? They're threatening to fine us for holding up the ship!' He hobbled down the gangplank to them. Only when Molly descended from the wagon with the basket full of crying babies did he seem to notice Robert was not alone.

'You there!' Mrs Bienenstock shouted up at the captain. 'If you're so goddamned worried about getting away, tell your men to bring this stuff on board. Standing there like a jackass won't help. Jesus H. Christ, do I have to do everything myself?' She continued to swear joyfully as she shepherded Molly on board.

William Lobb stared after them. 'Are you mad, Goodenough? Fifty-three trees, two babies and a woman to look after for three months on board a ship?'

'Maybe so. Anyway, I'll get those trees to Wales, and plant 'em for the gentleman. I'll let you know how it goes.'

William Lobb nodded. 'You do that, lad.' Then he smiled, his teeth bright against his dark beard. It was a sight so unusual, especially since Lobb's illness, that it made Robert smile too. They shook hands. 'Have yourself a Pitmaston Pineapple or two while you're there,' he added. 'You know Pitmaston is only sixty miles from where the redwood grove will be.'

'Really?'

'The world is not so big after all. Now, don't forget to set aside water for the trees, make sure there's enough for the whole voyage. Don't let the captain fob you off with rainwater they've captured – there's too much sea spray in it, it'll kill the trees.'

Even as Robert was hauling the rest of their

things onto the *Star of the West*, Lobb was shouting instructions after him: 'Don't take the seedlings all out on deck at the same time: split 'em into two groups and take 'em up on alternate days. When you cross Panama, make sure the trees get their own wagon – don't let them tuck the pails in with other goods, I've seen that before and the boxes shift and crush the seedlings. If that happens, though, don't throw away the tree – there's still a chance it can recover at the other end. And when you reach Cardiff, send a message ahead so the gentleman knows you're coming with the redwoods. Look after those trees,' he finished, as Robert paused and looked down at his employer. 'They deserve better than to perish at sea. Site them well, plant them carefully. Make them stars in their new land.'

Mrs Bienenstock had gotten Molly and the babies settled into a cabin, and gave Robert a brusque clap on the shoulder before she left. 'God help you all,' she muttered. 'What a lot of trouble!' But she was whistling as she strode down the gangplank, and she waited with William Lobb to wave to them as the ship steamed away from the quay.

'Goodbye, goodbye!' Molly cried, though she couldn't wave back with her arms full of babies. 'Think of us on the other side of the world!'

Molly finally got to see the ocean. It did not take long for the *Star of the West* to clear Seal Rocks and head out into the Pacific. As they stood on deck watching the waves churn beneath them, Molly thrust both babies into Robert's arms, held her own out wide and whooped, making the passengers near them smile. 'All this water!' she cried, laughing. 'You never told me it was this big! How long do we get to be on it?'

'Two to three months, with a week on land crossing Panama. From there we head up to New York, then change ships for Cardiff. Mr Lobb said we'll get tired of it.'

'Bah, I don't listen to that Englishman. I hope the whole country ain't like him.' Molly leaned against the railing and gazed out over the water unfurling before them.

The ship began its long turn from the afternoon sun towards the south so that eventually they would be following the California coast. Robert felt himself lurch inside, as if he was breaking off and taking a path where a compass would be no help.

He could not linger on this feeling, though, for Sarah was squirming and nuzzling at his arm, trying to find something to suck. He had never known a man or a woman or a horse as demanding as these babies were. 'Can you feed Sarah?' he asked, glad to have someone with him to ask.

Molly took their daughter and got her latched on to a breast while keeping her eyes on the ocean. 'Look!' she cried. A mile or so west of them a plume of water was sprayed high into the air, followed a moment later by the dark back of a whale arcing through the water. It was impossible not to be infected by her enthusiasm. Robert found his eyes glued to the ocean, watching for signs of the whale's progress – the plumes of water, the humping back and the curved tail flashing and then sliding back down into the water. He shouted when he saw the tail, which made Molly laugh and grab him in a kiss, the babies sandwiched in between.

Later when Jimmy and Sarah were asleep in their cradle and Robert had checked on the trees, he and Molly leaned against the railing and watched the sun set. There were no clouds and little haze to soften it as it dropped down its burning path. It at least was certain of where it was going.

'What are you worryin' about now, Robert Goodenough?' Molly was studying his profile as he looked out at the fiery water.

Robert shrugged. 'I haven't gone east ever in my life. I don't know what I'm going to do back there.'

Molly's skin was orange in the evening light. 'I'll tell you what you're gonna do. You're gonna plant fifty trees—'

'Fifty-three,' Robert corrected. 'There are fifty redwoods, three sequoias.'

'You're gonna plant fifty-three trees in England—'

'Wales.'

'—Wales, and make sure they grow so there's a redwood grove as good as any you got here. Then you're gonna take me to London and see the sights.

347

Then you're gonna find me one of them Golden Pippins you've talked about so much—'

'Pitmaston Pineapple.'

'—A Pitmaston Pineapple, and I'm gonna taste it for myself.'

Robert was beginning to warm to Molly's list. He felt in his pocket for the Golden Pippin seeds Martha had brought him. They were still there. Seeds could keep for a long time. All they needed was the right place to take root. He would know it when he saw it.

AUTHOR'S NOTE

Inspiration

Sometimes ideas for novels come to me in a flash. One second I'm thinking of what to cook for supper; the next, I see a painting or a cemetery or a museum display and think: That. Other times a novel slowly forms from disparate ideas that fit together like pieces of a puzzle. *At the Edge of the Orchard* took the slower route.

The first piece of the *Orchard* puzzle is my interest in trees. I have always loved trees. Who doesn't? It would be like not loving chocolate or bread or sunlight. Impossible. Several years ago I edited a collection of stories called *Why Willows Weep* for the Woodland Trust, a charity working to plant more trees in the UK. The book was a collection of fables written by contemporary authors who each chose a native British tree to write about. My story was 'Why Birches Have Silver Bark', and I enjoyed writing it a lot. It planted the seed, so to speak, and I began to contemplate how I might write more about trees.

The second piece of the puzzle came from

someone else's work. When I was researching my previous novel, *The Last Runaway*, I read *The Botany of Desire* by Michael Pollan. It's about our relationship with certain plants, and is divided into four sections: Apples, Potatoes, Tulips and Marijuana. I focussed on the Apples section, which was mostly exploring nineteenth-century Ohio, where *The Last Runaway* is set. What I learned about apples in Ohio made me picture in my head a scene: a husband and wife are locked in a battle over apple trees. He wants to grow sweet apples for eating; she, sour apples for making liquor. How would this battle affect the children of the family, and how would that be reflected in their relationship to the trees around them? I couldn't use this scenario for the novel I was working on, but it became the basis of the next.

There was one more puzzle piece I brought in, and it is what made *Orchard* about migration, about movement rather than stasis. In thinking about trees, I kept remembering one of the most surprising tree experiences I'd had. Over twenty years ago my husband and I were staying in mid-Wales and were told there was a grove of redwoods along Offa's Dyke on the Welsh-English border. We went to see the Charles Ackers Redwood Grove, which was planted in the nineteenth-century, and it was amazing to walk among trees so different from their surroundings. All those Californian trees in a British forest: as an American transplant myself, I was tickled.

Many years later, while researching *Orchard*, I kept recalling those redwoods, wondering how and why they came to the UK. Then I got to thinking that I wanted Robert Goodenough to go and see some redwoods in California. He would love those big trees, and they might help him. Not only that: I'd learned from Michael Pollan that apple trees are not indigenous to either the US or the UK. They come originally from central Asia. It seems trees move around just as people do.

Put all of those pieces together, and the jigsaw puzzle that is this novel emerged.

Apple Trees

Given how common and popular they are, it's surprising to discover that apples did not originate in the UK; they seem so British, as if they've always been here. But no: apple trees originally grew in Khazakstan, and were brought south and west with traders over hundreds of years, through Persia, Greece, and to the Roman Empire. It was the Romans who introduced apples to Britain.

When an apple seed is planted, you never know what sort of taste you will get, and most often the fruit will be sour. If you find a variety you like, the only guaranteed way to replicate the flavour is to take a branch from that tree and graft it onto the root stock of another. So apple varieties all stem from a specific tree. The Cox, the Russet, the Granny Smith can each be traced back to one tree. For instance, the most common cooking apple in the UK is the Bramley. The original Bramley tree still exists, in a cottage garden in Nottinghamshire, having reached its 200th birthday in 2009. All trees producing Bramleys came from grafts from that tree, or grafts of grafts. That Nottingham tree is the Eve of the Bramleys.

This makes those original trees hugely important. The tree that produced the popular Golden Delicious apple in West Virginia, for example, was considered so valuable that during its lifetime a cage with an alarm attached was erected around it to protect it from thieves.

These days apples have become major commercial products. In shops now there are often only 3-4 varieties available, and the overriding taste is simply sweetness, with much emphasis placed on an even appearance, a crunchy texture and long storage time. In the nineteenth-century, there were hundreds of varieties of apples in the UK, with varying tastes and textures. Apples were more interesting then; eaters were not quite as sweet, but had undertones of interesting flavours – such as the Pitmaston Pineapple. Some of the emigrants from Britain to the New World brought branches and sometimes whole trees of their favourites, taking the taste of home with them. It is another reminder that while an individual tree may be rooted to one spot for its whole life, the species moves around with people.

Johnny Appleseed

Every American child learns in school and from picture books about Johnny Appleseed, an folk hero who distributed apple trees throughout Ohio and Indiana during the nineteenth-century. An odd man, he went barefoot, dressed in sacks, wore a pot on his head for a hat, and canoed up and down the network of rivers and streams with sacks of appleseeds, handing them out with advice about eating an apple a day and appreciating nature. He was apparently America's first eco warrior.

Johnny Appleseed was undoubtedly one of life's eccentrics, but he was not quite what children's books make him out to be, and in his apple chapter of *The Botany of Desire*, Michael Pollan debunks these myths. While it's hard to argue with the message Johnny Appleseed has been used to promote, the reality is much stranger, more interesting, and less sickly sweet: as an apple, he was more of a spitter than an eater.

John Chapman – the real name for Johnny Appleseed – grew up in New York state and moved west, setting down (literal) roots in Ohio in 1803, the year it became a state. Lots of Americans were doing the same thing. Chapman anticipated their arrival by a few years; everywhere he thought people might settle, he planted apple tree nurseries, then sold the seedlings to the new arrivals. To claim land in Ohio, you had to agree to plant an orchard of 50 viable fruit trees, and Chapman was simply taking business advantage of that requirement. He was not an eco warrior or a pantheistic promoter of the good life. He was making money.

Why he was making money is the strange part, worthy of a different novel. John Chapman was a Swedenborgian – one of literally a handful of American followers of Emanuel Swedenborg, a Swedish scientist and theologian who had unusual interpretations of Christian beliefs. Chapman went around selling trees and talking about all kinds of strange ideas to the Ohio settlers, who let him sleep on their hearths and leave behind impenetrable tracts on Swedenborg's ideas, which most of them professed not to understand. Chapman ploughed all his profits back into buying more leaflets and supporting the Swedenborgian way. None of that made it into the children's story books.

Nor did an important botanical point. Apple trees grown from seeds mostly produce sour apples only good for making cider and applejack (a rough brandy). If you want to produce sweet apples, you have to graft a new tree from an existing sweet producer, as James Goodenough does with his Pitmaston Pineapples. Johnny Appleseed was *not* actually promoting a healthy lifestyle. He was selling people the wherewithal to get drunk and dull the pain of harsh settler life.

After his death, his story was gradually mythologized, softened and sweetened; John Chapman was turned into an eater. The Women's Christian

Temperance Union went after apple growers for making alcohol out of the fruit. (Remember, this is a country that managed to prohibit alcohol from 1920 to 1933.) Growers were forced to promote apples for healthy eating, and Johnny Appleseed was the chosen poster boy.

When I brought him into the Goodenoughs' story, I was glad to have the chance to give John Chapman back his strange, gnarled shape and his much more interesting taste.

California Goldrush

On 24 January 1848, at Sutter's mill on the American River in California, a carpenter named James Marshall reached down and picked up a chunk of gold the size of half a pea. That moment changed California, and arguably changed America too. The California papers caught up with the story a few months later (news moved slowly back then), and within months Americans everywhere knew about the discovery. By the end of the year, would-be miners were heading to California to look for gold themselves. In 1849 that turned into a flood of prospectors from all over the world, nicknamed 'Forty-Niners'. People made the long journey by ship all the way around South America or via Panama, then sailing up to San Francisco. Or they took the difficult, months-long overland route across the States, often guided by hastily set up commercial companies. Many died along the way.

With this massive influx of newcomers in a short period of time, California grew from a population in 1848 of about 8000 immigrants (i.e. not counting Native Americans or Mexican 'Californios') to almost 100,000 by the end of 1849. San Francisco had been a small town of 800 in 1847; by the end of 1849 it had grown to 15,000, and by 1851 34,000.

The Goldrush, with its notion that you could go from poor to rich in a moment and radically changing your life, underpinned the American Dream. Indeed, though Californian gold in any substantial amounts is long gone, the Dream with its transformative power remains.

The reality of mining was rather different. Miners worked long hours doing backbreaking work in the cold and wet, for little return. It was relatively easy to find tiny flakes of gold by searching the mud and sand from rivers, and perhaps that is what kept people going, those glints always promising that a bigger nugget might soon be uncovered. When they collected enough flakes they could sell them, but miners soon discovered that in the remote camps they lived in, food, clothes, tools and other supplies were available only at vastly inflated prices. Indeed, those who grew wealthy from the Goldrush were usually the suppliers of goods and services to the miners rather than the miners themselves.

The dream of fortune kept prospectors going, though, as did – for some – the lawlessness of the place. Churches were rare, and the social glue of family and community was almost nonexistent. Men who had gone west with the intention of bringing fortune back east to their families sometimes decided to remain, preferring the looser social code. Gambling, prostitution and alcohol were all common, and that too is where a lot of miners' earnings went.

Into this chaos I couldn't resist thrusting Robert Goodenough, to see how he would cope with it.

Giant Sequoias

With Robert Goodenough in California, and the Welsh redwood grove still on my mind, I decided he needed to see these tall trees. Once I started researching redwoods, it wasn't long before I moved on to their cousins, giant sequoias, which also have thick, tawny red bark. Sequoias grow up to 300 feet high – not as tall as coastal redwoods, which can reach almost 400 feet. But sequoias have wider trunks, up to 30 feet in diameter. If redwoods are like basketball players, sequoias are like sumo wrestlers.

They were first 'discovered' in 1852 (by white people; Native Americans would of course already have known about them) at Calaveras Grove in the Sierra Nevada mountains by a hunter stumbling across them as he chased a bear. Later, other sequoia groves were found further south in what are now the Yosemite, Sequoia and Kings Canyon National Parks.

Calaveras Grove was quickly made into a tourist destination, and to this day it still has the 'Chip Of the Old Block' and the Giant Stump you can stand on (though I saw no one dancing when I visited). I could never have made up the detail that a bowling alley was built on the felled sequoia, and it is what lured me into including the trees in the book. Calaveras Grove is not far from some of the mining camps like Murphys, so it was easy enough to get Robert there to see these astonishing trees.

William Lobb

While researching giant sequoias and their discovery at Calaveras Grove, I came across a mention of William Lobb, and it felt as if he were the detail that linked everything else together.

William Lobb was an English gardener from Cornwall who, along with his brother Thomas, was hired by Veitch Nurseries in Exeter to travel the world, collecting plants and their seeds to send back to Britain. With global exploration introducing a taste for the foreign, Victorian gardeners were beginning to plant trees and plants from all over the world to make their gardens more interesting and exotic. Nurseryman James Veitch sent Thomas Lobb to Asia, while William travelled to South America, where he collected and sent back plant varieties of begonias, salvias, nasturtiums and many others, as well as the ubiquitous monkey puzzle tree still found in many a suburban front garden or park in Britain.

After his sojourn in South America, he moved north to the West Coast of the United States and began sending back seeds and seedlings of a wide variety of pines and fir trees. The UK has only the Scots pine, juniper and yew trees as indigenous conifers; Victorian gardeners demanded more variety, and William Lobb provided it.

In 1853 he heard about the giant sequoias discovered the previous year at Calaveras Grove, and hurried there to see for himself. He sketched and measured, then collected seedlings and cones and accompanied them back to England, for he knew he was onto a winner. Indeed, despite the seedlings being tiny, the giant sequoias captured the public imagination, and soon sequoias were being planted in country estates all over Britain. You can still see them today, getting bigger and bigger, though not sumo wrestler size yet – for that, give them another thousand years.

So William Lobb was at Calaveras Grove around the same time Robert Goodenough decided to visit the sequoias. Two men fascinated by trees: how could they not meet?

Sadly, Lobb's health was beginning to deteriorate, possibly from diseases caught from his travels. In 1854 he returned to California, eventually broke ties with Veitch, travelled less and less, and died in 1864. He is buried in relative obscurity near San Francisco. I like to think there was a tough landlady like Dody Bienenstock somewhere nearby to look after him.